"An enchanted place."

They broke into the small clearing. The ground was covered with leaf litter, and a few butterflies flitted here and there in the broken sunlight that filtered through the red and gold leaves.

"I used to come here to be alone. To me it is a little like a chapel. I always feel . . ." Amanda hesitated.

Jack's gaze had been roving the area. When she stopped speaking, he looked at her and lifted an inquiring eyebrow. "Close to God?"

"Yes." Her answer was a soft whisper, and she turned away, not wanting him to see that she felt near tears. *That remark completed your conquest, Jack. I love you.*

"Thoroughly enjoyable . . . a great read."
—Jo Beverly

Siege of
Hearts

June Calvin

A SIGNET BOOK

SIGNET
Published by New American Library, a division of
Penguin Putnam Inc., 375 Hudson Street,
New York, New York 10014, U.S.A.
Penguin Books Ltd, 27 Wrights Lane,
London W8 5TZ, England
Penguin Books Australia Ltd, Ringwood,
Victoria, Australia
Penguin Books Canada Ltd, 10 Alcorn Avenue,
Toronto, Ontario, Canada M4V 3B2
Penguin Books (N.Z.) Ltd, 182–190 Wairau Road,
Auckland 10, New Zealand

Penguin Books Ltd, Registered Offices:
Harmondsworth, Middlesex, England

First published by Signet, an imprint of New American Library,
a division of Penguin Putnam Inc.

First Printing, July 1999
10 9 8 7 6 5 4 3 2 1

This book is dedicated to F. D. "Mike" Behringer, who gave me a job at the end of my freshman year in college. He gave me so much more than that, though, for Mike knows how to praise, and gave me a much-needed dose of self-confidence, too. Whatever success I have had, in many endeavors, has sprung in part from his gift for giving more than just a paycheck for a job well done.

Chapter One

❧

"Tom, you clunch! Never say you have invited Maitland to your shooting party?"

The civilized clatter of cutlery and glass in the exclusive men's club halted; the rumble of masculine voices ceased as the portion of the *beau monde* taking their luncheon at White's turned their attention to a large round table positioned just under the grand chandelier. Tom Garfield and Viscount Maitland stood there looking down at Lord Penstock, who had just so loudly voiced his displeasure.

Maitland's golden-brown hair glinted in the sunlight pouring in the bank of windows behind him. His uniform hung upon his shoulders, which White's clientele had no difficulty understanding, for who in London did not know that the Earl of Chalwicke's son had been wounded while distinguishing himself for bravery during the recent Waterloo campaign?

The diners waited to see if Maitland would resent Penstock's rude remark. In this brief silence two of the three young men sitting with Penstock could be heard arguing. "A fiver says he challenges Winston," Richard Dremel whispered hoarsely.

Gerrard Linderhill whispered back, "You're on. He's no hothead." The two young men shook hands on the bet and then turned expectantly to see what the gaunt young man standing by their table would do.

John Stanwell, Viscount Maitland, known to his friends as Jack, lowered himself into the chair next to Lord Penstock, a taunting grin on his face. "What, Winston? Afraid I'll show up your marksmanship again?"

As he showed no obvious intention of taking offense at the rude greeting, conversation resumed, waiters returned to their tasks, and Dick scrawled his IOU on a piece of paper and handed it to Gerrard.

Tom Garfield took the chair next to Hal Bingham, the other man at the table, looking anxiously from the viscount to the sullen, swarthy face of Winston Ardel, Lord Penstock. "Never knew you for such a rudesby, Win. Maitland was invited by my brother Caspian. Comrades-in-arms and all that, and I'm honored to have him, b'gad!"

"Never mind, Tom," Hal said soothingly. "These two have been at daggers drawn since they were in short pants. They luxuriate in these kinds of pleasantries."

Winston showed no diminution of his truculence. "Thought you said you'd welcome me as a brother-in-law, Tom. How'm I to win The Beauty's heart when Jack is on the scene? Women take one look at him and fall for that fatal phiz of his. Bad enough before he became one of the heroes of Waterloo. But now . . . bah!" Winston turned sideways in his chair, giving his shoulder to the group and staring moodily out over the dining room.

"He's right, you know," Richard commented to Gerrard. "A tenner says The Beauty falls at Jack's feet." The two shook hands on the bet.

Jack's eyes narrowed; his posture stiffened. "Hold a minute. Thought it was a shooting party. Caspian said just some friends and his father. I'm in need of a safe retreat, not another frontal assault from the petticoat battalions."

"I assure you, Maitland, that we go to Yorkshire for the shooting," Tom Garfield replied. "I have two sisters, but . . ."

Bingham lowered his fork, his brow wrinkled with worry. "Hadn't thought of it, Tom, but Win's right. The ladies very nearly trampled me down last night at the Mainwaring's rout to get to him. He'll beat Win and me both out if he goes on this hunting party."

Jack surreptitiously massaged his left calf under the table. His full mouth canted in a half smile, half grimace. "I have no wish to beat anyone out. I am heartily sick of all of this female adulation. As I told Cass, I wish to rusticate. You'll get no competition from me."

Dick and Gerrard began whispering together again.

"Still at the constant wagering, eh, Dick, Ger?" Jack shook his head. There were times when the sameness of

London society seemed surreal to him after the carnage of Waterloo. "What did I say to set you off this time?"

Giving the two sporting gentlemen no time to answer, Penstock growled, "If you rusticate at the Garfields', you'll meet the fairest of the fair, and she can't help but have her head turned by you. She is the only reason I would consent to go into the country. Why don't you hunt your own coverts, Jack? You go into Yorkshire with us, and no matter what you say, I won't have a chance with The Beauty, though I swear she favored my suit when she left London."

"About to step into the parson's mousetrap at last?" Jack's eyebrows lifted in surprise.

"I am," Winston intoned in a reverent voice. "I mean to marry the most beautiful, the most delightful, the most elegant female it has ever been my pleasure to know: Tom's sister, Penelope Garfield."

"A diamond, eh?" Jack looked to Hal for confirmation.

Hal nodded vigorously. "Every word true, except that it is me she is considering marrying." Lord Penstock loudly objected to this, leading to a spirited discussion of various marks of The Beauty's favor to one or the other.

Richard and Gerrard did not participate in the discussion, but instead began negotiating odds on whether Jack would actually go to the Garfields' or cry off.

Jack ruthlessly interrupted these deliberations. "Tempting as she sounds, I'll leave her to you two. But I can't hunt my own coverts this fall. My father has a mind to see me legshackled before the year is out. If I go to Chalk Hill now, he'll invite half of the ton—the nubile female half, that is—to follow me there." The bitterness in his voice surprised the other young gentlemen, who were not privy to the Earl of Chalwicke's latest, most treacherous maneuver in his quest to get his son a wife.

After a moment of silent reflection, Jack continued, "Think I'll go to my hunting box in Scotland instead. Not in the mood to do the pretty now, even for a glimpse of such a remarkable beauty. Express my regrets to Caspian, will you, Tom? And Hal and Winston, may the better man win."

"Don't part with your blunt yet," Tom admonished Dick as he started to pass another coin to Gerrard. "Pay Hal and Winston no mind, Maitland. No need to do the pretty, none at all. We go there to shoot and nothing more, and my sisters know it. They won't expect us to dance attendance on them. In fact, Mother is planning to take them off to Brighton as soon as Penny has recovered a bit from all the attention this Season."

"Huh!" Jack's skepticism showed, but he stayed in his chair.

"If you like, I'll write to Caspian, tell him to encourage them to be on their way."

Winston's scowl returned. "Cass told me I could take the opportunity to press my suit with her, Tom. I don't care a fig for shooting."

Tom was beginning to tire of Winston's boorishness. In truth, he did not like the arrogant lord all that well, and wondered what Penelope saw in him. *Let Penstock cry off. Cass asked me to bring Maitland, and bring him I will.* Tom's younger brother, Caspian, on leave from Wellington's staff, had gone ahead of them to Yorkshire, eager to see his family again. He had urged Tom to be sure Jack joined the hunting party.

"Court her to your heart's content, Winston. Just don't expect the rest of the shooting party to trail after the petticoats. I know! You may escort the ladies to Brighton if you wish. That way none of us will have to interrupt our hunting to do so."

"I'll do it with pleasure," Winston declared fervently.

Jack allowed himself to be convinced, for he was truly desperate to escape his father's matchmaking. Yet going to his estate in Scotland didn't suit him either, for he dreaded the thought of being alone with his memories just now.

"Good! I am off to write that letter." Tom took his leave.

"I need to go to Tats to see what I can find to replace Beelzebub." Jack rubbed his hand over his brow, seeking to shut out a sudden picture of blood and flesh and shattered bone, and the memory of his faithful horse's scream of agony as the saber slash that had cut his own leg brought the valiant beast down.

Hal threw down his napkin and stood up. "I'll go with you. Wouldn't mind finding another hunter."

"And I," Winston said, standing. The other two at the table abandoned their luncheon, too, and followed Jack out of the club.

"Bet he buys old Grimmy's knockdowns," Dick challenged Gerrard as the two trailed behind the others.

"You're on. Jack's got too good an eye to fall for that showy chestnut, and the bay ain't up to his weight."

Jack laughed over his shoulder at them. "Don't you two ever stop?" As they strolled along St. James Street, he picked up one thread of their previous conversation. "Don't Cass and Tom have two sisters?"

Both Hal and Winston nodded but said nothing more.

"So what is the younger sister like?" Jack persisted. "Another beauty?"

"Not younger," said Hal.

"Oh. Older sister, then."

"Not older."

"Now how . . . Twins?" Jack halted momentarily, intrigued. "Twin beauties? Then why don't each of you marry one, instead of competing for . . . what was her name?"

"Actually," Winston said, "Penelope is a few minutes older. Or is it Amanda?"

"I'll wager a penny it's Penny," Hal quipped.

Jack groaned. "Not you, too!"

"Thought you weren't interested," Winston grumbled, eyeing Jack uneasily.

"Always have an eye for beauty, Win, you know that. Just not about to tie myself down right now." *I won't give my father that satisfaction,* Jack thought grimly.

"Can't each marry one. The other one's not beautiful," Winston asserted.

Hal agreed. "Just so. Pale imitation of The Beauty."

"Imitation! By no means," Winston exclaimed indignantly. "They don't resemble at all. You'd hardly believe the plain one is even Penelope's sister, much less her twin."

"Poor thing," Jack said, genuinely sympathetic. "Must be difficult for her." He had one beautiful sister and one plain one. He knew how such a disproportionate share of looks could affect a young woman. Indeed, the competition between Mary and Sarah had affected their entire family, especially after his mother died. She had always insisted on equal treatment of the two, whereas his father had blatantly favored Sarah, the beauty. Relationships had grown increasingly acrimonious as, for example, Sarah had stolen away her older sister's beaux. *Odd, how things work out.*

Jack smiled as he reminisced. Plain but vivacious Mary had married wealthy and handsome Lord Winbridge, whereas the beautiful, vain, and rather vapid Sarah had married Mr. Stratford, a man of modest fortune and even more modest appearance.

Dick and Gerrard stopped to put their heads together. "Not another wager! What did I say this time?" Jack groused.

"Never mind. We both wanted the same side—that you'd fall for the beautiful sister, not the plain one. Say, Hal, Win, don't suppose you would give us odds . . ."

Winston just snorted. Hal waved them off. "I'm no green 'un, to waste the ready that way."

"Cass!" A blur of pink muslin and suddenly Caspian Garfield's arms were full of sisters. He hugged them both, then lifted them up and swung them around exuberantly. "Oh, Cass, it's been so long," Amanda gasped as he set them down.

"We thought you'd never get here," Penelope complained. "Why did that beastly Wellington make you go on with him to Paris?"

" 'Tis a jolly good thing he did, Penny. A feather in the cap of any aspiring diplomat. Father!" He advanced to take the hand of Sir Edwin, who had been watching this tableau with a grin upon his face. After a moment's hesitation the two men left off dignity to hug and clap one another on the back. Then the sound of his mother's voice made Cass break away.

Lady Garfield approached him slowly, but her greeting made Caspian's throat swell. "I still have two sons," she whispered, stopping just in front of him, her hands raised prayerfully. "I could not truly believe it until I beheld you again. Thanks be to God." Great tears rolled down her cheeks, and Caspian engulfed her in a hug, afraid he would break into tears himself.

When the emotional scene ended, the five moved to the Chinese drawing room, where Caspian told his family over tea, "I bring more than just myself to gladden your day."

"Nothing more is wanted," his mother assured him, but Penelope pleaded prettily, "Oh, tell us! Tell us!"

"Tom and I have gotten up a shooting party. I've three guests to lay at your pretty feet, Pen."

"Three!" She clapped her hands. "Do say that Lord Penstock is one!"

"He is. Now, Amanda, your turn to guess."

His sister smiled slyly. "Why, I think from your triumphant look it must be the Prince Regent himself."

Penelope waved her hand at Amanda. "Oh, pooh! You know it must be Hal Bingham. Dear, dear Hal. But who is the third?"

"Now, *that* you shall never guess."

Penny bombarded him with possibilities, occasionally joined by their mother. Sir Edwin looked on complacently, as did Amanda, who knew it must be one of her sister's suitors, though she couldn't imagine who would please her as much as the two already named. When Penelope, exhausted by the social rounds, had left London before all of the many celebrations of the victory at Waterloo had ended, she had still been torn between the dark-haired, handsome Lord Penstock and the ordinary-looking, exceedingly kind Hal Bingham.

At last Caspian held up his hand. "I'll give you a hint. He's one of my comrades-at-arms. I wrote you about . . ."

Three female voices cried out in unison: "Viscount Maitland."

When he nodded, there fell a reverential silence of a few minutes' duration, broken by Penny. "Oh, I can't wait to meet him. When I read your letter about how he helped Wellington steady the Brunswickers and then joined Sir Hussey Vivian's light cavalry, though he hadn't the least need to, being an aide . . ."

Cass laughed heartily. "No need to retell the battle to me, Penny. I was there, remember."

"And just as brave as the viscount, though we had to learn of your conduct from others." Penny and her sister both looked at Cass with teary-eyed admiration.

Suddenly Lady Garfield wailed, "Oh, Cass, I almost wish you had not. I've never seen the boy, but I am told he is the image of his father, and the Earl of Chalwicke was quite possibly the handsomest man in England when he was young."

Their father showed no jealousy at this encomium. "Quite

so. Devilish glad he had already settled on Caroline Tennyson before Lucinda made her come-out! For she'd never have looked at me otherwise."

"But that is wonderful! Handsome as well as brave. Mother," Penny cried out dramatically, "why should you not wish him to come? I cannot wait! Or is it because he's an earl's heir? Is he too high in the instep for a baronet's daughter, Cass?"

"Certainly not, though I cannot say just how his father might regard an alliance with our family. But Jack is not on the lookout for a wife just now, I should warn you. In fact, I think he accepted my invitation partially to get away from the hordes of females laying siege to him in London. I know I can trust you not to make him uncomfortable, though, which is why I encouraged him to come here."

Penny instantly agreed. "It wouldn't do at all to flirt and flutter around him. And perhaps I shan't like him at all. But perhaps . . ." Her eyes took on a dreamy look.

Cass turned to Lady Garfield. "I, too, don't see why you regret the invitation, Mother."

"With such an eligible young man about, she'll never choose between Mr. Bingham and Lord Penstock," Lady Garfield wailed. But she didn't really seem distressed, joining in the general laughter at this observation.

Penelope jumped up to hug Cass, then snuggled by his side. "We must think of some entertainments for Viscount Maitland."

"Of course!" Her mother stood and began pacing. "And we must have a female guest join us, to make up the numbers."

"Now, ladies, I invited him to a shooting party," Cass protested.

"You cannot shoot at night, though, can you? And there will be rain sometime during his visit. We must be prepared. Come, girls. We shall put our heads together while your father and Caspian have a comfortable coze." She started toward the door.

To everyone's surprise Sir Edwin suddenly exclaimed, "Must have another gentleman in the party. One of Amanda's suitors. Which means two additional young ladies."

Amanda's heart sank. Well her father knew that she had only one suitor, and for all that Sir Edwin sang his praises,

Mr. Tittlecue did not interest her in the least. "That isn't necessary," she said. "You know I shan't think of marriage until Penny has made her choice. I am perfectly content . . ."

"Nonsense. Foolish notion of yours, that no one will court you until she is wed. A man of discernment is what you need. Not one of these young puppies who doesn't realize how unimportant a woman's looks are in the long run."

Amanda smiled somewhat wistfully. "When you married Mother, she was the Toast of London, Father, as you have often told us."

"Yes, and still a great beauty today," he asserted, causing his wife, who had retraced her steps and now stood at his side, to drop a quick kiss on his forehead. "Fortune smiled on me and made her as good as she is beautiful, but a mature man knows how rare that combination is."

"A mature man? Oh, Papa, you are not going to invite Mr. Tittlecue for Mandy, are you? Because I won't stand for it! He gives her the headache every time he calls." Penelope leapt from her seat and hastened to the chair where Amanda sat, throwing her arms around her sister in a dramatic protective gesture.

"Penny!" Lady Garfield called her daughter to order. "It is not for you to speak to your father thus of whom he invites to be a guest in his home. Besides, Mr. Tittlecue is perfectly amiable and very well fixed, too. Amanda could do a great deal worse."

"Amanda, say something," Penelope urged. "Don't let them foist that old grampus on you!"

Amanda twisted in her sister's embrace and smiled up at her. "Don't worry, Pen. It isn't as if they plan to force me to marry him. But Father enjoys Mr. Tittlecue's company, you know, and I don't wish to deprive him of it. When the younger men begin bragging about their racehorses and their hunters, Papa and Mr. Tittlecue can discuss the merits of mules to their hearts' content."

To herself, Amanda thought, *At least with Mr. Tittlecue on hand I won't be subjected to the humiliation of being the last chosen after Penny has sorted out which of the eligibles she will pair with before each event.* She suspected this was partly what her thoughtful father had in mind in proposing to invite Mr. Tittlecue, who seemed impervious to Penelope's beauty.

No more than any other member of her family did Amanda entertain the least notion that Viscount Maitland would fail to become Penelope's suitor. The thought that he would take an interest in Amanda never even entered her mind. After only two balls in London in the spring Amanda had chosen to return home, leaving the field to her sister. She had tired very soon of being foisted off on men who had clustered around to ask Penny to dance, or finding that someone who pretended an interest in her was only seeking to curry favor with her beautiful sister.

Her mother had taken her part when Sir Edwin had been reluctant to agree to Amanda's departure, explaining to her perplexed husband that it made perfect sense to give her a second Season once Penny was married. "Then her own agreeable appearance won't be eclipsed as it is now, my dear," she had reassured the fond, uneasy father. Penny, loyal and loving sister that she was, had pleaded for Amanda to stay, promising to make sure she always had partners, and not quite grasping why the idea of her beautiful sister blackmailing her suitors into doing the pretty held no appeal for Amanda.

"Well, now, what's to do?" Caspian Garfield held his brother Tom's missive at arm's length and squinted at it, as if that might favorably alter its content.

> When Viscount Maitland overheard Winston and Hal singing Penny's praises, he very nearly cried off our shooting party, for he is run to death by matchmaking mamas and their daughters. Encourage Mother to take Penny and Amanda to Brighton as planned, will you, bro? I promised him he'd have a respite from all the adulation he's getting here in London. Said he'd go on to his hunting box in Scotland otherwise.

Tapping the letter against his chin, Caspian considered the problem. He and Viscount Maitland had become friends during their brief but intense stint in Wellington's army. He knew that Jack's father had not forgiven his son for risking his life in the military when he had not yet married and produced an heir. While still in Belgium, Jack had mentioned how uncomfortable his return to Chalk Hill would be. When Cass had gone on to Paris with Wellington and the army, Jack had gone not to the family seat in Kent, but to rented lodgings in London to recuperate from his wound. Cass had called on him there upon returning to England, and Jack had seized eagerly on the invitation to join the Garfields, rather than joining his father at home for the fall hunting season.

"If I warn him of my mother's plans, he'll go off to Scotland on his own," Cass muttered, going to the window to look out across the deer park. "But he's got no business being alone with his thoughts right now." Cass knew better than anyone how dark Jack's thoughts must be. The things they had seen, heard, and done at Waterloo would haunt them both for the rest of their lives.

"It's for your own good, Jack," he said, crushing the parchment in his hand and tossing it into the wastebasket. "Indeed, I'm thinking the sight of Penelope's lovely face and bright hair might be just the medicine you need, whether you know it or not."

"Here, sir, let me help you." A stalwart gardener left off scything the lawn in front of Garfield Manor and hastened to where a bedraggled young man with a haggard face limped away from the departing post chaise he had just paid off.

Viscount Maitland first waved the gardener off, then reconsidered after struggling with the first three stairs. Once inside the entryway, he stood erect and smoothly slipped the gardener a coin. The man started to carry his tip to his mouth but decided not to insult the amiable gentleman by doubting the value of his money. Instead, he pulled at his forelock and bowed at the same time.

"Very good, Jones. That will do." A distinguished gray-haired man waved the gardener away, his expression suggesting he contemplated doing the same to the ragged gentleman whom he now beheld. Only the obviously expensive cloth of the torn clothes, added to the hourly expectation of the arrival of the Garfields' final guest, kept Bennington from doing so. Instead, he lifted a skeptical eyebrow and inquired, "Viscount Maitland?"

"The same." Jack smiled wryly at the senior servant's obvious puzzlement. Not for the first time that day he wished he had not refused to travel to Yorkshire with Tom. "Let me give the ladies time to make their departure," he had declared, setting his own exit from London for two weeks after his host's.

"Sorry to make such a poor appearance," Jack told the uneasy butler, "but my horse threw me just outside of Highton, and . . ."

"Bennington, show Lord Maitland into the Isis drawing room, please. And bring tea right away." A diminutive young female confidently issued these orders as she hastened down the stairs. "Unless you would prefer lemonade, my lord, for to be sure it is unseasonably warm, and Cook will have a pitcher made up," she added, looking inquiringly at him.

"Lemonade, then," Jack responded, smiling broadly. There was something in the young woman's aspect that made him want to laugh, not at her, but because of something he felt in her presence. Perhaps it was the way her mouth turned up at the corners? Or was it that such high-arched brows over large, light-colored eyes gave her a look of surprise and expectation?

She lifted those improbable brows higher in response to his expression, but returned his smile in full measure. It was not until she reached the bottom of the steps that she realized his condition and inquired anxiously, "Are you injured, my lord? Shall I send for the doctor?"

"No, I thank you, Miss . . ."

"I beg your pardon. I am Amanda Garfield."

He attempted to bow to her, but a shaft of pain through his left leg made him take his weight off of it so suddenly that he lost his balance and fell on his posterior with an undignified plop.

The sprite, for such he had immediately designated her in his mind, bent to help him, and between her and Bennington he managed to struggle to his feet, apologizing profusely. She ignored his stammerings, concentrating on piloting him, with the butler's help, into a sumptuous drawing room in the Egyptian mode that looked out through double French doors onto a portico with a magnificent view of the park.

As they lowered him onto a leather sofa, she murmured, "You are badly hurt. We must send for the doctor."

"By no means," Jack snapped. "It is but a strain. A little rest and I shall be . . ."

"Here. Put your leg on this footstool. Bennington, send for Dr. Bruce at once, if you please. Oh, and hand me a decanter of brandy before you go." When Jack started to protest, she primmed her rosebud mouth and pointed to his buff inexpressibles. "You are bleeding, my lord. I have rarely heard of anyone bleeding from a strain."

Chapter Two

Jack instinctively grasped his left calf, which only had the effect of further staining his riding breeches crimson. "Damnation, but I've opened it again!" The young woman started and frowned at his language. "Beg pardon, Miss Garfield, but I had no idea. Wounded there, you know. When my horse went down, I must have reinjured it."

"I expect that is so," she said in a calm voice. "Here, take this." She poured him a measure of brandy. "Would you care for some laudanum?"

Jack shook his head vigorously. "It would have to hurt a deal more than this scratch does, for me to muddle my brain with that nasty stuff."

She chuckled approvingly. "It *is* rather like a London fog inside one's head, isn't it?" He found himself grinning again, the pain in his leg forgotten.

She handed him the brandy. "I am sorry to be your only welcoming committee, but after nuncheon everyone rode out to look at Papa's excavations." She looked disapproving.

"You do not care for ah . . . excavations? What are they digging up, I wonder? Fossils? Antiquities? They haven't taken to robbing graves as a pastime, have they?"

Amanda laughed again. "Roman ruins. Papa is as proud of them as he is of his mules, and that is saying a great deal." Before Jack could pursue the reason she had looked so censorious for a moment, she asked, "Is there anything else I can do for you to make you comfortable until the doctor arrives?"

Jack scowled. "I wish you will not send for a physician. When my valet arrives, he can manage very well, just as he has done since Waterloo."

"Yes, I know." Amanda perched lightly on the end of

the sofa, like a small bird ready to take flight. "Cass told us about your valet turned batman. But he is not here now, is he? You need not fear that our good doctor will bleed you excessively or torment you with nasty potions. He is a very sensible man."

"Still, I had rather wait for my valet, if you don't mind."

Amanda frowned. "I am sure Bennington has already posted a footman by now. Will you tell me something? Cass told me quite an amazing tale about how you held off the surgeons at gunpoint when they would have . . . have . . ."

"Amputated my leg?"

Tears sprang to her eyes, and she looked away. "Dreadful to think of it!"

"And so I thought," Jack responded wryly. "Cass was a beast to distress you with that tale."

The eyebrows went up. "Why, no. I do not wish to be wrapped in cotton wool, which is a very good thing, with Tom and Caspian to contend with."

"Yes, Cass told me about some of the rigs he and Tom would run in their wilder days."

Her eyes sparkled with mischief. "I daresay you amused him in turn with some tales of your misspent youth."

"Most assuredly." Jack laughed again.

"But you did not answer me. *Did* you hold off the surgeons with a gun, or was Cass indulging his penchant for exaggeration?"

"Let us just say my gun gave a certain authority to my protest at what I thought was a hasty decision on their part." Jack winked at her. "Don't think I am unaware of your ploy, little schemer."

"I beg your pardon, my lord?" Amanda tried to look entirely innocent, but a dimple quivered at the edge of her mouth, giving her away.

"Changing the subject won't change my mind. I won't let myself be quacked, so you will just be putting your good doctor to an unnecessary amount of trouble."

"Well, then, he will not touch you, but you must tell him yourself, for I am persuaded he is on his way by now. He lives quite nearby. His land marches with ours, you see."

"A farmer as well as a doctor?"

"A gentleman farmer, at that." Amanda lifted her chin. "Dr. Bruce is my mother's cousin. His practice of medicine arose out of a deep interest in the subject and a desire to help others. You may rely upon him to do you no harm, Lord Maitland."

Jack surrendered. He began to perceive that this small female was a force to be reckoned with. "Very well. Do you think I might have another dram of brandy?" He dropped his head against the back of the sofa and studied her through half-closed eyes as she poured another measure of amber liquid for him.

Who is she? he wondered. He could not recall the names of the Garfield daughters. *Not The Beauty, to be sure.* He studied the young woman's profile as she carefully replaced the cut-glass stopper. *No one could claim beauty for that short, turned-up nose.* Her stature was too short, her figure too slight, her thin, delicately boned face too far from the perfect oval to pass for a beauty in a society that idealized Greek statuary. That the Great Artist, who never allowed Himself to be bound by human conventions, had saved her chin from being pointed by putting a small but decided thumbprint there, causing an intriguing cleft, would not have weighed with human arbiters of taste. Could Winston Ardel have been captivated by a woman who did not meet the fashionable definition of beauty?

No, Jack decided. Even if that were possible, both Win and Hal had praised their beauty's shining golden curls, and this sprite's hair, a non-nondescript brown, looked dull and lifeless. *The product of a curling iron and an excess of pomade, unless I miss my guess.* Flicking his eyes once more over the excess of curls that threatened to overwhelm her delicate features, he could not imagine why anyone would choose to torture her hair into a style so ill-suited to her.

And didn't he say her eyes were celestial blue? Jack could not have said what color Amanda's eyes were, but knew that they were very light in color, either pale green or gray. Decidedly not blue.

His brows knit together as he pondered the puzzle. *But she surely can't be the plain one. No one in his right mind would call her plain. She is quite appealing in her own way, with that pretty little mouth, those quizzical eyebrows and huge eyes, and that perfect porcelain complexion.* Jack decided she must be a cousin, a poor relation who had stayed behind to keep house for the men after Lady Garfield and her daughters departed for Brighton. The dress she wore argued for that conclusion, being of a color and cut entirely unsuited to her. *A hand-me-down, surely. But I never heard Cass mention such a relation.*

Despite the nonclassical features and the lack of style, as Jack contemplated the young woman, he felt a surge of desire, something he had not experienced since Waterloo. He shifted position and scolded himself into decorum.

Amanda felt his eyes on her, and bit the inside of her lower lip nervously. Never had she regretted her lack of looks so much as when she felt the handsome man beside her taking stock of her. In spite of strong, uncompromisingly masculine features, he could almost be described as beautiful, with that double row of long dark lashes over the long golden-brown eyes. He had a wide forehead, on which trailed golden-brown curls any girl would envy. His wide, firm mouth curved slightly upward in repose, suggesting a man of pleasant temperament, even though he had so far forgotten himself as to swear in her presence a few moments ago. His square chin and strong jawline suggested a man of strong character, perhaps even stubbornness.

Amanda had until this time felt very little jealousy of Penelope. Instead, she was inordinately proud of her beautiful and loving sister. But she found herself dreading the moment when Viscount Maitland first beheld Penny. He would never look at Amanda with such interest again. The mild, kindly expression he favored her with would be replaced by that delighted but predatory alertness that gentlemen inevitably displayed when in Penelope's presence.

This won't do, Amanda. She girded herself to resist Maitland's powerful pull upon her senses. She had no intention of breaking her heart over one of her sister's suitors. Until Penny was happily married, she intended never to open her heart to disappointment. Indeed, she doubted she would ever marry, for she had a certain proud turn of mind that made her want a husband only if he would love her and desire her over any other woman on the planet, including her sister. A female such as she seldom called forth such devotion. So it was very likely that she would simply remain a spinster, and indulge herself in the role of maiden aunt to her siblings' children.

Taking a deep breath, Amanda turned to the viscount, holding out the glass of brandy. "How did you happen to be injured today, my lord? I think I heard you say your horse threw you?"

"Not threw me—fell. Some cowhanded gudgeon who fancied himself a whipster passed my baggage coach too close and struck it. In the ensuing crash one of his wheels came off and rolled down the road. I was riding up ahead, and my horse reared and tried to get out of the way, but was caught on the hind legs. It bowled him right down. I'm dam . . . ah, extremely fortunate to have been able to jump free, but I suppose landing on my left side has reopened my wound."

Jack bent forward and tentatively explored the injury. *It seems not to be bleeding badly. Perhaps it is only a superficial break in the skin.* The thought of once again having to fight doctors for the right to keep his leg made him furious. He looked up to see the young woman watching his hand where he probed the wound, concern clouding her eyes.

"Shall I have someone assist you up the steps? I am sure you would like to stretch out and rest. I collect your baggage and servants remained behind with the coach?"

Jack nodded. "Which went into the ditch. The rear axle was broken. My valet is directing salvage operations, while my groom and footmen are seeing to the horses. I rode back to Highton on one of the coach horses to summon help, and then hired a chaise to bring me here." He stood up. "Now that I've rested, I'm sure I can make it up the stairs on my own."

Amanda rose, too. He smiled at her as she put her hands on her hips in the classic posture of a woman about to read a man a scold. "No, don't tell me what a fool you think I am. I know it already, but we men have our pride, you know."

"We shall see if pride can carry you up two flights of steps, sirrah!" She shook her head in mock despair. "Just like Tom and Caspian. They make a great fuss about the slightest illness, but an injury of any sort is seen as something shameful that must be hidden and ignored."

"You sound like my mother, God rest her soul. She had no patience with malingering, but little respect for those who ignore reality, either. Nevertheless, I am confident that

I can manage on my own." However, the jolt of pain when his weight came down fully on his left leg made him flinch, belying his words. Since his war injury, he had been subject to sudden, severe cramps in that leg, and this one dwarfed all the ones that had gone before.

"Are you prepared to face reality now, my lord?" The young woman's expression invited him to laugh at his own foibles, which he did.

"You win this battle, little general." The shared joke had the agreeable effect of reducing the sting to his pride dealt by having to submit to be flanked by two stout footmen and assisted up the steps. As they made their way up, he heard noises suggesting that the doctor had arrived, so he was not surprised to find such a person joining him in his room before he had even been settled in a chair.

He *was* surprised to see a relatively young man, surely not more than thirty, briskly greeting him and bending at the same time to examine the bloody leg.

"See if you can take those boots off without taking the limb with it," the doctor instructed one of the footmen. A quick dive into his surgical bag produced a scalpel with which Dr. Bruce cut the breeches away from his left leg from ankle to hip. The sight of the scalpel made Jack shiver, but he resisted the urge to physically assault the brisk, competent physician. Using the basin of hot water the second footman had brought—on Miss Garfield's order, Jack had no doubt—Dr. Bruce cleaned the blood away so that he could view the wound.

Jack bent eagerly to have a look himself, and heaved a sigh of relief. "It hasn't split open," he exclaimed.

"No, you've been a lucky lad in more ways than one. You fell on a stick when you hit the road. There are some splinters embedded beneath the flesh, but they are not very deep. I shall have to cut them out and cleanse the wounds, but you should be fine as fivepence in a few days." He ran an expert finger along the angry red scar that curved around Jack's calf. "Nasty cut, that was. The army surgeons wanted to remove it?"

"They did." Jack's mouth clamped grimly on his terse answer.

"I wonder how many fine lads left perfectly good limbs

in France because the army surgeons were too rushed to evaluate wounds carefully? I am Dr. Bruce, by the way."

Jack nodded. "I am sure my man can take care of this. If you'll state your fee, he will bring it around tomorrow."

Dr. Bruce stiffened. "It is not a question of receiving a fee."

"Ah, yes. I forgot. You are a gentleman, whose motives for practicing medicine are above filthy lucre. Plague take you, man, I don't want a physician. I'll not be bled. I saw many a man wounded at Waterloo, and none of them were the better for loss of blood!"

Dr. Bruce's eyes glittered with amusement. "I rarely bleed, my lord. I reserve that treatment, which I regard as outmoded, for those who have too much flesh, or whose energy is spent in fighting their doctors."

"You are a damned impertinent . . ."

"But I am sure you have too much sense to place yourself among their ranks. Now, your man, if he had the care of this battle wound, must indeed be competent to treat you. However, it needs to be treated right away, to lessen the chances of infection. I'll clean it and leave instructions for him for future treatment. If you will be so good as to stretch out on the bed?"

Jack looked into Dr. Bruce's determined face. He saw a sincere concern for his patient there and decided to capitulate. The fact that his whole leg hurt madly and was trying to draw up against his posterior influenced his decision. As he allowed himself to be helped to the bed, he asked, "Why does it hurt so plaguey much?"

"You would have had a painful bruise there even if that leg hadn't been previously wounded. Newly healed flesh is especially tender and subject to bruising, and will be so for many a month. That wound must have cut through muscle, and this new injury has triggered a muscle spasm, which I fear my treatment will only make worse, but it has to be done. Hmmm. Ummmmhmmmm." He probed the wound as Jack grimaced and ground his teeth to maintain a manly silence. The syringe of water with which the doctor sluiced it caused almost as much pain as the removal of the splinters. When the doctor straightened up and reached again for his bag, Jack warned, "Don't put any of your nasty poultices on there."

"I am not a purveyor of goat dung or dog urine, as you seem to think, Lord Maitland." With economical movements Dr. Bruce put a light bandage on the wound, and wiped his hands on one of the cloths the footman had brought along with the water and soap. "I see no need for stitches. All that is needed is to keep it clean and lightly bandaged. After that it will be up to your body to fight off infection. You look a strong lad; doubtless in a week or two you'll be on horseback again."

Jack opened his mouth to protest.

"Now, my lord, you can choose to ignore that scratch, in which case riding may enlarge it, and sweat and dirt may foster infection, thus inconveniencing you for weeks, or you may behave sensibly for a few days and be done with it."

"Bother! I came here to shoot!" But resignation was in Jack's tone of voice.

"In a few days, when it has closed over, you may certainly do so, as long as you are conveyed to the fields in a gig. In the meanwhile, I have no doubt the ladies will delight in entertaining you."

"The ladies have gone to Brighton," Jack snapped.

Dr. Bruce lifted skeptical eyebrows. "Was it the ghost of Miss Amanda I spoke to in the hall, then? Perhaps the invitation to dinner, which I gladly accepted a few days ago, came from other such specters. Well! That should make for a most interesting dinner party. Here is some laudanum for you to use. A few drops now and again before bedtime should . . ."

"I don't use laudanum."

"There is no end to your stoicism, I see. But you require educating, I think. Your muscle spasm will retreat sooner if you have relief from the pain. However, it is your choice."

In addition to the drawn, screaming muscles in his leg, Jack felt bruised all along his left side, so he gave in. "Oh, very well. But only this once." Jack grimaced as he swallowed the dose Dr. Bruce prepared for him.

"I bid *au revoir,* my lord. I shall look in on you again after dining with these pretty specters this evening, eh?" Dr. Bruce gave him a short bow, which Jack could only characterize as mocking, turned on his heel, and exited.

So the ladies have not gone to Brighton? That sounds ominous. Jack closed his eyes for a few minutes, listening to the sounds of the footman who had attended the doctor, clearing away his discarded materials.

With the aid of the laudanum, he dozed off as the spasm in his leg diminished. The sounds of his valet tiptoeing around the room awoke him. "Haskins, is that you?"

"Aye, my lord. Sorry to be so long, but the wheelwright in Highton said it would take two days to make a new axle and repair the other damage to the carriage."

"What about that cawker who caused it all?" Jack had left the offending driver in care of Haskins rather than give in to the overwhelming urge to strangle the creature.

"Badly bruised, but nothing broken. I left him at the Highton Inn in the care of an apothecary."

"And the horses?"

Haskins shook his head. "The young man's pair had to be put down. One of our leaders has a bad gash in his fetlock, and Triton's badly bruised and scraped all along his left side, like his master. He also has deep cuts on both hind legs just below the hock. The groom is to bring him here at a slow walk. I'd say the chances that he is still sound are not good. After I have seen to you, I will make up a liniment to try to bring down some of the swelling in his leg."

Disgusted at the misery caused to so many animals, particularly the one he had so recently paid a good price for at Tattersalls, Jack lashed out. "And while you were looking to the other driver and the horses, I suppose my baggage was left at the mercy of whatever brigands happened by."

Offended at the tone of voice as much as the suggestion that he might have abandoned the viscount's wardrobe and guns, Haskins frostily answered, "Transferred to a cart and brought here under my supervision, my lord."

"Ah. Of course. As usual, you are the perfect servant, Haskins." Jack pinched the bridge of his nose. "Forgive my bad temper, I beg of you. You know what a devilish bad patient I am."

Haskins nodded. "You are always cross as crabs when you are hurting. Shall I bring some liniment for you, too?"

"I thank you, but no. Your liniment is effective but gives off a distinctly unpleasant odor, and I have no wish to smell of the stable when I go down for dinner. Besides, it is an open wound. God alone knows what you put in that stuff, but it certainly shouldn't be applied to raw flesh."

"Then you do intend to go down, my lord? I wonder if clothing will not be painful and . . ."

"Don't be old-womanish, Haskins. I'll not lie abed because of a scratch. Besides, that plaguey physician talked me into taking some laudanum. I'll just chase it with a bit more brandy and close my eyes for a few minutes while you finish unpacking. Come dinnertime, I will be fit to go." He proceeded to make liberal use of the anesthetic qualities of medicinal alcohol.

Jack awoke to the sound of Amanda's voice, lowered to a careful whisper. She was inquiring of Haskins as to whether his master intended to come down for dinner. He opened his eyes.

"Yes, Miss Garfield, I shall join you this evening."

"I shall send our footmen to assist you down the stairs, then, my lord." Amanda started to leave.

"You most certainly will not. I'm dashed if I'll be carried about like a sack of meal."

She smiled. "Dr. Bruce said it was not a serious cut, but still, Lord Maitland . . ."

"A scratch, merely, though he advises me that it would be unwise to ride for a while. I plan to leave for my hunting box as soon as my carriage is mended."

"Why would you do that? We will be more than happy to nurse you for a few days, and then you may join the men in their hunting. Besides, I think you would be most uncomfortable in a carriage for some time, for you must be bruised all over."

"I won't put your family to the trouble of nursing me. It would be tiresome for the men, and would delay the ladies' departure for Brighton."

Amanda's dimples appeared. "Brighton? No, indeed! If that is your concern, you may lay it to rest. We had originally intended to go there for the hunting season, but since hearing of your plans to grace us with your presence, my mother has quite a different scheme in mind."

Irritation flashed through Jack. *Just as I thought! Whatever possessed me to accept an invitation from a man with two unmarried sisters?* The thought of feminine plots triggered a recent, painful memory, and Jack lashed out, "I am all too familiar with such schemes. I came here to escape from them for a while. In spite of the lady-authoress's widely quoted remark, not all unmarried gentlemen are in need of a wife."

"Lord Maitland, I resent your implication."

"I resent Cass and Tom's misleading me into believing this was to be a masculine party."

Amanda stared at Jack in amazement. His hitherto amiable countenance had changed: a fierce scowl and a bitter edge to his voice left his listener in no doubt of his meaning. She primmed her mouth. "I meant only that we wished to entertain you, my lord, not that anyone here intended to entrap you. If my brothers had known of your dislike of females, they could have warned us, and I assure you we would have been well away. Since you must not travel for a while, we must be the ones to leave." She lifted her small chin proudly. "I will tell Mama. She will cancel all of her invitations, and we will absent ourselves as soon as possible." Amanda turned and headed for the door.

The sight of her stiff back retreating filled Jack with remorse. She had gone to considerable trouble for him this day, and had the right to expect better treatment from him. "No! Wait, Miss Garfield. I did not mean to offend you."

She turned around, a strange look on her face. "That is the second time you have addressed me as Miss Garfield, my lord. I am Miss Amanda Garfield. I am the younger sister, you see, by a few minutes. You will meet my beautiful twin later."

The thought that occurred to Amanda then hurt her very much. *He thinks I am the older sister everyone says is so beautiful, and is disappointed. That is why he wishes to leave so soon. Once he sees Penny, he will change his mind.*

"Please excuse my rude outburst," Jack said. "I spoke harshly, and unforgivably. But can you find it in your heart to forgive me anyway?" Seeing no sign of such a dispensation in her expression, he tried to explain himself. "I do not dislike females. It is only that I have need of some time to recruit my strength. I found London's gaiety overwhelming after the grimness of war. The very fact that I would speak so rudely to you must tell you that I am not fit for the company of ladies just now. I need a respite before launching myself into the *ton* again. Will you accept my apology for expressing myself so clumsily? After I have had a few weeks to myself, I will welcome the opportunity to know all of your family better. Doubtless we shall all meet in London next Season.''

Amanda studied him gravely. He was a charming man; his coaxing voice and rueful smile drew her irresistibly to lay down her irritated pride. He seemed sincere enough; perhaps he deserved her compassion rather than her censure. But she would reserve judgment about his sincerity. Doubtless he would change his mind about leaving once he saw Penelope.

"Very well, my lord. I understand. You will not wish to come down to dinner after all, as mother has invited half the county. She can inform our neighbors of the need to cancel our other engagements after we dine." She curtsied formally, and left the room.

Jack watched her go, damning himself for a churlish fellow, for in spite of her words, in her stiff posture he read hurt pride. To have offended Amanda distressed him greatly. He spoke no more than the truth when he told her his behavior was a measure of just how disaffected he was, for ordinarily he enjoyed the company of women, and was never clumsy in his address toward them.

His dislike for her mother's plans remained. He did not wish to meet the county, nor to be entertained. He especially did not wish to dance attendance on The Beauty. *If Amanda is plain beside her, she must be a beauty indeed, with all the spoiled self-centeredness that implies. I must surely disgrace myself if I have to deal with such as her in my current unpleasant state of mind.*

In spite of regret at offending Amanda, he felt a great sense of relief that he had carried his point. He was glad to be spared a journey into Scotland anytime soon, for his bruised flesh ached fiercely, and the roads that led to his hunting box were little more than rutted paths. *Not a journey I care to make in this condition. Miss Amanda had the right of it on that score.* He wondered if he would still be welcome to hunt with the Garfields, though. Sir Edwin would be understandably inhospitable to a man who had snubbed his daughters.

Chapter Three

"But what am I to do?" Lady Garfield moaned. "I have plans for almost every evening of this week, and have accepted on his behalf several invitations from the neighboring families."

"You will have to tell them the truth, that Lord Maitland does not feel able to participate in society at this time. They will attribute it to his recent fall." Amanda twisted her hands in her skirt, feeling great sorrow at her mother's distress. "They will understand."

"Well, I don't understand." Sir Edwin, usually so mild in manner, struck his fist angrily on his knee. "It is as good as ordering my wife and daughters out of the house. Very high in the instep, he must be, to think he can do such a thing."

Caspian put his hand on his father's shoulder. "Not in the least, sir. He has been blue-deviled lately, that is all."

"Didn't I tell you?" Tom said. "Pity you did not get my note, Cass, in time to prevent Mother from planning these things." He took his mother's hand in his and patted it. "I did ask you not to go ahead with your plans, you know."

"I should have listened to you, Tom." Lady Garfield put her handkerchief to her eyes. "Well, I certainly shall go to Brighton, or perhaps abroad, for I won't ever dare to show my face in this county again."

"You shan't leave, I tell you! My wife will not be insulted in this manner. I'll speak to this young puppy myself."

"No, Papa." Penelope stood up, her arms flung out dramatically. "That poor, poor man. He must be very unhappy. We must do just as he asks, and let him have his rest. I shall count it an honor to be inconvenienced for such a brave man."

Caspian winked at Amanda. They often laughed fondly

at Penelope's excessive sensibility. "I have a confession to make. I did receive Tom's letter. I simply decided to ignore it. You see, I felt that the last thing Jack needs is to withdraw from society. He mustn't be allowed to turn reclusive. Father, you remember William Turner? You told us he became a hermit after returning from America. Something happened to him there, you said, that changed him forever. It is my belief that Jack is in danger of a similar existence, or worse, if he is allowed to sink into despondency. I am determined he shall neither remain here to sit by himself while we men go hunting, nor go to his hunting box. What is wanted is precisely the social activity he seeks to avoid. What is wanted is Penelope's pretty face looking admiringly at him, inviting him not to think about the dark past, but to focus on a bright future."

Amanda did not resent this slight of her own person, being all too well aware of the vast difference between herself and her sister in their effect upon males. But she felt her brother should be put into possession of all of Lord Maitland's objections. "I should warn you that he suspects us of conspiring to make a match for him," she said. "In fact, he took up the word 'schemes,' which I used to describe Mama's plans, as if they referred to some sinister plan to entrap him."

Penelope's nostrils flared at this. "I have no need to scheme for a husband!"

"No, you don't, and so he will know the minute he lays eyes on you." Cass laughed and flicked her cheek with his finger. "Which is going to be right now. Come, sister. We go to rally the hero." He held out his hand to Penelope, who glanced at her father and mother. They made no objection.

"Amanda, what do you think? You have talked to him."

Amanda surrendered her reservations. "I think Cass is right. Go to him, Penny. You cannot help but cheer him up."

So Penny allowed herself to be led upstairs on a mission of mercy, while Amanda watched, dreading but not doubting the outcome, and feeling a bit blue-deviled herself, to once again face the fact of her plainness. *I had no cheering effect on him whatsoever,* she thought, biting her lower lip. *In fact, all he could think of was departing, but I feel sure he will change his mind now.*

Tom raised no protest to their scheme, but after the pair had left he said, "I shall feel guilty whether he stays or goes, for I promised him he would not have to do the pretty. He isn't high in the instep, Father, but if you had seen how the females were falling all over him, you would understand his wish for some masculine society."

Sir Edwin frowned. "Once he can get about again, he shall have it. How long did Dr. Bruce say he must wait, Mandy?"

"A week or two before he can go about on horseback. But he did say he could join your shooting party in a few days if we transport him to the fields in a gig."

Lady Garfield emerged from her brown study. "I wish Penelope had not gone up to him. If he thinks we are scheming to attach him to her, it might make it impossible for her to . . . to . . ."

"Attach him to her," Tom and Amanda finished for her in unison. Everyone began to laugh, and in perfect good humor left their family conference to dress for dinner.

Jack stirred restlessly in the bed. Tired of watching his valet look as if he smelled something disgusting, he inquired, "What is it, Haskins? Am I still in the doghouse for having mistrusted your devotion to my baggage?"

"It is not my place to criticize you, my lord."

"When has that ever stopped you?" Jack shook his head. His valet was something of a law unto himself. Originally a groom and then a footman in his father's house, he had served Jack devotedly from the day the viscount promoted him to valet, determined to have one servant who was loyal to himself instead of to his father, the Earl of Chalwicke. As a groom and footman Haskins had always been the one he could count on not to carry tales to his father, the one who would help him elude the constant, stifling supervision that his father felt necessary for his only son. Those occasional few hours of freedom, Jack often thought, had saved him from becoming a candidate for Bedlam.

Haskins expressed his opinions freely, criticizing, scolding, and praising as if Jack had been his nursling instead of a grown man and his employer. Jack stood for his imper-

tinence because in addition to his loyalty, the man could
do just about anything, from turning him out to perfection
in the latest fashions, to cleaning and loading his guns, to
doctoring his favorite horse when the head groom had
given the animal up. When Jack had decided to join
Wellington in Brussels in defiance of his father's orders,
Haskins had insisted on coming with him, and had proven
himself steady under fire, too.

"Come, man, speak up. You think I have blotted my
copybook, don't you?"

"To behave so to any young woman would have been
reprehensible, but particularly to such a kind lady."

Jack sighed and sat up. "You are right, of course. But I
simply don't want to . . ."

"Do anything that your father might wish you to do. I
quite understand, my lord. His actions just before Waterloo
were most unethical. But Miss Amanda won't lay siege to
you the way the ladies in London did."

"No, not she. It is The Beauty I am concerned about."

"From what I have heard, it is she who is besieged by
suitors."

Jack swung his leg carefully out from the edge of the
bed, then slid down to test his weight on it. "I devoutly
hope so. At any rate, I owe Caspian better, though I do
feel a bit betrayed by him."

*The spasm has gone. I suppose Dr. Bruce's laudanum
worked,* Jack grudgingly admitted to himself.

Haskins left off buffing Jack's boots to turn his penetrat-
ing blue eyes on his master. "My lord, I think you are
wounded elsewhere than in your leg. I only hope you may
not become one of those men who can never again trust
anyone because their trust has been betrayed once."

"I hope so, too." Jack took a couple of experimental
steps, wincing at the pain that once again shot through his
leg. Suddenly Haskins was at his side, looping Jack's arm
over his shoulder.

"Back to bed, my lord!"

"Oh, leave off, man. I shall do." Jack impatiently tried
to pull away. It was in this posture that Caspian found them
when he came to the viscount's bedroom door.

"Here, let me help," he said, hastening across the room.
It has been easy enough to forestall Haskins, a small man,

but Cass was more than a match for Jack, who found himself once more in bed in spite of his sputtered protests.

"Plague take both of you. I'm bored to flinders. I mean to dress and make my bow to your parents."

Cass lifted a knowing eyebrow. "Blue-deviled, aren't you? And injuring yourself again can't have helped. But we shan't let you leave us, you know. I'm of the opinion that you need to be around people and not off by yourself moping."

"Exactly what I was saying to him, sir." Haskins nodded and put one finger to the side of his nose.

"That will be enough," Jack snapped, embarrassed at his valet's free speech in front of his friend. "You may go find your dinner, Haskins."

"Not until I have found yours, my lord." Haskins bowed and started for the door.

"I told you I meant to dine downstairs."

"Then I must stay and see to dressing you in a manner that does me credit, in spite of that bandaged leg."

"Haskins . . ."

"I will see where the rest of your baggage has gone." Another thing Jack's valet knew was when to make a strategic retreat.

Cass laughed. "Being an invalid is not something you do well, Jack."

"And glad I am of it. Nothing I despise as much as a malingerer. So, traitor. You participated in this scheme to 'entertain' me, for my own good, of course."

"Of course!" Cass sat on the side of the bed. "Look here, Jack. If you find we are not to your taste, of course you will leave us once you are recovered from today's fall, but I think it would be a mistake. As I said . . ."

"I know, I know. Cass, do you ever dream about it?" Jack's voice dropped, and he looked away.

"God in heaven, yes. At first, I didn't, because my duties as Wellington's aide in Paris kept me busy. But here, every so often I wake up in a sweat, fighting the battle all over again."

"Ah!" Jack's eyes met Cass's. "But do you find images of it rising up at you in the midst of daily activities? Sometimes I think I am going insane. When my horse reared today . . ."

"Right back in it, weren't you? The first time I went out shooting with my father and brothers, I could barely control my trembling well enough to aim."

"Yes, that is how I fear it will be with me. But at least it will be among men. I am no fit company for ladies right now. Your sweet little sister Amanda can testify to that."

Cass nodded, understanding in his eyes. "All the more reason to join them, do the pretty, and accustom yourself."

"You think so?"

"I know so. And a pretty face is a wonderful antidote to those grim memories, I have found."

"Yes, I heard how you physicked yourself with that French countess. But you won't wish me to take that draught here among your family."

Cass threw his head back and roared with laughter. "You damn well better not. Pity your injury prevented you from going with me to Paris to take that dose. No, I am afraid you will have to content yourself with the milder medicine that gently bred females can administer."

"Oh, very well. If you really want such a surly guest."

"Excellent. My sister is waiting outside, hoping to have a word with the hero."

"To comb my hair with a stool, no doubt."

"Not Penelope! She was quite indignant to hear how I had lured you here under false pretenses. If you show the slightest aversion to her, I fear she'll bully Mama into packing and leaving at first light."

"Which would put me forever in her debt. But I meant Amanda. She was considerably insulted, and I don't blame her."

"Oh, Amanda." Cass waved his hand as if to brush away a gnat. "She will follow Penny's lead. You will quickly find who rules the roost here, but she is a most benevolent dictator. Shall I bring her in?"

Jack sat up in the bed, tucking his brocade robe firmly closed over his nightshirt and pulling the covers across his legs to block the sight of his limbs, to say nothing of his scars, from the sight of a young lady. "I hate having to be seen like this."

"Believe me, it can only make you more romantic in her eyes." Cass moved toward the door, and in seconds Jack found himself in the presence of the most beautiful creature he had ever seen. Here indeed was the perfect oval face, the classical nose, the vivid blue eyes and guinea-gold curls that Winston and Hal had described to him. They had not exaggerated her other charms, either. Miss Garfield possessed a fine bosom, which the V-neckline of the deep blue dress she was wearing displayed beautifully.

Jack noted with pitying amusement that Amanda had been wearing an exact copy of this dress. The color and style had not become her, but Miss Garfield they suited to perfection.

He took her shapely, slender hand in his as they were introduced. "If anything, Mr. Bingham and Lord Penstock understated your beauty, Miss Garfield. You quite take my breath away," he said, and meant every word.

Penelope shook her head, making bright golden curls bounce around her oval face. The fine blue eyes misted over. "It is you who take my breath away, Lord Maitland. To think that I am in the presence of the hero who almost single-handedly steadied Vivian's line . . ."

Jack schooled his features. This kind of adulation was just what he disliked. His voice carefully modulated, he responded, "My role has been drastically overstated. Every man on that battlefield was a hero that day. I wish you will say nothing more of it. It is in the past. Instead, I prefer to look forward to this opportunity to be dazzled by your beauty."

"Why, he is a flirt," Penny laughed. "From your account of him, Cass, I thought him a serious-minded fellow. So you do not intend to leave us? I am so glad!"

Jack dared to kiss her hand. "Your pleasure makes my joy complete. I am told by my keepers that I must not join the men for a few days, but suddenly I am glad. It will give me more time to further our acquaintance, which I find I greatly desire."

Penelope lowered her eyes demurely. "I, too," she whispered, quite as if she had never received such fulsome praise before. Then her natural vivacity reasserted itself. "I shall see that you are not bored. Since you cannot join us tonight, after dinner we can bring the party to you."

"Now, Penny, that will be doing it a bit too brown," Cass objected.

"You are very kind," Jack responded gallantly. "But I intend to join you downstairs."

"Oh, no. I won't be the cause of your risking further injury. I could never forgive myself."

In most other young women, Jack would have found her effusiveness, her histrionic manner, annoying. But it was difficult to be annoyed by such a breathtaking beauty, especially when it was clear that she was utterly sincere in every word she said. He smiled indulgently as she clutched at her brother's sleeve.

"We shall have my practice piano brought up. Lord Maitland shall have music, and cards, too, if he likes." She seemed almost to bounce with excitement. "Or forfeits, or . . ."

"Enough! Pen, you will frighten him into bolting. Come, it is time to go and allow the stubborn fellow to dress for dinner, for I see he means to forestall your plans." He took his sister by the elbow and began steering her out of the room. She called back over her shoulder, "One way or another, we shall see you shortly, shan't we, my lord?"

Jack smiled and nodded his head. When the door had closed and silence settled into the room, he sighed. Penelope Garfield was a beauty, and delightful. Moreover, she did not seem to be the selfish, self-centered creature he had expected. Could such a thing exist as a woman as beautiful on the inside as on the outside? *Cass, I shall have my revenge on you if you have found me a wife, for I had meant to make my father squirm for some time before I married.*

Amanda felt a flush rising to her cheeks at the news that the viscount would stay. It wasn't pleasure or embarrassment that brought the color, though, but anger. Not at anyone in particular, just at the way of the world. She had expected no less than for Viscount Maitland to change his mind about leaving after meeting Penny. After all, Penny was beautiful, and he was a man. Men wanted beautiful wives if they could get them, and Jack Stanwell could get any woman he wanted, merely with that smile and perhaps a few melting looks from those tawny eyes. Even more so could Viscount Maitland, heir to the Earl of Chalwicke, a title that could make a much less attractive man than he irresistible to the ambitious. *Not that Penny is ambitious,*

Amanda scolded herself. *But neither is she unaware of the advantages of rank.*

The greatest part of her anger, she realized, was reserved for herself, for feeling anything but indifference toward the viscount. She knew better: after all, didn't she have a mirror? She could see her mousy hair, thin face, colorless eyes, and turned-up nose as well as anyone.

Fortunately for her equanimity, no one noticed her agitation. When Cass and Penny, after changing clothes, joined them in greeting their invited guests, everyone turned eagerly to them to discover the outcome of their visit with the viscount. The rest of the family exchanged relieved glances when Cass announced that Maitland had changed his mind and would stay. Lady Garfield was in transports when she learned he even intended to join them for dinner. The other guests, who knew only that he had taken a spill, murmured their pleasure at this news, especially Kathryn Majors and Barbara Satterfield, Amanda and Penny's closest friends, who were to stay with them for a few weeks. They yearned to make the acclaimed hero's acquaintance at the earliest possible moment.

Chapter Four

❧

When Lord Maitland entered the Chinese drawing room where the Garfields' guests had assembled before dinner, all eyes turned toward him, staring avidly as he limped his way across the room. *Surely the most uncomfortable entrance I have ever made into a drawing room,* he thought. *Now I know what Byron experiences all of the time.* Tension tightened his shoulder blades as Caspian introduced him to Sir Edwin and Lady Lucinda Garfield. He expected no less than the frosty air with which Lady Garfield acknowledged him, but was pleasantly surprised by Sir Edwin's hearty and unmistakably genuine welcome. The short, dark-haired baronet proudly led Jack around the room, introducing him to upward of a dozen of the local gentry.

The Garfields' guests included a retired general whom Jack had met before. After the formal round of introductions had been completed, and Jack had taken a small glass of sherry, General Draycourt approached him and began to explain all of the mistakes Wellington had made at Waterloo. Since Jack knew that Draycourt had been one of Wellington's harshest critics during the Peninsular war, he felt more irritated than enlightened by the general's opinions. While nodding and murmuring soothingly to the elderly man's diatribe, he surveyed the room, admiring the way the decorator had managed to incorporate the current fashion for Chinese decor without making the room look garish. As he scanned the room, he saw the divine Miss Garfield.

Unsurprisingly, she was the center of a large group of young people who all seemed to be laughing and talking at once. She wore an ivory satin dress that draped most seductively over that magnificent bosom. The neckline was

once again a deep V, and under the bosom a wide cummer-
bund of bright gold further accented her womanly figure.
Jack idly looked around for Amanda. Surely she wouldn't
dare to wear such a dress!

He found her at the periphery of the group, smiling as
she listened to the others talk, but saying nothing herself.
Jack sighed as he saw that she had, indeed, dressed identically to her sister. Her slight figure did not show to advantage in such a style, and the color made her skin look
sallow. *I wonder whose idiotic notion it is to dress her like
her twin—her mother's, or hers?*

His sigh offended the general, who snapped, "I see I am
boring you, sir."

"I beg your pardon, General. I am not really a military
man, you know. These technicalities are beyond me. I admire your grasp of strategy, though."

Somewhat mollified, the general drew breath to begin
again, when they were joined by Sir Edwin, who charged
right into a new conversational gambit. "Came a cropper
today, eh, my lord? A bad business, bad business indeed.
Nervous animals, horses. I daresay you never would have
been thrown had you been riding a mule, Lord Maitland."

So unexpected and outlandish was this declaration that
Jack could only stare.

Sir Edwin chuckled at his guest's astonishment. "Thought
my boy might have told you that I breed the finest mules
this side of Spain. Likely better, though I plan to travel
there and see for myself. Now that they have lifted the
embargo on their giant jacks, we shall see fewer spills such
as you took today, for I expect the riding mule to replace
the horse. You look surprised, sir. But cross a Spanish jack
with a fine Arab mare and you have the best riding animal
that may be! Excellent gait, stamina, calm disposition.
When their saddle is fitted properly, no horse can beat
them."

"Pfaugh. You and your mules!" The general turned on
his heel and went in search of more congenial company.

Jack did not voice his reservations, as he had no wish to
offend his host again. Sir Edwin saw through him, though.
"You have a very expressive countenance, Lord Maitland.
I see that you doubt me, though you are too polite to say
so."

"I know the value of mules, Sir Edwin. I have seen them pull baggage carts at twice the weight a similar team of horses could manage. But I confess it is difficult for me to imagine how a mule could have avoided a flying wheel, any more than my horse could."

"But if you knew how devoted mules are to their own safety, you would understand. Your mule would have had his eyes open and those long ears working forward and back, on the lookout for danger. He'd doubtless have heard the crash, spotted the wheel rolling toward him, and taken evasive action on the instant, whereas all your silly horse ever thinks to do is rear and squeal in terror."

Since this was exactly what Jack's newly purchased hunter had done, he could not really deny this indictment of equine folly.

Sir Edwin was high on his hobbyhorse and pressing hard. "Your horse will take risks for you all day. Put him at a high brick wall, and he'll jump it without knowing what's on the other side. He'll take your word for it that he may land safely. But your mule is a thinking beast. He'll look at that wall, calculate his odds of surviving the jump to a nicety, and if they do not seem to him to be in his favor, that's an end to it."

And to you, Jack thought, a vivid picture forming in his mind of Sir Edwin sailing over the head of his mount. His mouth curved skeptically. "Excuse me, sir, but that does not seem to be an advantage. A balk at the wall can be dangerous. I suppose that is why mules aren't ridden in the hunt."

"Not ridden in the hunt! Not ridden in the hunt!" Sir Edwin's voice rose, causing several people to turn and look inquiringly at them. "There you are far out, m'boy. I ride my Cleopatra to hounds every year, and I'm never late for the kill. She'll take the jumps if she knows they are safe, and why should I risk my neck when they are not? She forces me to exercise better judgment about where to jump. That's why I insist my daughters ride them." Sir Edwin paused a second, and Jack thought something like sadness shadowed his eyes for a moment. "My boys did, too, when they were young and inexperienced. Now, of course, they must have horses, being gentlemen of fashion." Sir Edwin's tone grew indulgent. "When they have settled a bit and have families to live for, they'll want the safest mount again."

Caspian, who had joined them several minutes before, put his hand on Sir Edwin's shoulder. "Sir, I have no doubt you will convert Jack to your way of thinking before the end of this visit, but for now he needs sustenance. Mother informs me we must go in to dinner or our cook will resign and return to London."

Sir Edwin's eyes widened. "An alarming thought. Next to talking about mules, Lord Maitland, my dinner ranks a very close second for my favorite activity." He beamed up at Jack. "You shall reap the benefit, for my François is quite the best cook ever to pretend a French accent!"

Jack laughed. *What a charming man,* he thought. *I know where Caspian gets his easy address, and where Penelope gets her vivacity.* A moment's reflection and he realized Sir Edwin was also the principal contributor to Amanda's stature and facial features, so different from the magnificent Penelope's. He glanced across the room at Lady Garfield. *Yes, she is the source of Cass and Penelope's height and coloring, while Tom and Amanda favor their father.*

It was Jack's duty to take Lady Lucinda Garfield in to dinner. The statuesque Lady Garfield was still very striking, her blond hair little touched by gray. She was also exceedingly cold toward him, so he set himself to charm her out of her frosty air. He could not have hit upon a better subject than to praise her elder daughter. "I must tell you, my lady, that Penelope's beauty is quite astonishing. Has Sir Thomas Lawrence taken her likeness yet?"

His hostess immediately launched into a detailed narration of the eagerness with which any number of portrait painters had painted Penelope. "You must allow me, when your leg is better, to take you up to the long gallery. We have pictures of her from the time she was in the cradle. She was a beauty even then, you know."

"I don't doubt it. Of course, she has a beautiful mother, whom she nearly resembles."

That demolished whatever remained of Lady Garfield's reserve. She tucked her chin down and tilted her head to one side in a universal feminine gesture that said, "I am too modest to agree, but of course you are right."

"And Miss Amanda is a very attractive young lady as

well, though I collect she takes after her father's side of
the family."

Lady Garfield murmured, "You are very kind, Lord
Maitland. Poor Amanda. However, she has many excellen-
cies, sir, and will make someone a wonderful wife."

Jack had been sincere in his praise, and felt a strong
surge of indignation on Amanda's behalf. Fortunately for
their newly created rapprochement, they had now gained
the dining room and Lady Garfield turned to her duties as
hostess, indicating where her numerous guests should sit,
as if name cards did not grace all of their places.

Dinner very nearly put Jack in the megrims again. He
had been seated between Miss Barbara Satterfield and Miss
Kathryn Majors, friends of the Garfield sisters. With a sinking heart he learned that they were also houseguests for
the next few weeks. *More females to entertain and fend off,*
he thought morosely.

Miss Satterfield would have been considered a diamond
of the first water in any gathering, her dark clouds of ringlets framing a face almost as perfectly Grecian as Penelope's. Miss Majors, like Amanda, was attractive though not
a beauty. She quickly found an excuse to inform Jack that
her red hair should be described as Titian. A few freckles
bespoke a battle with the sun that had not quite been won.
Both young ladies alternately flirted, simpered, and pitied
him until he felt he must roar out his displeasure.

He glanced down the table enviously toward where Penelope sat, with Lord Penstock on one side and one of
the local gentry on the other. *Lucky Winston*, he thought,
watching The Beauty's animated countenance enviously. In
a pause between onslaughts from his dinner partners, he
turned his attention to Amanda. She was seated across the
table at about the halfway point, next to a balding man in
his late thirties, a substantial if not yet obese man with the
peaches-and-cream complexion of a young girl. This worthy, who had been introduced to him with the unlikely
name of Tittlecue, seemed to be explaining something of
importance to Amanda, who looked down as if deeply absorbed by her dinner. She nodded from time to time but
did not appear to be making any other response.

Prosy bore, Jack concluded, from her manner and the
look on her face. *Hal should rescue her.* But Hal Bingham,

her other dinner partner, ignored her to stare across the table at Penelope, straining to hear what was said.

He shook his head, smiling. *Hal is overmatched, I fear, for Winston, whatever his flaws, can charm when he exerts himself.* Darkly handsome, with a title as well as a fortune, Lord Penstock was almost as eligible as Jack. Reflecting upon some unsavory incidents from the past, Jack wondered just how enthusiastically the Garfields would receive Lord Penstock's suit if they were aware of his frequenting of low gaming houses and prostitutes. Certainly they would have no idea that he had been suspected of underhanded dealing in assorted horse races.

He wondered if he should give the Garfields a hint, but rejected the idea. *Perhaps Win has reformed. After all, he is thinking of marriage, which he certainly never did before. And if I decide to court Miss Garfield myself, it might seem I was being underhanded, seeking to eliminate a rival by carrying tales.*

Jack knew he needed no such gambits. Based on his past experience with the ladies, he had confidence that he could win Penelope if he tried.

As for poor Hal, he stands little chance with The Beauty, Jack thought, *whether or not I join the contest.* Untitled, prosperous but not wealthy, Hal could only be described as passable in looks, with a rather bulbous nose and thinning dark blond hair. His considerable height was not accompanied by a proportional amount of flesh, giving him a gaunt, hungry look. Worst of all, when with the ladies Hal had no conversation. A very talented poet, he became utterly tongue-tied when required to keep up his end of a fast-paced discussion. He was more likely to admire from afar than to actively court a woman, as his rival Lord Penstock was doing.

Reflecting on the expensive but tasteful decor of the Garfields' handsome Palladian mansion, and the air of prosperity that hung over the estate, Jack knew that the Garfield misses, though the daughters of an obscure baronet, would be well dowered. Baron Penstock, who had no parents to please in his selection of a wife, would find no obstacle of birth or fortune to prevent him from marrying Penelope.

I wonder what my father would say to her. A moment's consideration, and Jack knew that the Earl of Chalwicke would regard the Garfields as barely eligible, in fact, a step down if not an actual mésalliance, for his son and heir. *No, indeed!* Jack's mouth turned down as he remembered his father's machinations, attempting to shackle his son to the daughter of the Marquess of Ridgewell, whose chief attraction was her long, distinguished pedigree.

"Don't you agree, Lord Maitland?" Sir Edwin's voice drew his attention again to his end of the table.

"I am sorry, Sir Edwin, I was not attending."

"No, of course not. Had your eyes on my girl, eh? Well, she is a treat, I admit." The fond father beamed at him. "I asked you what you thought of these new corn laws?"

Jack shook his head. "I am sorry, Sir Edwin, but I take little notice of politics. It all seems to me to be much argufying and little accomplishment."

"The problem as I see it is that this administration is accomplishing too much. The six acts, the corn laws . . . If we are not careful, all of our English liberties will be lost. Thank heavens this war is finally over, for the need for security has been the government's cloak for this attack on the British constitution."

"But, Sir Edwin," Barbara Satterfield said, "we cannot allow these common laborers to take over the country. Papa says . . ."

Kathryn Majors put her hand on Jack's arm to draw his attention. "For my part, I do not think it seemly for a female to put herself forward in a political discussion, do you, Lord Maitland?"

Jack smiled. "Perhaps Miss Satterfield is better informed in the matter than I."

"Pooh! She only parrots what her father says. Do you like to be read to, my lord?"

"Well, I . . ."

"Because I know you will be bored to flinders these next few weeks, with all of the men off hunting. I am told I read charmingly, and I would be most happy to keep you entertained. I have brought one of Mrs. Hannah Moore's wonderful books with me." She leaned a little closer and whispered conspiratorially, "I fear that Miss Garfield is inclined to light reading, such as must offend a man of your consequence. Why, she has read Byron's *The Corsair.* Would you credit it?"

Jack suppressed a deep sigh. While he composed his answer, which he hoped would be both polite and utterly quelling of her wish to read him improving literature, he lifted his wineglass, from which he had already been partaking much more liberally than usual.

Fortunately, just then their hostess stood and invited the ladies to join her in the Chinese drawing room, while the men discussed their politics, horses, and hunting over their port. Jack appreciated the general female withdrawal. That feeling of being under siege had washed over him again. *This is going to be every bit as bad as I had feared. As soon as I can tolerate riding, I am off to Scotland, in spite of The Beauty,* he promised himself.

Chapter Five

～

To Jack's regret, the men did not linger over their port. Sir Edwin rose after no more than half an hour of desultory conversation, saying, "I know you young bucks are all impatient to join the ladies." Certainly he spoke the truth as regards most of the young men present. Winston and Hal led the charge back to the Chinese drawing room, where they found all of the younger women clustered at one end of the room, looking through fashion magazines, and the older generation at the other, discussing subjects maternal and wifely.

Both groups quickly broke up when the gentlemen joined them. Several new groups formed, the largest of these clustered about Penelope, who sought Jack out, a mischievous grin on her face; she wished to know what he thought of women shooting. "If you approve, shall we join you at your hunt, Lord Maitland?" she asked provocatively. The mischief in her eyes told him she had a fair idea of his thoughts on the matter without asking.

Jack looked down at the lovely face turned up to him. "I am in a great perplexity as to how to answer that. If you are keen to learn to shoot, nothing would please me more than to be your gun bearer. But in general, the thought of the fairer sex armed with guns is more alarming to me than any number of French regiments."

Amid laughter and words of support from the other young men, Penny responded, "Gallant toward me, but not toward my sex, Lord Maitland!" She tossed her head. "As it happens, I do not wish to hunt with the men. Poor little partridges. And it quite breaks my heart to think of anyone shooting the beautiful pheasants. But Miss Satterfield's brother has taught her to shoot, and she recommends it to me as an exciting pursuit."

"I am as good a shot as my brother, Lord Maitland," Barbara Satterfield asserted in response to his obvious skepticism. "And shame on you, Penny, for pretending to pity the partridges, for I am sure you ate your partridge pie with relish this evening."

Lord Penstock, who had looked daggers at Jack during this discussion, bid for The Beauty's attention. "If you decide to learn to shoot, Miss Garfield, please give me the honor of teaching you. I have no fear of stray bullets, you see, for you have already wounded me fatally with those beautiful eyes."

Penelope batted those fatal eyelashes at him, clearly delighted by his tribute.

Amanda stood at the back of the group, listening to Lord Penstock praising her sister, a fond smile bringing her dimples into play. "What of you, Miss Amanda?" Jack asked, seeking to bring her into the conversation. "Do you wish to become a Diana, or to form a league to suppress shooting parties?"

Surprised at being singled out, Amanda found no witty words at the tip of her tongue, so she could only state her feelings prosaically. "I am very fond of partridge, Lord Maitland, and François can do wonderful things with pheasants that I would be loath to do without, so I cannot in good conscience deplore hunting them. But I prefer not to contemplate the living animal too much when I am dining, so I would not wish to shoot them, or even be present when they are shot."

This pronouncement was met with a chorus of bravas or objections. Penny demanded of her sister, "But wouldn't you enjoy learning to shoot, Amanda? You love archery, and you are very good at it. I should think you would find firing at targets would suit you to the ground."

Amanda nodded her head, but before she could speak, Mr. Tittlecue, the substantial man who had sat next to her during dinner, and who now stood behind her looking down a disapproving nose at the company, weighed in. "As for shooting game, the thought of gently bred females engaged in such a sanguine activity offends every feeling. Moreover, the hunters and their servants will be much safer without the distraction of female participation or audience. And Miss Amanda will certainly not wish to participate in target shooting. What could be more disgusting to a delicate female than to soil her hands and stun her ears with firearms?"

Amanda clearly wanted to reply, but he gave her no opening. "It is an entirely unfitting occupation for young ladies, as I should think your father would have told you, Miss Satterfield. But the Satterfields have ever had a careless attitude toward their daughters, permitting them to learn Latin and ride astride and engage in all sorts of unseemly activities."

This long-winded pronouncement, spoken in a chastising tone as if he had been routing a group of naughty schoolchildren, caused a sudden quiet among the heretofore lively group. Since no one wished to give him a setdown and complete the destruction of the festive atmosphere, he continued unchallenged, delivering himself of a diatribe against modern females and modern manners. While he spoke the group began to dissipate, edging away one at a time, until only Amanda, Penelope, and Jack were left at the pink pomposity's mercy. Curiosity held Jack in place. He could see that Penelope was furious, for her face had grown flushed, and those magnificent eyes flashed fire. He almost held his breath as he waited to see whether she would give Mr. Tittlecue the sharp side of her tongue.

Amanda, however, forestalled the setdown her sister looked ready to pronounce. When Mr. Tittlecue was at last forced to draw breath, she seized her chance. "Perhaps we should organize some games, Penny, or a musicale? We have several accomplished musicians among us, Lord Maitland. We even have a small chamber orchestra that rehearses assiduously during the winter months."

As Amanda made polite conversation, Penny obviously struggled with herself to tamp down her anger and behave as she ought. To Jack's admiration, she won the struggle, and fixed a smile on her face as she excused herself to arrange entertainment for their guests.

Jack resisted the desire to follow her, out of pity for Amanda. *Bad enough she had to listen to this prosy bore during supper. She shouldn't have to entertain him alone, or rather, to listen to his sermonizing, after dinner as well.*

The obnoxious Mr. Tittlecue seemed oblivious to the havoc his remarks had wrought. He regarded Jack from under lowered brows. "Heard you discussing mules with our good host before dinner. Are you a mule fancier, Lord Maitland?"

"I have little personal experience of them, sir, but I know that his Royal Highness the Duke of Cumberland had some especially fine mules for his baggage train. I had the pleasure of seeing them on parade during the recent celebrations. Very impressive."

"Yes, I saw them, too. Sir Edwin has bred better, though. My haymow is pulled by a pair from his Spanish jack and my shire horses. None can equal them for strength, I can tell you! But mules can excel in any arena that the horse can. As Sir Edwin said, if you had been mounted on a mule, you would likely have escaped injury today."

Jack glanced at Amanda to see how she received this preposterous statement. Her lips were compressed, but her light eyes flashed with amusement, and she looked away as soon as they met his, to avoid breaking out in laughter, he guessed.

"As I told Sir Edwin, I do not see how, Mr. Tittlecue. Unless the beasts can fly?"

"Ah, you can speak with levity of a situation that your sad condition makes all too clear is not a fit subject for humor. You young blades are all alike. You think that a gentleman of fashion wouldn't be seen riding a mule. Well, let me tell you, my lord, I have some pretensions to fashion myself, and I am proud to be carried by my Giselle. She is by Hercules out of a thoroughbred mare, and can be counted on to lead the hunt! Takes the highest jumps . . ."

"Mr. Tittlecue, I beg you will take pity on Lord Maitland and say no more on this topic this evening," Amanda said, touching his forearm briefly. "Between you and my father, he has probably already learned more about mules tonight than he cares to know."

Tittlecue drew himself up, a thunderous expression on his face. Jack sought to forestall the diatribe he saw coming. "I certainly intend to look over his stock while I am here."

"Ah, but will you ride one? I challenge you to do so, my lord, when you are able to sit a saddle again. You have proved your bravery in battle, but are you brave enough to appear before yon posturing young cocks on so unfashionable a mount?"

Jack bristled. How dare this pompous nodcock speak to him so?

"I say, Amanda," Tittlecue went on before Jack could find a suitable setdown, "if we could but convince a man of the ton such as Lord Maitland to ride one of your father's mules in Hyde Park, it might serve to bring them into fashion, eh?"

He looked down at Amanda with an air both conspiratorial and proprietary. Suddenly Jack realized why Tittlecue had ranged himself with the young people instead of joining his host and the other more mature guests, and why he seemed so truculent toward Jack. *He fancies himself her suitor, and sees me as a potential rival.* It was a bizarre thought. Not only was the man too old for her, and a bore besides, he was a huge man, several inches over Jack's five feet eleven inches and fully fleshed besides. In another ten years he would be massively obese, Jack guessed. The idea of him as dainty Amanda's husband was distasteful in the extreme. *It would be a shire horse covering a Shetland pony.*

Caspian appeared at his elbow and prevented him from crossing verbal swords with Tittlecue. "Penelope has organized a musical evening for us, Jack. I protected you, though, assuring her that you could neither play nor sing."

Jack welcomed the intervention, for he felt a strong desire to come to cuffs with the obnoxious Tittlecue. A few sarcastic comments upon the self-proclaimed man of fashion's puce and green waistcoat, which gave a hint of his notion of sartorial splendor, would have given Jack a welcome relief for the anger that had been building up in him. *Miss Garfield mastered her emotions, can I do less?*

"You spoke true, Cass. My voice is about as melodious as that of Sir Edwin's mules."

Amanda and Cass laughed; Mr. Tittlecue looked as if he might defend the vocal abilities of mules, but before he could make the attempt, Amanda distracted him. "Did you bring your violin, Basil? I certainly hope so."

"Come, let us sit down," Cass urged Jack. "I am persuaded that your leg is paining you."

Jack tried to refuse, but Cass insisted. "The musicians among us will begin their performances soon. Let us claim seats well away from the piano while they are still available."

"That sounds ominous," he replied. Amanda laughed at the same time that she shook a scolding finger at her brother. She led Tittlecue away, and Jack allowed himself to be escorted to a large, comfortable chair, but shook his head at the offer of a footstool. From this vantage point he watched Amanda walk to the piano on the arm of her huge admirer. *Does she care for him, I wonder? Does she have any intention of marrying him?* The thought of the sprite under the control of that boorish, insensitive man troubled him. *She did not behave fondly toward him,* he reassured himself. *And surely her parents wouldn't force her?*

The Garfields' guests displayed the usual range of musical ability for a gathering of this sort, from the barely tolerable to the sublime. To Jack's surprise, Mr. Tittlecue's performance on the violin fell in the latter group. Miss Satterfield performed credibly two of Thomas Moore's Irish melodies, and Tom unself-consciously displayed a magnificent baritone to good effect in a musical rendition of Ben Johnson's "Drink to Me Only with Thine Eyes," his own eyes never leaving a very young, very pretty girl seated nearby. After everyone who could be dragooned into performing had done so, the company began to demand a duet from Amanda and Penelope.

The sisters, so dissimilar in appearance, had voices so much alike that it was difficult to tell who sang which part. All he knew was that they blended together so perfectly that he felt pure bliss as they performed a duet from *The Marriage of Figaro*. Penny accepted the enthusiastic applause that they garnered as her due, while Amanda, pink-faced with embarrassment, turned away.

Jack prepared to drag his bruised body out of the chair, thinking that surely had been the grand finale. But Amanda replaced Tom at the piano, and accompanied her sister as she sang "Ach, ich Fuhlis" from *The Magic Flute*. Singing solo, Penelope displayed a magnificent, beautifully trained voice, soaring effortlessly to the high notes. More, she actually performed the song, acting it out without inhibitions. It was a stunning performance, well worth the thunderous applause that greeted her final notes.

While not musical himself, Jack enjoyed well-performed music very much. All thoughts of speedy removal to his hunting box disappeared. *I must know more of this beauty,* Jack thought. *She is intelligent, talented, kind, generous, very spirited, and yet has self-control. I begin to believe I cannot leave such a treasure to be won by the likes of Winston Ardel.*

He regretted happening upon Miss Garfield at this time, for he had no wish to gratify his father by marrying so soon after the earl's treachery of a few months before. Then a comforting thought occurred to him: *If I decide to marry her, at least I shall have the satisfaction of knowing that my father will consider that I have married beneath me!*

Chapter Six

As the young men at last made their way to bed that evening, long after everyone else had retired, Hal followed Jack to his room. As soon as the door was closed, he demanded, "Well, what do you think of her?"

"Miss Amanda is a delightful sprite. Miss Satterfield is a bold minx. Miss Majors is a bit of a Puritan. Now, let me see, whom have I left out?" Jack slanted a mischievous grin at his friend.

"Do you mean to have her?" Hal's expression was so lugubrious that Jack took pity on him and left off teasing.

"I don't know, Hal. But I mean to know her better. You and Win did not exaggerate her charms, and she has many good qualities that have nothing to do with beauty."

"I knew it." Hal slumped into a chair in Jack's sitting room. "No man could look at her and not want her. I knew you would go after her."

"Cheer up, Hal. Even if I decide to court her, that doesn't mean she'll have me. A diamond like her will be very particular, I expect."

Hal dropped his head into his hands. "You were not given the sobriquet 'Irresistible Maitland' for no reason. Before Waterloo every eligible female set her cap for you, especially as you would inherit an earldom. And now you're a war hero, too. She'll have you!"

Jack dropped a comforting hand on Hal's shoulder. "Don't be a gudgeon. We may not suit at all. I do not intend to single her out until I have observed her for a while. My intentions were not to marry for some time yet, so she will have to suit me right down to the ground before I'll offer for her. Until then, I'll be most evenhanded in my dealings with these four charmers, lest I end up in parson's mousetrap before times. You will have more than ample time to attach her yourself."

"Attach her?" Hal raised his head. "I can barely talk to her. All I can do is gaze at her! That and write poems about her. But what woman ever preferred a poet to a handsome viscount?"

"You're being too pessimistic. Look at how the females swoon at Byron's feet!"

Hal stood and lifted miserable eyes to meet Jack's gaze. "But I ain't Byron. Not a romantic thing about me. Not handsome, no title, no tormented past, no deformity, nothing!"

"Too bad I can't give you my injury."

Hal scowled. "Forgot about that. One more attraction to your credit. What woman can resist ministering to a man wounded in action? You'll rack up here and spend your days courting her, while I waste shot trying to hit Sir Edwin's partridges." He stalked out of the room.

As he allowed Haskins to undress him, Jack found himself thinking, *What the devil is so desirable about tortured pasts or deformities? Or even battle injuries? I would have a low opinion of a young woman who would be swayed by such as that. If any of those things give me an advantage with Miss Garfield, Hal can have her!*

While Hal and Jack discussed the young women, the daughters of the house were discussing the young men, or more to the point, one man. Amanda and Penny lay in their bed side by side, reviewing the events of the day as they always did.

"What do you think of him?" Penny demanded without preliminaries as soon as their maid had withdrawn.

Unlike Jack, Amanda did not pretend ignorance. "You bowled him over, as usual, Penny." She kept her eyes focused on the Bible she always read for a few moments before retiring. Her pride dictated that she not reveal her strong attraction to a young man who was obviously swept away by her sister's beauty.

"That's not what I asked. I think he is handsome, and charming, and there is a touch of mystery about him that is very intriguing. What do you think?"

"The handsomest man I ever saw," Amanda could but

agree. "And kind, too. Did you notice that he stayed with
me instead of following you as he would have preferred,
only to save me from Mr. Tittlecue's conversation?"

"I hadn't noticed that. Any man who is kind to my dear
sister is my friend already!"

Which perhaps is why he was kind, Amanda thought. But
she did him the justice of rejecting the notion. Unlike some
of the men she had met in London, Jack seemed to her to
be honest about his likes and dislikes, as his rude outburst
earlier in the day demonstrated all too clearly.

"But what about him hints at mystery, my gothic nov-
el–loving sister?" Amanda rolled over on her back and
stared up at the ceiling.

"Oh, I don't know. His eyes look sad. And why has he
not married? He must be quite as old as Tom."

"Who also isn't married," Amanda pointed out. "And
twenty-five is not a great age for a man to remain single."

"Tom hasn't wed because his chosen bride has been in
the nursery until this year. No, I think Lord Maitland has
been jilted. He is a man with a broken heart."

"Penny!" Amanda laughed, a low, indulgent chuckle.

"Well, he is. Or his true love died, or . . ."

"Lord Maitland has reinjured a leg that was so badly
damaged the surgeons wanted to cut it off. He was in a
great deal of pain this evening, and feeling embarrassed for
his previous uncouth behavior besides. I think any dark
shadows you saw in his eyes are well accounted for."

"Mandy, you have no romance in your soul!" Penny
flopped over with her back to her sister. A few moments
of silence ensued. Then, "But you do think he liked me?"

Amanda had no hesitation in reassuring her sister on this
point. "Extremely. Did he not change his mind about leaving the instant he saw you?"

Penny sighed dreamily. "That's true, isn't it. Oh,
Amanda! I may have found my husband at last."

"I knew you would be infatuated with him, but surely
you don't intend to give up Lord Penstock and Mr. Bingham on the basis of so brief an acquaintance?"

"Oh, no, but . . ."

"Penny! Mother's fears were justified. You really cannot
marry three men, dearest."

A giggle preceded a sudden movement as Penny turned

and swatted her sister with her pillow. The spirited fight that ensued, so totally lacking in feminine delicacy, would certainly have startled the young gentlemen in the opposite wing had they been able to witness it.

The Garfields' two gentlemen guests, Mr. Tittlecue and Lord Maitland, had their suite of rooms on the third floor of the east wing, near Tom's and Caspian's rooms. As the other men prepared for their day of hunting early the next morning, the bustle filtered through to Jack, awakening him from a deep sleep. Immediately the aches and pains that sleep had temporarily held at bay demanded his attention, making further rest impossible.

Ringing for Haskins, he got out of bed, groaning as he forced his stiff, sore body into action. When his valet entered the room, a tray with steaming tea and toast in his hands, he greeted his master with "Never say you are going to join the hunting party today!"

Jack kneaded his left thigh ruefully. "No, I think not. My whole body feels as if I had been thrown from a horse. Fancy that."

Haskins smiled. "Indeed, sir. I cannot think why. But since it is so, why do you rise so early?"

"I plan to escape before the young ladies put into action their good intentions for entertaining me! A long walk on the grounds will loosen me up and begin the process of healing. Lying abed, I fear I will ossify." He gulped the tea but left the toast in favor of a more hearty breakfast in the morning room. There he greeted Sir Edwin and traded barbs with Tom and Caspian in the manner of young men everywhere, while Mr. Tittlecue occasionally cast condemning looks their way.

After the other men had gulped down their repast and departed, Jack lingered over his breakfast. He feared no feminine intrusion, the hour being so early. He was mistaken in his complacency, however. He had barely begun the second page of the *London Times,* which Sir Edwin had left behind for him, when Penelope and Amanda entered the room. Today both girls were identically dressed in white sprigged muslin. For once Jack thought the chosen garment suited neither sister, in either color or style, being excessively trimmed with ruffles and lace.

Penelope's attention was on her sister, and she waved her hands about in her dramatic way as she talked. Thus Amanda saw Jack first and momentarily checked, before continuing into the room.

Her eyes scanned his face swiftly. With a satisfied nod, she said, "Good morning, Lord Maitland. You are looking much more the thing today."

Penelope rushed to his side. "Why, you poor man, to be up so early. I expect your injuries made it impossible to sleep in. But why did your valet not bring your breakfast to you, my lord?" She looked as if she would personally fire the negligent servant. *Belligerent and utterly adorable,* Jack thought. Although her dramatic solicitude did not annoy him as it might have done coming from a lesser beauty, he did not wish to play the invalid.

"I am accustomed to rising early, and preferred to come downstairs. And yes, I feel pretty stout today," he replied firmly.

"You see, Penny. He will not tolerate cosseting any more than Tom or Caspian will, so you had better give it up." Amanda helped herself to tea, ham, and toast from the sideboard and took a seat across the table from him. Penny took only a slice of toast with jam and some coffee, and sat down beside him.

"Oh, I know it," she admitted. "We must put our heads together and find some way to keep him from overexerting himself."

"You need not be concerned. Dr. Bruce, who is as excellent as you represented him to be, Miss Amanda, said I might walk, though he advised me not to ride for a day or two."

"A week, surely," Penny challenged him. "Come, Amanda, tell me what Dr. Bruce really said."

Amanda laughed. "He told me a week or two. Now, do leave Lord Maitland to his paper, Penny."

Since it seemed such a good idea to Jack, he lifted the paper again, girding himself to resist Penny's disappointed look. *Best to begin as I mean to go on,* he thought. In his opinion the first domestic duty of a wife was to leave her husband to his paper at the breakfast table.

After they had broken their fast, the girls announced their intention to gather the few remaining roses and then proceed to the succession houses to find enough flowers to freshen up the flower arrangements. Both of them seemed to relish this task; Amanda confided that her mother rarely allowed them the pleasure, as it was her favorite housekeeping duty.

"She welcomes our participation in every other aspect of housekeeping, but ordinarily guards the flowers like a dog with a juicy bone," Penelope added. "But she has so very much to do right now, she said we might. Would you like to accompany us, Lord Maitland?"

"How could I refuse such a charming invitation," he replied. "But only if you will call me Jack. Mind, I do not insist on your reciprocating if you feel it is too soon."

"We should be delighted," Penelope crowed, accepting for both of them. "And by all means, let us drop our Misses, too!"

Amanda looked worried. "You should realize, sir, that if we begin calling you Jack, everyone will."

"That is agreeable. It is largely a family party, after all. I don't wish to be the only person hauling around last names and titles!" Jack had noticed that Penelope addressed Winston as Penstock, and felt smug at succeeding in moving ahead of his old rival. "Shall we be off, then?"

So it was that Jack, who had intended to avoid female companionship that morning, spent it carrying a large basket for Penny and Amanda to fill with flowers, and found it a very agreeable occupation indeed to observe them companionably arguing over who got to pick which rose, or whether a blossom had passed its prime.

They are both charming and intelligent females, he thought. He was especially pleased to see the loving relationship between them. His own sisters had quarreled constantly, jealously comparing their looks, their suitors, and their husbands. Now whenever they came together, their rivalry was renewed over their children's accomplishments.

They had not yet made it to the succession houses by eleven o'clock, as Penelope and Amanda had gladly responded to his request to view all of the pleasure gardens, which included a very impressive statuary and topiary garden. There they sat for a while on a stone bench, one girl on each side of him, admiring the statues in stone and leaf and talking of everything and nothing, when suddenly Barbara Satterfield and Kathryn Majors descended on them. The four young women made a great din greeting one another. The Garfield sisters quizzed their guests for being such slugabeds, and Kathryn and Barbara in turn scolded them for stealing Lord Maitland and hiding him away in the enclosed garden.

Jack began to feel overwhelmed by so much female company. The delight had gone out of the morning, so he was not sorry when their friends reminded the sisters that they were to ride over to have luncheon with the hunters.

"Mr. Bennington was supervising the placement of the hampers in the cart when we left the house. Do hurry, Amanda, Penny, for you are not even dressed for riding."

"I shall stay and read to you if you wish, Lord Maitland," Kathryn said, looking hopefully up at him.

"Much as I appreciate the offer, I need to go round to the stables and have a look at my horses. Several of them were injured in yesterday's accident, you see."

"Will your injury allow you to walk so far?" cried Barbara. "I shall sit with you if you wish to remain here."

"Actually, the walking I have done thus far has been most beneficial, just as Dr. Bruce said it would," Jack replied firmly.

Having repelled these attempts to scale his defenses, he walked with them back to the house, watched them climb the stairs with a sigh of relief, and went through the offices and out the north door, which Bennington had informed him would be the closest path to the stable area.

Chapter Seven

Jack watched as Angus McLean, his groom, walked the bay gelding back and forth. The horse moved carefully, favoring his left hind leg. "You have done a good job, but I think it will prove a fatal injury to Triton in the end," he said as he eyed the bay's battered legs. The thought of putting down such a fine animal made him sad.

"He won't hunt again, that's for sure," McLean responded. "But Mr. Haskins' liniment seemed to ease him somewhat. He may recover enough for a country mount."

Jack nodded. "Then we'll give him a little more time."

McLean led the gelding back into his stall and shut the door before turning to his employer. "What do you think of Sir Edwin's mules?"

The two men stood in the center of the stable block, looking down the rows of stalls. In most of them the inquisitive animals peering out at them had long ears that swiveled back and forth as if trying to eavesdrop on the two men's conversation. "I've not had the opportunity to examine them," Jack replied. "Are they impressive?"

"I've never seen the like," McLean said. "You must go have a look at that Spanish jack of his. Sixteen hands if he's an inch!"

After walking down the corridor and studying the various mules, Jack followed McLean into the next stable block, where the largest jackass he had ever seen brayed at them as they approached. "More like fifteen hands," he said, holding out a carrot for the astonishing animal. "Quite a beast, though. Well, I am impressed, but don't think I will want to adopt mules as my riding stock."

McLean grinned. "You should have seen Sir Edwin, though, up on his riding mule. Proud as a peacock. Calls him Thor."

Shaking his head and laughing, Jack emerged from the stables and blinked in the sun. It was past noon, and hunger had begun to gnaw on him, but somehow taking nuncheon with Lady Garfield, without the buffer of any other company, daunted him, so he sauntered over to the succession houses. He had always had a lively interest in matters horticultural, and if the quality of fruits and vegetables on Sir Edwin's table last night was any indication, the baronet employed a master gardener.

When he entered the first greenhouse, he was surprised to find Amanda there, conferring with an elderly man while the gardener who had assisted him into the house yesterday stood nearby, gently swinging two baskets of produce to and fro. A large basket of hothouse flowers sat on the ground at his feet.

Amanda's eyes widened when she saw him, and she left off her conversation. "Lord Maitland! I made sure you would spend the morning in the stables."

"Jack," he reminded her.

Stepping close enough to whisper, she put her finger to her mouth. "Shhh. Not in front of the servants. T'would give rise to speculation, I fear. Besides, Mother said we were to address you by your surname, that anything else would be encroaching on so recent an acquaintance."

Jack frowned. *Lady Garfield is a high stickler,* he thought.

"Were you looking for me? Is there something I can help you with?"

"No, I thought you had gone with the other ladies. I wanted to see the succession houses. Perhaps you will give me a tour?"

Amanda seemed curiously reluctant. "Mr. Bliss could give you a more informative one."

Jack studied her carefully. "You haven't quite forgiven me for yesterday, have you?"

Amanda hotly denied it. "It is only that I thought you would prefer masculine company."

"Which only proves what I said—you haven't forgiven me. I am wounded to the heart." He struck his chest over that organ forcefully.

"Gracious! Penelope would appreciate such theatrics, sir, but I beg you will spare me." But she smiled, and motioned him to follow her. "Jones, please take the baskets to the

house and put these flowers in water right away. Oh, and
you must speak to François, and ask him if he particularly
requires anything else. Mr. Bliss, I won't keep you from
your work any longer." The head gardener nodded and
excused himself.

They started walking down the aisles of the greenhouse,
Amanda giving a well-informed commentary on both its
contents and their culture as they went. When they reached
the orangery, she sat with him on a bench and looked
around herself with much satisfaction. "Uncle Jasper sent
me the orange and lemon trees from Spain, as well as numerous specimens of exotic plants. They are my mules, I
am afraid."

Jack lifted his eyebrows in surprise. "I've heard plants
and trees described in many ways, but never as mules."

"I mean that I am quite as mad about exotic plants as
Father is about his mules. I am forever botanizing, you
see."

"You will never get me to consent to calling a passion
for botany a madness! We have that in common," Jack
assured her. "My special interest is fungi." He reached up
to caress one of the lemons hanging from a nearby branch.
"I never thought one could ship living trees so far."

"Nor did I," Amanda responded, eyes sparkling with
pleasure at his interest. "A grateful Spanish don sent them
in huge tubs, because Uncle rescued his daughter from a
most unpleasant situation at Badajoz. Don Carlos also gave
him Hercules, and helped him smuggle the animal out of
Spain, which at that time would not permit their large don-
keys to be exported."

"Hercules would be the mammoth jack, I presume."

"Yes. Did you see him?"

"Indeed. Very impressive. Is he a bad-tempered beast?"

"Surprisingly, he is not. For all the pampering he re-
ceives, he is quite manageable. He came with his own
groom, you know, who is utterly devoted to him. Hercules
is quite affectionate toward Sergio."

"Your father told me that you ride mules. Do you also
hold them to be superior to horses?" He could not keep
his amusement at this ridiculous notion out of his voice.

Amanda turned her head away, but Jack could see that
color mounted her neck and into her cheeks. He could not

tell whether she was embarrassed or angry, so he turned her around gently by grasping her shoulders, and found her red-faced and teary-eyed with suppressed mirth.

"I know I should be offended, hearing my dear father ridiculed, but he does become terribly enthusiastic, doesn't he?" She took a tiny handkerchief from her sleeve and dabbed at her eyes. "It has become a mania with him." More soberly, she said, "I wish he would not become a figure of fun, for I do not want to see him hurt."

"I am a beast! I hadn't meant to ridicule your father. For all I know he is a visionary, and the mule will be the accepted means of transportation in the future. In fact, I fully intend to try riding them myself. It is just that with their long ears and those peculiar tails . . ."

Amanda grinned. "Those ears are very expressive, though. If you pay careful attention to them, you will always know what a mule is thinking. I know they are not as aesthetically pleasing as horses, of course. You are not alone in your opinions. Almost everyone thinks them ridiculous-looking. I sadly fear Father will never bring them into fashion, at least not for Hyde Park."

Jack chuckled. "Well, he has a disciple in Tittlecue."

At that reminder Amanda went off into whoops. "He did try to enlist you last night, in his own inimitably charming way!"

"Do you and Penny mind that your father requires you to ride a mule?"

"Penny does. She and Father are always at daggers drawn over it. This spring when we made plans for our Season, she declared she would be mortified if she had to ride a mule in Hyde Park. She begged and pleaded, but could not talk Father into buying us both horses, so she refused to ride at all during her London sojourn."

"I have noticed a certain rebellious spirit in her," he said in a voice that suggested he admired rather than deprecated this trait. "But you do not mind riding a mule?"

"Certainly not! If you must know, I ride a very fine white mule. Actually, Hippolyta is cream-colored, and I think she is very pretty, as well as being a gentle, well-behaved mount. They are very affectionate, you know, if reared with gentleness. Most people mistreat them from an early age in the belief that they are stupid and stubborn by nature, and must be abused to get them to obey." She broke off to put her hands to her rose-tinted cheeks. "Oh, I am being so silly to run on this way. You will think me as mule-mad as my father."

"I do not think you silly. I am fascinated. Please go on."

She searched his face for signs of merriment, and finding none, continued. "They need to be handled a great deal when young, and even when grown and trained must be frequently worked to keep them attuned to their owner, else they will grow to like the company of their own kind too much and be unwilling to leave their barn or pasture. But I adore my Hippolyta. She is very surefooted, which is needful when riding on the dales. She has a wonderfully comfortable gait, too."

"I would have thought that the mule's high spine and sloping withers would make it uncomfortable to ride."

"Not if properly tacked with a breast collar, crupper, and carefully fitted saddle. I . . ." Amanda stood up abruptly. "She is an excellent mount. That is all! Shall we continue our tour?"

He caught up to her. "I had begun to think you didn't ride. You weren't with the family on their expedition yesterday, and you didn't ride out with the young ladies this morning."

"I ride." That look of disapproval he had seen on her face the day before was back. "And I am not in the least afraid to be seen on a mule, let people laugh as they will. But Penny had cajoled a groom into saddling a horse for her yesterday, declaring she would be forever humiliated if her London beaux saw her on a mule. Father let her do so rather than make a scene, and so today she also rode a horse. She wished me to follow her lead, but . . ."

"You were torn between two loyalties. You didn't want to embarrass your sister, nor disappoint your father." He smiled down at her tenderly. "Does Penny know why you aren't riding?"

That smile almost cost Amanda her composure. It had been a sweet torture to show Jack around the succession houses, for she liked all too well to look at him, to talk to him. She yearned to see him look at her with that mixture of awe and desire with which he looked at Penny. But it would never happen, so she felt the necessity of keeping her distance from him. It was difficult, though, as they walked down the narrow aisles together, their shoulders brushing, their hands sometimes touching as she picked up a plant to show him. She bit down on her lower lip, schooling herself to remember it was Penny he was interested in, as his question made clear.

"Of course not. She would feel miserable about it if she did. I don't know whether she would quit riding, too, or go back to riding her mule, but I don't want either one to happen. I want her to enjoy herself. So I have made excuses. I said I had the headache yesterday, and today I said I had too much to do. The management of the succession houses and the kitchens fell to me this month, so it is not too far from the truth." At his puzzled look, she continued, "Mother wants Penny and me to know how to manage a large household, so we take turns supervising various portions of the housekeeping staff. Pen has the care of linens and furniture this month."

Jack had not known of the necessity of training a woman to manage a household. He had never given it any thought, in fact. His mother certainly had not done so with his sisters, perhaps because of failing health. *Which probably explains why their homes are always so chaotic,* he thought.

"But don't you miss riding? It seems a shame . . ."

"I do, of course. While we have guests, I plan to ride only in the early-morning hours when no one is about to see us. But I haven't had a chance to do so for the last two days, so Hippy is very likely dreadfully bored, poor dear."

You are the dear, Jack thought. The more he knew these two sisters, the better he liked them. Penny's beauty and spirit fascinated him; Amanda made him feel calm and lighthearted. *They are indeed the medicine I needed,* Jack thought, silently thanking Cass for convincing him to stay. The dreadful memories of battle had not plagued him once since arriving at the Garfields'.

Jack silently followed Amanda into the next greenhouse, where flowers were blooming out of season. As she explained their growing requirements, she picked quite a few to put in a long basket she carried. When it was full she said, "I've talked you into total ennui, I expect. You will be wanting some lunch."

Taking the full basket from her, Jack responded, "I am

not at all bored. I have enjoyed every minute. You and Penny are very close, are you not?"

"Oh, yes. She is the best of all sisters, too."

"Then why did you not stay in London to be presented this last Season? Was it because you did not wish to be caught between her and your father over the mules?"

Amanda avoided Jack's eyes. She did not wish to discuss her appearance with him. Bad enough that she was so plain, without focusing his attention on it. But he clearly intended to have an answer. He put his knuckle under her chin and lifted it so that she had to look at him.

"Why, Amanda? Is it from shyness? Did you fear you would be overlooked by everyone? I cannot wonder at it, the way your family dotes on Penelope. Doubtless it causes you pain, though you hide it well." Jack thought that if Amanda were receptive to this line of conversation, he would just give her a hint about her hairdo and her style of clothes, both of which were unsuccessful copies of Penelope's.

"You are fair and far out there, my lord. They couldn't overlook me. You see, Penny would insist that I have partners, or she wouldn't dance. It's the same thing she has always done at the local assemblies. It is meant kindly, but I find it humiliating. If I cannot get a partner on my own, I prefer to have none at all."

"I think you would find that if you put yourself forward a little more, you would attract your own admirers. You are a very pretty young miss, Amanda."

"Huh!" She started walking away from him.

"I mean it. And I am something of a connoisseur."

"Now, why do I doubt you, my lord?" Amanda glared at him. "When you first arrived, you could hardly bear the thought of staying. I could see it in your eyes, the minute you learned I would not be going off to Brighton. You had arrived expecting a great beauty, and found 'Miss Garfield,' as you thought me to be, a sad disappointment. Yet when you clapped eyes on Penny, you changed your mind."

"That was not how it happened, Amanda. No, don't go away." He put a restraining hand on her arm. "Hear me out. I had already changed my mind before I met Penny. You may ask Cass, for it was he who talked me into staying. When I first saw you, I was quite perplexed. I had been led to expect . . ." He hesitated, not wanting her to know that she was routinely dismissed as "the plain sister."

"A beauty, which I clearly was not," she finished for him.

"A blonde." He shook his head emphatically. "A tall, willowy blonde with blue eyes. I found myself in the presence of a very fetching young lady, but she was a diminutive creature with light eyes and brown hair."

"Fetching! You know I am not. I beg you will let me go. I assure you I do not repine for my lack of looks. I have a loving family and a busy life. If I do not marry, I will enjoy being a doting aunt and a comfort to my parents in their declining years."

"Gammon! And shame on you for not appreciating how blessed you are. I have seen some truly plain young women in my day, and they would give a great deal to have your beautiful skin, as smooth and fair as a baby's, your perfect teeth, and that sweet little mouth." As he spoke, Jack gently drew his fingers along her jawline and traced the outline of her mouth. "I declare I wanted to kiss those shapely lips yesterday, even when my leg hurt like Hades."

Amanda froze stock-still when he touched her face. She felt a surge of warmth through her, warmth that differed from any other sensation she had ever felt, warmth that centered itself in a portion of her anatomy where it was surely a sin to feel *anything!* She looked into his golden-brown eyes and thought she saw honesty. *He wanted to kiss me!* Amanda's heart raced. She yearned to believe him, but could he possibly be telling the truth?

"And those eyes! So expressive, and . . ."

This compliment broke the spell. If there was anything Amanda was sure of, it was that her eyes were her worst feature. "Yes, indeed, my beautiful eyes," she snapped sarcastically. "If you admire them so much, I am sure you can tell me what color they are, Lord Maitland. I hope you can, for no one else has ever been able to come closer to them than 'odd' or 'murky.' "

"Murky! Each time I notice them they fascinate me, but until now I have not been able to study them and determine their color." When she would have turned away, he prevented her with one hand on her shoulder. With the other he lifted her chin again. "Look at me, Amanda. Ah, yes. Mostly gray, of course, like your father's. A very light gray. But with flecks of pale blue, green, and even a little bit of brown. If they were darker, they could be called hazel, but as it is . . . ah, I have it! They remind me of a mountain spring where the water flows fast over mossy rocks."

Once again, her heart pounded at his touch. Amanda felt herself in serious danger of throwing herself at him, of begging him to kiss her. *I must do something to stop this before I make a cake of myself!*

She pulled away and laughed up at him. "I am eternally grateful to you, for at last I know what my eye color is. Lichen! Watery lichen at that! Come, Maitland! Why are you exerting yourself to charm me? Are you one of these men who is not content unless every woman is his slave?"

"Your sister has always been petted and made much of, hasn't she?"

"Well, and why not? She was a beautiful baby, a beautiful child, and is now a beautiful young woman. Please do not try to set us against one another! I have never seen her as a rival, and she has never queened it over me."

"I speak to you as a friend, a concerned friend who sees a charming, desirable young woman shrinking from society because of her family's careless cruelty. Your family probably hasn't really looked at you in years. They grew into the habit of thinking her the pretty one because she is blond with blue eyes, like your mother, who was a great beauty, and still is a most attractive woman. Every compliment to Penny rebounds to your mother's credit, since it is obvious and much remarked upon that Penny closely resembles Lady Garfield. And your father is attracted to blue-eyed blondes, or he would not have married your mother, hmmm? So that is his standard of beauty. But there are other types, just as attractive."

Amanda looked at him. Saw his lips move. Even heard the words he spoke. But nothing made any impression on her, for she kept hearing, over and over like a death knell to the barely formed hopes she had tried so hard to repress: "I speak to you as a friend." *What else, Amanda, you silly chit!*

"Come, then, concerned friend," she said with a forced smile. "Let us go in to lunch before I perish of hunger."

Chapter Eight

When the young ladies returned from lunching with the hunters that afternoon, Kathryn again offered to read to Jack. Of course, Barbara quickly volunteered to assist her. He submitted, partly because his leg was giving him some pain and partly to avoid an appearance of particularity toward Penelope until he was ready to declare himself. The twin sisters joined them in the library and settled down to listen.

To his relief, Penny emphatically refused to hear anything by Hannah More. "She is so sanctimonious, Kathryn, not to mention a dreadful bore. I am sure Lord Maitland would prefer something more exciting. Have we not *Mansfield Park* here? It is by the same woman who wrote *Pride and Prejudice,* which I enjoyed wonderfully." She placed the book in Kathryn's hands, ignoring her flustered protests about improper novels.

"Fustian," Penny laughed. "I'm sure it is as proper as Mrs. More's book, for it is written by a lady, after all." She carried the point, of course. She and Barbara worked on embroidery while they listened; Amanda appeared to be sorting through some drawings at a card table nearby.

Jack found the book a dead bore, but stifled his yawns and pretended interest, for fear another one might be even worse: a book of sermons, for instance. After a while, Kathryn began to sound hoarse, and took a break to drink some water. Barbara said she would read next, and Kathryn reluctantly surrendered the book.

While the two young women were negotiating, Jack left his chair to stretch and walk about. Curiosity drew him to Amanda's side, where he found that she was poring over some botanical drawings. He studied them silently as she shuffled them. Their quality was excellent, clearly the work of a talented naturalist. That they were original watercolors made him suspect she had done them.

"I daresay you think me demented," she whispered, for Barbara had taken up the book and begun reading again.

"These are very good drawings," he said. "But I am curious . . ."

"I am attempting to classify them."

"Really, Amanda, if I am to read, you must be still," Barbara exclaimed crossly.

"Sorry." She smiled wryly at Jack and gathered the papers into a stack, leaving him to wonder why she did not simply take out Dr. Darwin's botany book and classify them according to the Linnaean system. Surely someone capable of making such sophisticated drawings could do so. It was a mystery that went unsolved, however, for she moved away and took up a small piece of embroidery, though with no great appearance of enthusiasm.

That evening Lord Penstock came into the drawing room before dinner limping dramatically. He explained that he had tripped and wrenched his ankle, and very likely would not be able to slay any more partridges the next day. Jack and Hal exchanged amused glances at this transparent bid for some of the female attention his rival had been garnering.

"Oh, you poor man," Penny cried, instantly and excessively solicitous.

Jack winked at her as he said, "That is a deal too bad, Winston, for you will be left to entertain yourself. The young ladies and I have already planned an expedition into Highton to get some supplies for silhouette making. Miss Majors has offered to make our portraits."

"I will be well able to ride in a coach," Penstock declared through clenched teeth.

Penny patted his arm soothingly. "But Highton's streets are steep and narrow, and everything is cobblestone and ruts. We will have to leave the coach and walk around to the various shops. It would be a very difficult town for you to hobble about in. No, dear Lord Penstock, I must insist that you stay here. Highton is no place for a sprained ankle." The sparkle in her eyes spoke of a clear understanding of Penstock's tactic and a delight in quizzing him.

Winston looked dourly at Jack. "Then Maitland and I

must keep one another company, for he surely cannot manage such an expedition."

Dr. Bruce, who had hunted with the men and returned to take his dinner with them, spoke up. "I have prescribed walking to Lord Maitland, to stretch and condition his injured muscles. Shall I have a look at your ankle after dinner? Perhaps some ice packs and a night's rest will restore you to health."

Winston let go of his cherished vision of Penelope sitting by his side, exerting herself to comfort and entertain him as he imagined she had been doing with Jack all day. "I would appreciate that, Doctor," he responded as graciously as he could.

"Where is Mr. Tittlecue?" Amanda asked, suddenly realizing her suitor, always the first to answer the dinner bell, had not yet put in an appearance.

"He has gone home," Sir Edwin replied. "Some sort of emergency having to do with his mother. He said that he would return soon."

"Ah." Amanda and Penny exchanged glances, then turned away to avoid laughing, for Mrs. Tittlecue always had an emergency when her son left her side for more than a few hours. Unfortunately, the family lived less than an hour's ride away, so Amanda could not hope that he would be away long.

The next day as the young men gathered around the breakfast table, Winston declared himself recovered but in need of a change of pace. The outing to Highton would be just the thing. Hal, giving him a sour look, then allowed that he had a few notions to purchase. At that point Tom, eyes twinkling, proposed that they all make the trip. "It will give me a chance to take Sylvia for a drive," he noted, winking at Cass. With his usual good humor, Sir Edwin fell in with their plans.

"Excellent notion. I have some estate business to attend to as well. We'll take a break from hunting. Perhaps Lord Maitland will be able to join us in the fields tomorrow."

"I feel sure I will, sir," Jack agreed. "My leg is very nearly healed." This was not precisely true. The several cuts had closed over and showed no sign of infection, but his bruises were deep, and his leg muscle still seemed inclined to go into spasms at the least excuse. Nevertheless, further inactivity would be torture to him. Even if it hurt, he intended to join the men at their sport soon.

The bright sunshine of a warm late-September day shone on a large party that as it left Garfield Manor and followed the winding road two miles into the market town of Highton. The parade was led by the Garfields' carriage, with Penny, Amanda, Jack, and Winston inside. Tom drove his fiancée, Miss Sylvia Destrey, in his curricle, while Cass and Hal followed in a barouche with Kathryn and Barbara.

As usual, Amanda and Penny were dressed alike, in green-and-white vertically striped muslin dresses topped by short, close-fitting green spencers. Also as usual, neither the color nor the cut of the dress exactly flattered Amanda, though it suited her much better than anything else Jack had seen her wear.

On the carriage drive, Amanda had little to say, allowing Penny to direct and dominate the conversation, which consisted mostly of her teasing Lord Penstock about his ankle. Penstock took it in good part, turning his malingering into a compliment to her. Penny tried without success to draw Amanda into the exchange, and Penstock ponderously seconded her, but it was so clear that he lacked any interest in her responses that she withdrew even further.

As Jack observed this interplay, he pondered the relationship between the sisters. They had enjoyed one another's company yesterday, he knew. Amanda had been animated as the three of them picked flowers in the garden. He thought it good of Penelope to try to draw her sister out in company, but lamented the obviousness of her efforts, which only had the effect of making Amanda look more awkward.

At least she tries. She is not deliberately cruel, as my sister Sarah is. That drew Jack to Penny even more, but somehow it was Amanda who occupied his mind.

She seemed such a self-confident person when first I met her, he thought. *But in the presence of men like Penstock, she becomes completely spiritless.* He felt a certain satisfaction in remembering how well Amanda had opened up to him in the succession houses yesterday. *Perhaps I can help bring her out of her shell and into fashion.* He promised himself that he would befriend her, whether or not he decided to marry Penny.

An hour saw the completion of all their errands, so the party entered the Golden Bell, Highton's best inn, seeking refreshments before the return home. The day continuing fine, they chose to eat out-of-doors. Mr. Makepeace, the innkeeper, had placed several tables on a small terrace with a picturesque view of Lake Ellersmere.

"Is that the same lake that I can see from the Isis drawing room at your home?" Jack inquired.

"Our dock is situated on a finger of it," Cass confirmed. "We also own the largest island."

In the middle distance they could see the dam and a large waterwheel turning majestically beside it. Just below them there was a pleasant cove with small rowboats tied to a floating pier, and on the water several young men were rowing their ladies about.

Jack watched the scene hungrily. "Remember our rowing days, Win?" he asked.

"How can I forget?" Penstock responded through clenched teeth.

"The memory does not seem as sweet to you as to Maitland," Penny observed, nipping her lower lip to keep from laughing.

"Our team inevitably beat theirs," Jack responded, grinning. "Anyone game for a turn about the lake?"

An enthusiastic chorus greeted this suggestion. "I have a capital idea," Caspian said. "Instead of eating here, why don't we have Mr. Makepeace prepare a hamper of refreshments for us? We can row up to Xanadu for our lunch, and then on to the manor. The servants can take the boats back tomorrow."

"Wouldn't Xanadu be a bit far to row?" Jack teased. "I thought Kubla Khan's seat was in Mongolia."

"Blame Penny for the fanciful name," Tom said, chuckling indulgently. "She had just read Coleridge's poem when Father had the summerhouse built, and since he designed it to look like an Oriental palace, the name seemed to fit."

"Sounds intriguing," Winston said in a bored voice. "But Jack, I shouldn't think you could row very far in your condition."

Jack bristled. "Nothing wrong with my arms."

"Well, you shan't monopolize Miss Garfield," Winston growled. "You'll let me row you there, won't you?" He looked pleadingly at Penny.

Penny looked at Amanda, a tiny line between her eyebrows. "I don't know," she temporized. "We must consider the best way to pair up."

Swifter than thought, Jack knew what she was worried about: that with Mr. Tittlecue absent, her sister would be left for her brother Cass to escort. He didn't want to see Amanda hurt, either; at the same time he felt a flash of annoyance at Penny's assumption that Amanda would be the last one chosen. Almost before the words were out of her mouth, he asked, "Amanda, will you do me the honor?"

Amanda lifted her chin proudly. "Thank you, Maitland, but I must go back with the coach. François needs those spices for our evening meal."

"Nonsense," Tom said. "John Coachman can transport our purchases home."

Cass added, "You know you love a boat ride, Mandy. And how can you pass up a chance to ramble around the island on such a warm fall day?"

"Say you will go, Amanda." Jack put his hands together in an extravagant imploring gesture. "Otherwise I shall have to make a third, and be rowed about. I do not know if my manhood can survive such a humiliation."

Amanda could not help but smile at his theatrics. Every word they said was true. The coachman could deliver the spices, she did love to be rowed about, and she loved rambling on the wooded end of Xanadu. It would be particularly beautiful this time of year wearing autumn colors. Of course, she knew she should refuse Jack's escort, being far too much in danger of losing her heart to him to spend so much time in his company. But she found as she looked into his smiling gold-flecked eyes that she simply couldn't resist the opportunity.

"Very well. I must go to the stationers, in that case, and purchase a sketch pad and some charcoals to take with me."

Within half an hour everything was arranged and the small boats moved out of the cove. Winston ignored Jack's shouted challenge; he had Penelope to himself for once, and intended to improve upon the opportunity. Hal was sufficiently insecure as a rower that he never even looked over as Jack passed him.

"You look absolutely blissful," Amanda observed as she watched Jack expertly maneuver the boat. She felt blissful, too, sitting opposite this handsome man. The sight of him, his golden hair gleaming in the sun, his long legs stretched out so that it seemed they might touch her, caused a fluttering sensation in her heart.

"I am. This is one of my favorite activities, and I am so weary of lying about. I need this exercise."

She reveled in the sight of his muscles rippling beneath his jacket as he strained against the water. "Yes, such a layabout. You were still for almost two hours yesterday afternoon listening to Kathryn and Barbara read. Oh, and you sat at cards for almost an hour last night before going off to play at billiards. Terrible of you to give way to your infirmity so completely."

He grinned. He liked her in this teasing mood. "Not to mention all the time I spent sitting at the dining table!"

They laughed together, and then fell into a companionable silence enfolded in the many soothing sounds of the lake. The waterwheel could still be heard behind them, the oars made a liquid whisper as they glided over and into the water, and sounds of birds calling and people laughing drifted over the lake.

Looking over his shoulder from time to time as he navigated, Jack saw a tiny, rocky bit of land ahead of them. "Is that the island?" Disappointment laced his voice.

"No, there are several small ones like that, but ours, though narrow, is fairly long, with a tiny cove and swimming beach along the west side." She leaned forward in her seat. "There it is."

"Ah, I see the roof now! It does look like something Kubla Khan would build."

"Father loves architectural and interior design novelties, as I am sure you have realized by now."

Jack smiled. "Yes, but at least he does not carry it to the point of the ridiculous as so many do."

"I think that is Mother's moderating influence. She has a wonderful sense of style."

Too bad you do not consult her while choosing your clothes and hairstyle, Jack thought.

As they passed between Xanadu and the shoreline to the west, Jack broke his silence again with an exclamation of surprise. "There is a strong current here."

"Cass and Tom have remarked on it, too. One of the streams that feeds the lake, the Trellbeck, joins it just above here, and apparently it funnels through this narrow stretch. Also the lake is drawn on now fairly frequently for water for the new canal."

When they were parallel to the summerhouse, Jack remarked upon the buoys that marked off a space in a small inlet formed by two rocky arms of the island. "That's the swimming beach?"

"Yes. What wonderful romps we used to have there." Remembered delight animated her countenance. "The buoys are there to mark the rocks, and to remind Penny not to swim out into the lake."

"Penny swims?" Jack's eyebrows arched. Though Lord Byron's devotion to swimming had brought it somewhat into style, the ability to swim was not universal among men, much less women.

"Like a fish," Amanda said proudly. "I could never learn to do more than paddle about, but she kept up with the boys when we were children. Of course, she is much too ladylike to swim now, you understand."

"Of course." Jack winked at her. "Where do we put in?"

"The dock is at the north end of the island. You'll see it as we pass these rocks."

Jack had been rowing at a leisurely pace. Spotting their destination, he decided to test his mettle. Their boat knifed through the water, passing first Cass, then Winston, who was too absorbed in Penny to pay any attention to them, and finally drew alongside Tom, who decided not to be passed.

Amanda held her breath as the boats sped along side by side. "Afraid?" he asked her. "If you are, I'll slow down."

"No, I love it!" She put her hands up to hold her hair in place, though. So time-consuming to create, the curls on her forehead were very quick to become disheveled and fall down into long, straight strings. *How I wish Mama did not insist on this style,* she thought. Her mother could never quite grasp that what suited Penny's curly hair and oval face did little for Amanda, with her straight hair and thinner features.

Jack shot past Tom just as they cleared the north end of the island. He gave a shout of victory, and Tom shook his fist at them. By the time Jack had turned the boat, all but Hal were ahead of them at the dock. Cass took the line Amanda tossed him, and then helped her out. To his intense annoyance, Jack discovered that his injured leg did not want to straighten out. He was forced to accept Cass's helping hand to get onto the dock.

Amanda walked beside him, concern in her eyes as he limped along the shore. "Perhaps this wasn't such a good idea," she said.

"Now, don't you start mollycoddling me. Until now you have been the only female to treat me like a grown man!" He smiled at her to take any sting from his words. "I shall limber up in a few steps."

Their first order of business was to fall upon their delayed nuncheon with sharp appetites. After Mr. Makepeace's picnic had been demolished, Jack felt the need to stretch his leg. While the others sat around the table joking and gossiping, he strolled around the exterior of the Oriental folly, admiring the carvings and the onion-shaped pinnacle. To his surprise, Penny joined him as he rounded the rear of the building; they were alone, and he had the feeling she had contrived it deliberately. This was the first time she had made such a point of being alone with him. Warning bells went off in his mind, and he looked at her warily.

Chapter Nine

Jack greeted Penelope with a formal bow. "Miss Garfield."

"You *are* angry with me! I knew it! I could sense it at the Golden Bell."

"I cannot think what makes you say that," Jack responded, genuinely puzzled, for he had forgotten about his momentary annoyance.

"When you most emphatically named Amanda as your chosen companion, you looked daggers at me."

"Oh, that." Relieved, and no longer sensing an attempt to entrap him, Jack relaxed and offered her his arm. *These young ladies are not connivers,* he scolded himself. *I fear Haskins was right. I have become too suspicious.*

"You see, Penelope, I have noticed that you and your family are in the habit of ignoring Amanda, or assuming that she will have no suitors, or even any partners, unless you manage matters for her. For her part, she finds it humiliating, and I find it incomprehensible. She is an attractive young woman; if she had more confidence, she would be even more so. But how can she develop confidence when her family constantly undervalues her?"

"I . . . we . . . no one could value Amanda more than I!" Penny's face flushed with anger, and Jack had the rare opportunity to observe The Beauty when she was not at her best. "She is the dearest, sweetest, kindest . . ."

"I know, I know. You value her inner beauty as you ought. But none of you seems to have the least awareness that she also has personal charms that may appeal to men, too. Just because she is not your identical twin . . ." Jack broke off, aware that he had said too much. *A wonderful way to woo The Beauty,* he scolded himself wryly.

Penny stared at him for a very long time. "You prefer Amanda to me?" she asked at last, in a very small voice.

Jack passed his hand over his brow. "I didn't say that. I only . . . oh, hang it. I do not see why I should have to explain my wish to row her instead of you or one of your female guests."

"N-no, of course you should not. Why, how proud, how conceited I must seem to you." Penny hung her head with shame. Jack hastened to recover lost ground by comforting her and assuring her that he did not consider her conceited. "I think rather you are excessively solicitous of her."

Unaware that their steps had carried them into view of several of the party, including Lord Penstock, he patted her hand, then lifted it to his lips. "You are so excessively beautiful you could never have too high an opinion of yourself, but yet you are as modest and unassuming a female as I have yet to meet. That is part of what makes you such a delight to know." Jack smiled down at her.

Much relieved, Penny returned the smile. "Thank you for calling to my attention my treatment of Amanda. I shall be more careful and less managing in the future."

They were distracted by the sounds of new arrivals. Looking toward the dock, they saw Sir Edwin and Mr. Tittlecue clamber up the steps, followed by two servants carrying hampers of food and wine and fishing rods. "John Coachman told us about your adventure, and Tittlecue wanted to join you," Sir Edwin called out by way of explanation. "I thought some of you might like to try wetting a line or two."

Jack and Penny stood by Cass, watching the elder Garfield climb the slight incline toward them. "I expected that," Cass laughed. "Mother would not allow her girls to spend the afternoon on the island unsupervised."

"Well, I think it quite unnecessary of her," Penny cried indignantly. "After all, you and Tom are here!"

"Do not cut up rough with me, my girl. I have no fear that anyone here would cross over the line with you. If you feel you have a grievance, you must take it up with the parents."

Jack kept silent but made a mental note that he must speak to Cass about Winston, who was by no means as reliable as he seemed to think.

The fishing program seemed to please everyone but Amanda, who stood back as the rods were handed out. Jack looked questioningly at her. "I do not wish to fish," she explained. "I much prefer to explore the island." She looked around. "Now, where did I put my sketch pad?"

"Exploring and sketching sound very agreeable to me," Jack said, offering her his arm again.

"Oh, no, you need not. Indeed, you don't." Amanda grew quite flustered. She, too, had seen Jack kiss Penny's hand. Her lack of enthusiasm for fishing grew in part out of a desire to be alone. "You are very kind, but you have done your good deed for the day. Follow Penny and keep an eye on Penstock, for I cannot like the way he has been looking at her."

"The only good deed I have done this morning is to secure for myself the companionship of a delightful young female. I hope she will not deprive me of more pleasure." Jack looked challengingly down at her, and Amanda felt a blush mounting her cheeks. She took his arm with a shy smile.

At that moment Mr. Tittlecue sauntered up to them and offered his arm to Amanda with a proprietary air. "I shall sacrifice my pleasure for you, Miss Amanda, for I know you do not care for piscine sport," he announced magnanimously. Jack showed no intention of relinquishing her. Indeed, he received Tittlecue's presence coldly.

"I say, am I *de trop*?" the older man asked Amanda, looking meaningfully at the hand that rested on Jack's arm. Clearly he expected her to hasten to his side to reassure him.

Jack covered Amanda's hand with his own, preventing her from withdrawing it. "By no means, Mr. Tittlecue," he responded before Amanda could. "I have already asked Miss Amanda to show me the island, but I am sure Sir Edwin will be desirous of your company—that is, if you do not talk too much and scare the fish."

Tittlecue glowered at Amanda, but she only smiled weakly at him, so he bowed formally, his pink face flaming with anger, and left them.

"There! I think *now* you may regard me as your champion," Jack said.

She smiled at him. "Indeed I do, sir. I have given him

so many hints, but he continues to think himself my received suitor." They watched the others sort out their gear for a few moments. "But you certainly may change your mind. There is no danger on the island. I have often rambled it alone while the others fished. In fact, I look forward to these occasions." She took her hand off his arm and started for the table where their packages sat. "There is my sketchbook!"

"Let you go alone and have Mr. Tittlecue follow you and cut up your peace? No indeed!" Jack took up her sketch pad and pencil box.

"I shall just wait until everyone is looking elsewhere and tiptoe away."

"And deprive me of the opportunity to see this point you spoke of that has such a magnificent view?" Once again, Jack offered her his arm.

"Oh, very well, if you insist." Amanda tried to sound irritated, but in fact she felt thrilled at his apparently sincere desire for her company.

So they strolled off, leaving the others to their fishing. Jack already knew that he and Amanda shared an interest in wild flora and fauna. She was able to give him the common names of every plant he was not familiar with, and gladly learned from him the correct species names of those he recognized. They argued amiably over the correct common name for a butterfly she had always called the golden wing, while he had known it as the yellow darter. This led to a discussion of the usefulness of a scientific nomenclature.

"I do wish Mama would allow me to study scientific classification," Amanda said wistfully.

Jack frowned. "I thought botany was held to be a highly suitable discipline for females."

"I do not understand it, but she says the Linnaean system is not fit for a decent young woman to know."

"Ah!" Enlightenment almost made Jack laugh; she was referring to Dr. Linnaeas's division of the plant kingdom into male and female. Then he thought of some of the more lurid metaphors this had given rise to in the works of the good doctor and his followers, notably Dr. Darwin, and sobered. "True, there are some things about it that might make it more suitable for a married woman."

"As you are blushing, I cannot doubt from your lips what seemed to me so excessively strict from Mother's." Amanda's eyes traveled lovingly over his face for a moment, then she looked hastily away. *You goose! Flirting with him, openly admiring him that way. Is there no end to your folly?*

"Surely I am not?" Jack looked startled. Embarrassed, he glanced away, and so did not notice Amanda's brief unguarded look of adoration.

By this time their steps had carried them through the woods to the rocky point at the southernmost tip of the island. Higher than the other end, it gave a very fine view of the lake and the surrounding countryside. They stayed there for quite a while. She divided her sketch pad with him, and he took a charcoal from the pencil box she had brought. While he propped himself against a boulder and sketched the small, twisted tree that grew in a depression halfway down the cliff, she took out colored pencils and busied herself drawing one of the plant species that he had indicated was new to him.

When she had finished it to her satisfaction, she offered it to him. "A wonderful job," he said. "I have seldom seen better botanical drawings in the finest natural history books."

Amanda blushed with pleasure, but demurred. "You don't think it plain and unimaginative?"

"No, it is as it should be, when your purpose is to illustrate the characteristics of the plant. Then, accuracy is far more valuable than artistry." He hesitated a minute, decided she might find that less than complimentary, and added, "Though I know you are capable of both, having seen your sketchbook. This drawing will make an excellent addition to my collection. Its careful attention to detail will aid me in classifying it."

Amanda's face pinked becomingly again, and Jack smiled at the realization that the "plain sister" looked much prettier when her color was up, whether in embarrassment or anger, than The Beauty.

"Did you say there was a bluebell wood?" he asked, when it seemed she had become flustered. *Praise puts her entirely out of countenance. Poor child, she has had so little of it.*

"Oh, yes. In the spring it is the prettiest one I know of.

But at this time of year, all we will find are mushrooms and toadstools, I expect."

"The fungi are a particular interest of mine." He held his hand out to her and pulled her to her feet. Tucking their sketches underneath his right arm, he offered her his left. Instead of accepting it, she took him by the hand and led him onto a very narrow path that could only be walked single file, instead of down the wider one that had brought them to the point. They dodged low branches and pushed through undergrowth for several moments, Jack admiring how gracefully she moved, her gown tucked close against her slender body to avoid the snags. *Like a wood sprite,* he thought, remembering his first impression of her.

"An enchanted place," he said when they broke into the small clearing that was their destination. The ground was covered with leaf litter, and a few butterflies flitted here and there in the broken sunlight that filtered through the red and gold leaves.

"I have always thought so. I used to come here to be alone. Penny never liked it except when the bluebells were blooming. She thinks it depressing in the fall, but to me it is a little like a chapel. I always feel . . ." She hesitated.

Jack's eyes had been roving the area, an inscrutable look on his face. When she stopped speaking, he looked at her and lifted an inquiring eyebrow. "Close to God? For that is how it makes me feel."

"Yes." Her answer was a soft whisper, and she turned away, not wanting him to see that she felt near tears. *That remark completed your conquest, Jack. A conquest you don't want and would be embarrassed to know you have made. But it is too late. I love you.*

For a few minutes they just stood there together, letting the peaceful scene sink into their souls. A robin's arrival broke the spell. It launched itself into the clearing and almost as soon as its feet touched the ground realized human beings were there and exploded into panicked flight, causing them both to laugh. They began searching among the leaves for mushrooms, and soon found several varieties.

When they found one Jack was not familiar with, he bent over it eagerly. "What is this bright yellow one with the upturned cup?"

"Don't touch it," Amanda advised him. That is the Fly Agaric, and it is poisonous."

"Excellent! Will you draw it for me?"

She sat on the ground next to it, and soon forgot her consciousness of the man beside her as she concentrated on her drawing. Jack lowered himself to the ground, too, grunting slightly in pain as he did so. She didn't look up, not because she didn't hear him, but because she knew he wouldn't want her to notice.

Jack stretched out to his full length and propped his head on his hand to study her as she worked. *There is something about her that exerts a calming influence on me,* he thought. *She is easy to be with. Penelope is more like me—restive and full of energy. Not that Amanda isn't energetic. She just seems more in control. I wonder how Penny would have reacted the first day when I arrived so mussed and bloodied?* The thought of the volatile Penelope's probable response made him chuckle.

Amanda looked up from her work. "What?"

"Nothing. Give me the other half of the sketch pad, will you?"

She complied, then held out her drawing. "Will this do? Of course, I can make a watercolor of it later."

"Excellent. Do you mind drawing the others for me? Yours are more accurate than those I have."

Cheeks once again pink with pleasure at the compliment, Amanda moved closer to another mushroom and soon lost herself in her task, which was just what Jack had intended. He lightly sketched in the glade and began working on a likeness of Amanda. *Such a charming picture she makes.* Using artistic license, he created for her a hairstyle that left her delicate features uncluttered. As he did so, he felt a flash of desire for the second time in her presence, and that turned his thoughts in an entirely new direction.

Perhaps I am considering marrying the wrong sister. He lifted his pencil from the pad and tapped it against his lower lip, wondering why he had put aside his determination to delay marriage as long as possible. *I suppose knowing the Garfields has given me a more attractive picture of what a family can be. Certainly my family held out no such example, at least after Mother died.* Caution whispered in his ear, *Best not marry either, until you know them better.*

But Jack knew the time to marry Penny was running out. She was like a rare object presented for auction: the bidding was fast and furious, and no one who hesitated could hope to win her. The competitiveness that was so much a part of his nature reasserted itself. *Can't let Winston have her; she is too good for him by half.*

Sir Edwin disapprovingly watched his younger daughter pair up with Jack. *What is she about, wandering off with the viscount? She should be making it possible for Penelope to spend time with that young man, to see if she wishes to marry him, for he will offer for her soon. And Tittlecue would make Amanda an admirable husband, but he has his pride. She will ruin her chances playing such games with him.* He almost sent Cass after them, but seeing his younger son kneeling head to head with Miss Majors as they sorted their tackle, he held back. *There would be the perfect match,* he thought. *Nothing could please me more than for him to marry a local girl who would tie him to us, for that boy has wandering ways, I fear.*

The lively party clambering around the rocky edges of Xanadu had little luck with any fish, though all but Mr. Tittlecue and Sir Edwin had a wonderful time. Sir Edwin was distracted by his concern for his various offspring, and Tittlecue nursed wounded pride over Amanda's defection.

Tittlecue, always on the lookout for storms, called their attention to a line of clouds approaching. "See how dark it has become in the north? And the wind is kicking up," he announced. Sir Edwin picked up the refrain, and soon there was a general exodus to the boat dock. The footmen loaded the remains of their picnic, along with their fishing paraphernalia, into one of the two larger boats and shoved off first, followed by Sir Edwin and Mr. Tittlecue, whose fear of storms was emerging in a rising hysteria. Sir Edwin called back to Tom and Cass to look after their sisters.

Cass and Hal had their hands full with Barbara and Kathryn, who had taken some of Mr. Tittlecue's panic. Their attention was taken up with getting the alarmed females into their respective boats. Hal shoved off immediately.

"Penny, are you going back with Penstock?" Tom asked as he helped his fiancée into his boat.

"Yes, but wait for Amanda," Penny cried. "She and Jack are likely still at the point. They could not see the storm approach from there, nor notice the wind, very likely."

Cass looked back, harassed, just as he was about to step into his boat. "The devil. We very nearly forgot them." Tom had already shoved off and was bending to his oars.

Penstock hid his vexation at Penny's inability to forget Jack's whereabouts. He had seen their *tête-à-tête* earlier in the afternoon, and had drawn upsetting inferences from it.

"I am delighted to be able to be of service to you, Penelope," he said, catching her hand to kiss it. "I'll go for them."

She withdrew her hand and exclaimed irritably. "Oh, stop. This is no time for your fustian."

"Pardon me, my dear. You are quite right." Penstock called to Cass, who still hesitated at the edge of the dock while Kathryn called insistently for them to be off. "I'll go for them, Cass. Wait here, Penelope."

"You don't know the way," Penny said. "I'll go with you."

"Let Penstock go on," Cass ordered. "He can go more quickly without you. Just follow that path, Win." Cass pointed out the obvious, well-trodden path into the woods. "It leads directly there."

"I'll see to it," Winston assured him. "You go on before Miss Majors has the vapors." So saying, he took off at a trot, leaving Penelope standing anxiously on the dock, observing her guests and family departing in their various boats.

Chapter Ten

As Lord Penstock trotted up the path, he was prey to sour thoughts. Penelope had spent much of the afternoon with him, and he had gone his length trying to please her, but she had seemed abstracted. He knew the source of her abstraction: the man he now sought. *Damn Jack. He always knows just when to advance and when to retreat,* Penstock thought. *Choosing the sister over Penny today was a stroke of genius, for it has piqued her interest as nothing else could.* Penstock hardly saw the path before him, for he saw only the sight of Jack and Penny in deep conversation, private conversation, behind the summerhouse this afternoon. Fury swept through him every time he recalled Jack kissing her hand.

When he arrived at the terminus of the path and found only the overlook, with the lake beyond, his anger grew. *Where the devil are they? I've no wish to spend a cold, wet night on this benighted island.* The wind had already whipped up little whitecaps on the water. Penstock was an excellent oarsman, but he couldn't swim. He wanted to be away before the water grew any choppier than it already was.

A vindictive thought came to him. *It would serve Jack right if I took Penelope and left him here to compromise the little drab of a sister!* As he started to retrace his steps, his eyes fell on the little path that led off into the woods. The broken twigs and disturbed leaves told a tale of a recent excursion into the most deeply wooded part of the island. *Perhaps he has already compromised her,* Penstock thought, grinning gleefully. *If so, I must make sure they have a witness.*

Cautiously he picked his way down the path, making as little noise as possible. The murmur of voices warned him to stop before he was seen. He crept forward just far enough to make out Jack's and Amanda's figures through the screen of branches. To his disappointment, their activity was utterly innocent. They were both sketching, and so immersed in their work that they clearly had not noticed him, or the change in the weather, or anything else.

Mind working furiously, Penstock backed silently away. *If I manage things just right . . . But how to get Penny to leave them here?* When he reached the main path, he trotted back to the dock as quickly as he could. "Did you find them?" Penny called anxiously.

"Yes, they're coming. They had to gather up their sketches. Let's go. The lake is becoming dangerous."

"We can't leave without them," Penny protested.

"We aren't. They'll be here any minute. Jack is a bit slow afoot, you know."

"We must stay. He might have difficulty getting into the boat. Cass had to help him out when we arrived."

"We'll let him take ours. It is tied right next to the stairs. Just let me get something from it." He climbed down the ladder and leaned over the boat, his back to Penelope. In seconds he had untied the rope that anchored it to the dock, leaving it hanging loosely through the iron ring. Turning back to Penny, he pretended to be stuffing something into the inside pocket of his jacket.

"Here, I'll hold our boat. Climb in," he said as he knelt at the end of the dock. Suiting action to words, he maneuvered their intended vessel sideways and then held out his hand to Penny. She stood back, a mulish expression on her face.

Penstock looked up at her. "The wind is increasing, Penny. Hurry."

"Not until I see Jack and my sister safely in their boat."

Frustration and anger filled Penstock. *Jack! Why must they always choose Jack?* But he made his voice gentle, cajoling. "Come now, Penny. We must be off. What is the worst that could happen? If they cannot leave the island, Amanda shall have a future earl for a husband. You'd be doing her a favor."

"Amanda would not want a husband gotten in such a way. And the worst that could happen would be that Jack would fall trying to get into that boat, capsize it, and drown both of them."

"It's not their safety you care about, is it? It's Maitland. You don't want him to have to marry Amanda. You've decided in his favor already, haven't you?"

The bitterness in her suitor's voice alarmed Penny. "I've decided nothing, Winston, except not to abandon my sister." Her chin jutted out even farther. She folded her arms and glared at him.

Desperation clawed at Penstock. *If I don't get her in this rowboat in another few seconds, she will see that I've untied their boat, and then all is lost.* He stood and walked toward her, still striving to keep his voice even. "Penelope Garfield, I am responsible for your safety, and Maitland is responsible for Amanda's. He was the best oarsman in our college. I wish I might see the boat he couldn't handle! And he won't wish to linger, for he has no mind to marry Amanda. Now, come along." He took her arm, and when she resisted, gave her a sharp tug. "Get in that boat or I'll throw you in."

Penny slapped at him and struggled, but he wrestled her into the boat, stepped in after her, and untied the rope. With swift, economical movements he propelled them away from the dock. "They're right behind us," he said, hoping to soothe her.

"You brute!" She rubbed her arms. "Take me back this minute!"

"I'll do no such thing. My one thought is to get you safely to land. How far is your father's dock?"

"If you really think there is danger, let us go back. We can stay in the summerhouse." As she spoke, Penny turned from one side to the other, trying to see past Penstock to determine if her sister and Jack had arrived on the dock yet. Suddenly she gave a shriek.

"Their boat. It's loose!" She pointed. "It's drifting away!"

Penstock said nothing, but plied his oars with grim vigor.

"Lord Penstock, if you don't take me back immediately, not only will I not become your wife, I will never speak to you again!"

She hadn't called him "Lord Penstock" since the early days of their acquaintance in London. He knew that he had lost the game. "You won't marry me. I see it in your eyes. I've lost you, but at least he shan't have you, unless you are so selfish as to marry the man who has ruined your sister." With each word Penstock's oars bit deep in the water, carrying them farther and farther from Xanadu.

Ignoring her arguments, he began talking half to himself. "That is the answer! I shall compromise you, too. We shall make it a double ceremony, perhaps!"

"You are mad!"

"You had best not speak so saucily to your future husband." With a deft twist of the oars he changed their direction. "That little island should do nicely. Not exactly a 'stately pleasure palace,' but it's only for one night, and we can keep each other warm." He leered at her.

Penny turned her head. They were rapidly approaching one of the small islands that dotted the lake, the one that the locals called Swan Island after the birds that nested there. "You had best not row any closer. There are submerged rocks . . ."

"Fine! I wouldn't mind having the boat damaged. It would give a certain respectability to our presence there. Don't want to scandalize society too much!" He deliberately aimed toward the rocky part of the shore.

In obedience to his wishes, a sudden scraping sound preceded an upwelling of water in the bottom of the boat. He gave one more mighty pull on the oars and wedged the vessel between two large rocks.

"Don't be afraid. I'll help you across the rocks to the shore." He stepped off the sinking boat and held out his hand to her.

Penny had already stripped off her spencer. Ignoring his outstretched hand, she bent over and took off her half boots, then dove into the water.

"What the devil are you doing?" Penstock screamed.

"Going back to Xanadu. Have a pleasant night."

"You crazy female! You can't swim that far! And I can't rescue you, for I can't even swim."

"Good!" Penny paused to wrestle her petticoat off. Already shivering from the cold water, she nevertheless swam resolutely away from the little island.

The line of clouds that had been a dim menace on the horizon an hour ago was almost overhead, and the wind had worked the water into small whitecaps. In the waves, she couldn't see Xanadu. The first spattering of rain fell, and lightning illuminated the scene. Suddenly Penny realized that swimming in an open lake during a storm was a vastly different proposition than swimming on placid, sun-kissed water in their cove. Instead of swimming to rescue her sister, or to save herself from Lord Penstock, she was swimming for her life.

"The light is going," Amanda said, looking up in surprise from her sketch pad. "I had no idea we had been here so long."

Jack looked around him, blinking owlishly. "Yes, 'Our idylls now are ended,' I fear." He struggled to his feet, then held out his hand for Amanda. "We'd best rejoin the others."

It wasn't until they had made their way through the woods to the point that they realized it wasn't the waning sun that accounted for the rapidly dimming light. "Gracious, I do believe it is going to rain," Amanda said, clutching her sketch pad to her chest tightly. "I am amazed someone has not come to fetch us before this. Poor Mr. Tittlecue must be terrified."

Jack looked questioningly at her as he took her half of the sketch pad and tucked it under his arm along with his.

"He is terrified of storms, even when he is in his own home," she explained. She told him an anecdote about her suitor's fears, hoping to lighten the serious look on his face.

Jack only half listened to her. *Why the devil didn't I realize how dark it had gotten?* He thought Sir Edwin a very careless parent not to have ordered a general evacuation of the island long since.

With dramatic timing, the first thunder rolled over them just as they reached the edge of the woods. They both stopped in astonishment, their eyes scarcely able to take in the sight of the empty boat dock.

"Oh! Oh, my!" Amanda trotted out onto the dock and looked over the end, hoping their boat still bobbed in the water. But all she saw were waves rising and falling. "They've gone off and forgotten us. Oh, how could they?"

Jack followed her, his eyes scanning the area. "How indeed? And even contrived, somehow, to take our boat with them." *Why the devil did I go off alone with her?* He answered his own question, a painful knife twisting in his heart at the realization of how deceived he had been: *Because you trusted her, you fool.*

Amanda looked sharply up at him. Instead of concern, his voice shook with anger, and his expression was dark and dangerous.

"Very clever! How excellently contrived. And you, looking so innocent as you led me into the woods, and now so convincingly amazed as you emerge to find yourself marooned here with me. A marvelous performance, m'dear. When you realize that your conspiracy hasn't worked, perhaps you will join Mrs. Siddons on the stage."

Bewildered, she stepped away, almost fearing he might strike her, so fierce was his expression. "What do you mean? You act as if you are angry at me. I don't understand."

"Act? I am not acting, you little schemer! I am furious! Furious, do you hear me!" He slammed down the sketchbooks and the pencil box. The wind snatched the sketches and tumbled them end over end through the air. The box broke open, and the pencils rolled hither and thither on the dock.

"Penny thought she saw me slipping away from her, so you joined forces in this desperate plan."

Frozen in horror as she realized what he suspected, Amanda stared blankly at him.

"The spit of land that shelters your swimming beach is closest to the shore of any point on the island, isn't it?" Jack grabbed her arm and shook it to bring her out of her frozen state.

"Y-yes, but . . ."

He turned and walked back up the dock. Amanda followed him as his long legs ate up the distance as if he had never been injured. He sat on a bench and pulled off his boots. "This is the best place to swim across?" he asked her, gesturing with his chin toward the spit of rocks that formed the northern boundary of the swimming cove.

"Maitland, you shouldn't try to swim that. Remember the current? And what about your leg?"

"Lord Maitland to you," he growled. "Of course you warn me against swimming away. I know you would not like your little plot upset, but Lady Maitland you will never be!"

"Lady . . . ! Oh! How could you think that of me!"

He glared at her, a betrayed look in his eyes. "Until a few moments ago I would never have believed it of you." Bitterly Jack recalled how he had been wary of Penny, yet never had the least qualm about going off alone with Amanda.

"I trusted you! I liked your decent, close-knit family and had begun to hope to be a part of it. Little did I know the Garfields' true nature! I see why it was you they chose to leave behind with me. Penstock is head over heels for Penelope. This way they think that each of you will marry a title. Well, I shan't be taken so easily." He stood and started for the water.

"Jack, you won't make it!" She grabbed at his arm. "Stay here, please! There was no plot, and I won't expect you to marry me. Indeed, the whole notion is silly. In just moments my family will realize we've been left behind and send someone after us."

"Ha! So I should wait, while the last of the light fades, for this rescue. Nice try." He brushed her hand off as if it had been a loathsome insect.

"At least take your jacket off. You cannot swim fettered like that."

He looked down at her again, his eyes steely. "I thank you for the reminder. Here. Wrap it around yourself and go into the summerhouse. It will be a while before anyone can get back here with a boat for you. Though it would serve you right to spend the night here alone."

She took the garment he handed her and folded it to her chest, tears streaming down her cheeks. "Oh, Jack. You'd rather die than marry me. But I would never marry you under such circumstances, I swear it. If they try to make me, I will . . ."

But he did not heed her. Stepping to the end of the rocks, he lowered himself into the water, and when it reached his chest, leaned forward and launched himself into the waves.

Before he had gone a quarter of the distance, he found himself in trouble. A severe spasm wracked his left leg, leaving it useless. The jolt of pain caused him to double up at first, sinking beneath the water. When he emerged sputtering, struggling to recover control over his body, he heard Amanda screaming in terror. He turned around in the water, for whatever his opinion in the matter, his healthy young body was not willing to die rather than marry her. Unable to kick effectively, he used his arms in a powerful breaststroke to plow through the water toward the shore, while the wind, waves, and current battled to deny him his objective.

Amanda had disappeared from view when next he looked up to get his bearings. Grimly he struggled to regain the spit of land he had launched from, but the current had already carried him parallel to the island far enough that in just a few more feet he would miss the southern arm of rocks that sheltered the swimming beach. Once past it, he would have to swim much farther to reach the island. He knew his chances of surviving would be poor in that case. *Wonder what odds Richard and Gerrard would give me now.* He put all of his strength into each stroke of his arms.

"Jack! Here!" He looked up again, panting for breath, to see Amanda running into the water. She had something in her hands. As he struggled toward her, she began pulling herself along the line of buoys.

He had no energy to express his feelings, compounded of fear for her life and annoyance at her illogical assumption that a tiny woman who couldn't swim could do anything but drag him to a watery grave faster. Exhausted, he prayed, "Dear Lord, let me reach those buoys!" Just when it looked as if he would miss the last of them by no more than a foot or two, something splashed into the water in front of him. Instinctively he grabbed for it. His hand closed over a shuttlecock bat.

The devil! What use is that! He almost let it go, when he saw the white material snaking out from it. He clutched it, pulled, and felt resistance. He had no idea what it was tied to. Praying it would hold, he grasped it with his other hand and began hauling himself toward the shore. It was then he realized she had tied it to the buoy to which she was now clinging, the last one before open water. As he hauled himself in, his weight pulled the bobbing marker underwater, submerging Amanda along with it, but both bobbed to the surface almost immediately. Amanda sputtered and choked.

Just as the bit of material gave way, he gained the buoy. His weight sank it again, and when he emerged it was with a handful of Amanda's dress in his hand. She sputtered and struggled as she surfaced.

Ducking under the rope, he clung to the buoy with her for a few moments, getting his breath. Then he waved Amanda ahead of him. "Let's go, before we are both too cold to move."

Amanda started pulling herself back along the line of buoys, with Jack following close behind. When his right foot touched solid ground, he once more became aware of the excruciating pain in his left leg, which was so cramped it was doubled up. Amanda, a few feet in front of him, had found solid ground, too, and struggled toward the shore. Jack hopped on his right leg for a few feet, then stumbled. He found that the water was sufficiently shallow here that he could crawl up a gradual sandy embankment.

When Amanda could stand unaided, she turned and helped Jack to stand, then supported him to the shore.

They collapsed there, both of them breathing stertorously for several minutes. When at last he could speak, he hiked himself up on his elbows and looked at her. She lay facing him on her side with eyes closed, pale as paper, her small bosom heaving. She had removed her spencer, and the thin muslin gown she wore was plastered to her skin in a most indecent way. Her hair hung straight as a string down her back and in her face.

"Are you all right?" he asked. "Amanda?" He touched her cold cheek, and her eyes fluttered open.

"Yes," she breathed. "Was it your leg?"

"Yes." He sat up the rest of the way and began massaging the offending limb.

"Does it hurt terribly?" She leaned toward him, her eyes full of concern.

"Enough to reassure me that I am still alive. And that I owe to you." He left off his massaging to touch her cheek again. Her head jerked back; she sprang up and started for the summerhouse.

In a few moments she returned with a rustic walking stick. "Here," she said. "Let me help you up."

He struggled to his feet with her help, then hobbled after her, for she turned her back on him the instant he had balanced using the walking stick. She walked back along the shoreline to where he had entered the water, collected his jacket, and headed for the summerhouse. There was a fireplace there, with remnants of the fire they had used that afternoon to heat water for tea. Amanda very competently stirred the damp ashes.

"As I feared, the servants are far too good at their work. No trace of fire here. But at least there is firewood." She scooped the wet ashes to one side and began laying a fire while he lowered himself into a chair and massaged his leg.

When she took the tinderbox from its place beside the firewood, he leaned forward. "Here, let me," he said.

Amanda complied with relief, for she always had difficulty with the flint, and there was only a tiny compartment for tinder, meaning the spark had to be expertly aimed. Within moments Jack had a glowing ember, from which he lit one of the slender sulphuric matches tucked into one side of the tinderbox. He carried this to her kindling, and soon they had a fire.

"Not before times," he said gruffly, urging Amanda close to it. Her teeth were chattering too much to speak, but the way she pulled away from him told him her feelings more eloquently than words.

"I am sorry," he said, pulling his chair close to the fire. "I said things I shouldn't have."

"Things you believed, nevertheless." She glared at him. "You accused us of scheming to entrap you before you had been five minutes in our home. I suppose that sort of thing must often happen to you." She bit her lower lip and turned her head away. At that moment she thought she must surely hate him, so filled with bitterness was her very soul.

"You saved my life, in spite of your justifiable outrage. Thank you, Amanda. Tying my neck cloth to that racket was very quick thinking, and going into the deep water when you can't swim was very brave."

"I had the buoys to hold on to." She shrugged and held her hands out to the fire.

"Still, it was risky. Indeed, when I tugged on the racket, you got a bad dunking. Very brave, my girl. I never saw a soldier braver. You needn't fear I will shab off, no matter what I said before. You will make me a very fine viscountess."

"No, I shan't," she said emphatically. "In fact, if you wish to repay me for your life, you will promise me . . ."

"Anything."

"That no matter what happens, you won't offer for me. It would be pointless, for I won't accept, but it would be a good deal less distressing to my family and myself if you simply assumed what they will, namely that we were far too busy trying to survive to indulge ourselves in any compromising behavior."

"I can't promise that, Amanda . . ."

"Besides, they will be here as soon as the storm lets up. There was no conspiracy!"

"Amanda, please listen to me."

"Will you honor my request?" She speared him with an icy glance from those light eyes.

Jack saw again the strong will he had run up against at their first meeting. His equally strong will refused to yield. "Only if it can be managed without compromising you, which I doubt."

"I will never marry you, not if I have to remain a spinster, no, not even if my family casts me off, which they will not. But I had as lief not tell them of your insulting suspicions, so please don't offer for me. That is all I have to say."

And it was. Though he attempted to engage her in conversation several times through that long evening, she remained mute. She huddled near the fire, looking over her shoulder frequently through the door of the summerhouse, toward the dock, seeing only darkness and rain, but expecting rescuers to arrive at any moment.

Jack watched her and brooded upon his cruel remarks, for he no longer believed that she, at least, had planned to maroon them together. Had Penny done it on her own, on the spur of the moment? Had her father and brothers been involved? No matter. He had every intention of marrying her. Thus it was with a proprietary air that he noted how well it became her to finger comb her hair back away from her face as she had done. The long braid she usually wore coiled on her crown she had tied at her neck with a ribbon

from the sleeves of her dress. He smiled as he thought of
the excellent view he had had of her before her dress had
dried by the fire and she had put her spencer back on. He
quite liked the sweet curves of her small bosom, the deep
indentation of her waist, the womanly flare of her hips. He
had seen her legs, too, and found them to be very shapely,
with nicely turned ankles. In all, he found her person
pleasing.

*I like her. Wasn't I thinking, just this afternoon, that she
might suit me better than Penelope? We deal well together.
It is not what I planned, but she won't be a bad wife for
me—a good deal better than the one my esteemed father
tried to trick me into marrying!* He knew he had his work
cut out to convince her, but had no doubt he could bring
her around, provided she survived the dunking, for she continued to shiver in spite of the fire, and refused all efforts
on his part to put his arms around her. She wouldn't even
accept his jacket, shrinking from it with as much disdain as
she displayed toward him.

Finally, she fell asleep, and he could lay the jacket over
her. He moved his chair by hers, gently tipping her so that
she rested against his shoulder. She murmured but did not
wake as he enfolded her in his arm. Then he dozed, too.
Not long after that the sound of voices woke him. They
were far off, but when he turned his head he saw lanterns
swinging. He nudged Amanda awake.

"Wh . . . Oh! Are they here yet?" She turned her head,
too, and then sprang to her feet and ran out the door and
down the summerhouse steps. "Over here! We're here,"
she called, flying toward the dock as fast as her feet could
carry her. Jack followed at a more leisurely pace.

Two large boats approached the dock, each holding several men. In both boats four men had lanterns on poles,
and held them out over the water. Two rowed vigorously,
and in the first boat Sir Edwin called out over and over,
"Amanda! My darling Amanda!" He sprang up the ladder
the instant the boat drew alongside, and was followed by
Cass, who had been one of the lantern bearers.

"Is Penny with you?" Cass asked Jack, as Sir Edwin took
Amanda in his arms.

Jack's eyes widened. "No. She went ahead of us, with
Penstock, I assume."

Cass called to the second boat, "Not here. Search around the island." It veered off and began moving slowly parallel to the shoreline.

Amanda leaned back in her father's arms. "I knew it! I knew you would come. But what is this about Penny?"

Sir Edwin hugged her almost hysterically, and then held her away from him, tears streaming down his cheeks. "I still have one daughter. Oh, God, I still have a daughter."

Amanda put both hands to her mouth. "What did you say, Papa?" Her voice came out as a horrified whisper.

"Penelope is out there somewhere. In the water."

Chapter Eleven

Amanda looked with terror into the inky night. "In the water, Father? For how long?"

"Since just before the storm hit. Apparently Lord Penstock's boat struck the rocks near Swan Island to the north, and she . . ." Sir Edwin's voice broke.

Cass completed his sentence. "She dove into the water and swam away, rather than be marooned there with Lord Penstock."

Penny was in the lake, trying to swim during all that wind and rain? Amanda felt her legs turn to rubber. Sounds reached her through a buzzing in her head that robbed her of the ability to speak. Her knees failed her, and she slumped against her father. Cass took her from him and carried her to the boat, where he handed her to one of the oarsmen. He instructed two of the estate workers who had been carrying lanterns to search the island, especially the shoreline. "I'll send this boat back for you as soon as we land Miss Amanda and Lord Maitland," he promised.

As Jack, Cass, and Sir Edwin took their places in the boat, Jack asked for more details on the accident.

Amanda struggled back to consciousness. "Yes, Father, what happened?"

"According to Penstock, he struck against the rocks and she could see that they were going to be marooned. She dove into the water with the intention, he thought, of swimming back to Xanadu."

Amanda gasped. "Why would she do such a thing?"

"We don't know," Cass said, his jaw set in a grim line.

"She voluntarily dove into the water in the teeth of a storm?" Jack's eyebrows shot up. He had been told that Penny could swim, but not that her skill equaled Byron's!

Sir Edwin took up the tale. "About the time we realized

the four of you were not just behind us, the storm hit with
such force we had to wait it out before returning for you.
When we did, Penstock saw our lights and hailed us from
the island. He seemed certain you two were still on Xanadu, and that she would try to swim here. I can only hope
that whatever her intentions, when she realized how dangerous her situation, she would have headed straight for
the west shore. She might have a chance in that case." Sir
Edwin shuddered involuntarily, and hugged Amanda to his
side. "Thank God you are here, safe and sound."

"I say!" He held her at arm's length again. "You've
taken a wetting." Glancing at Jack, he added, "Both of
you. Did your boat capsize?"

Dreading Sir Edwin and Cass's response to his desperate
effort to escape what he had thought to be a trap, Jack
briefly described his aborted attempt to swim to shore. All
the time that he spoke, he watched Amanda, waiting for
her to expose him. She paid no attention—she was anxiously searching the water, her eyes haunted.

When he had finished his narration, the Garfields made
no comment upon his motives for such a dangerous attempt. At the moment they probably were pondering the
unlikelihood that Penelope would be able to do what he
could not.

Amanda drew a deep breath and straightened her back.
"Penelope isn't dead," she declared. "She isn't! We must
join the search. Don't waste time taking us back to the
dock!"

But her father and brother both vetoed the idea. "I'll
not lose you to exposure, my dear, now I've found you safe
and sound." Sir Edwin felt her forehead. "No fever yet,
but we can't take chances. Besides, now we know Penny
isn't here, we must go back and enlist all of our tenants
and neighbors in looking for her. I'll see that every inch of
Ellersmere's shoreline is searched."

In spite of Amanda's pleas, the boat continued through
the dark water toward distant lights that marked the dock
in the Garfields' private cove. Above them the last of the
clouds dissipated, to be replaced by stars and a crescent
moon.

Icy dread gripped Jack at what the searchers might find.
Is it possible for a slip of a girl to swim any distance at all

in such conditions? he wondered. He leaned over to ask Cass, sotto voce, if the current was as strong all along the west shore as it was opposite Xanadu.

Cass shook his head. "Not if she managed to cross before she reached the mouth of the Trellbeck. That's where the current is strongest." This tiny shred of good news did little to lighten the load of fear in Jack's heart. He felt some responsibility for her plight, for he should have warned the Garfields that Penstock did not always behave as he ought. Penelope's flight suggested that he had misbehaved toward her.

While Lady Garfield, who paced nervously back and forth on the dock, took charge of Amanda, Sir Edwin and his sons left immediately to organize a search for Penelope. Jack wanted to go with them, but Sir Edwin insisted he go to the house with the ladies.

"You can hardly walk, sir, and have taken a good wetting, too. You don't know the countryside well, so there is no reason for you to expose yourself to more risk of illness. Stay here, please, and offer the ladies what assistance you can. And for heaven's sake keep poor Lord Penstock away from them. He is quite distraught and will do them no good with his lamentations."

Jack clenched his jaw to keep from saying Penstock would have something to lament, indeed, if he had been in any way responsible for Penelope's endangering herself.

When they reached Garfield Manor, Lady Garfield led Amanda away for a change of clothes. Jack found Haskins waiting for him in the door to his suite. As he assisted his master into dry clothing, his very silence told of his concern more than a dozen scolds or caustic comments might have done.

Jack made his way to Winston's rooms in a grim mood, to find that young man weeping and lamenting: "My fault! The best, the most beautiful, the dearest girl in the world, and I have killed her! I loved her, and now she is gone. I shall never forgive myself."

Hal was listening to him and trying, ineffectually, to calm the man. He turned to Jack eagerly.

"I hope you can quiet him, Maitland. He'll have a brain fever at this rate."

Jack had no patience with Hal's kindly pleadings. "Shut

up, Win," he commanded, clasping both of Penstock's shoulders in his hands and shaking him violently. "Shut up and stop wallowing in self-pity."

Winston gasped, choked back a couple of sobs, and broke indignantly from Jack's grasp. "The devil! Have you no sensibility, standing there so coolly? Penelope is drowned, don't you understand?"

"Did you attack her, Win?"

For answer, Penstock lashed out at him, and though Jack's reflexes were fast, he still took a glancing blow on the chin. The two traded several hard punches before Hal and Penstock's valet managed to separate them.

"You'll meet me for that, Jack," Penstock threatened.

"If you have frightened Penelope into swimming to her death, I will gladly meet you, but I expect I will have to stand in line."

"There wasn't the least reason for her to be afraid, but you know how excitable she is. The fool creature swam off before I had the least idea she meant to do so."

"But why?"

"Yes, why?" Hal seconded the question. "Can't make it out, unless you made advances. But in that storm?"

Penstock said nothing, only glared at the two men.

"So. You did frighten her, didn't you?"

"I didn't. I only said . . . well, it stands to reason we would be there alone together for several hours, as would you and Amanda on Xanadu. I only pointed out that we would have to marry. But I want to marry her. I love her to distraction. How was I to know she would take such a strong exception . . ."

"She preferred to risk her life rather than be forced to marry you?" Hal's voice was incredulous. "She must really loathe you. Never guessed. Thought it was a toss-up between you and Jack."

She must really loathe you. Jack suddenly recalled Amanda's words: "You would rather die than marry me." His head spun as he realized just how deeply he had insulted her when he waded into the water rather than stay and risk having to marry her. And yet she had risked her life to save his. Once Cass and Tom realized how he had insulted her and the entire family, they likely would decide to add his name to their dueling schedule! *They will prefer to kill me rather than have me for a brother-in-law,* he thought, *and I would be justly served.*

While Jack confronted his own sins, Hal had been thinking about the situation. "Now Jack will have to marry Miss Amanda. If you had behaved better, Penstock, you'd have lost your chief rival."

Jack's attention returned to Penstock, understanding sending a surge of fury through him. "Which is what you counted on, wasn't it, you bastard! You untied our boat, didn't you? Untied it and somehow got Penelope into the other one. You meant for us to be stranded there, to take me out of the competition. God in heaven, Winston! Your jealousy of me has put that gallant creature's life at risk. You've always hated losing to me, but this! This is beyond anything! Whatever the outcome of their search, I think I shall have to insist that I have first crack at you. And don't delope, for I promise you I won't!" He turned on his heel and walked from the room. He heard Hal berating Penstock loudly as he went back downstairs to watch for the return of the searchers.

Near morning a commotion in the front hall roused him from slumber on the long leather sofa in the Isis drawing room. He went to the door just in time to see Cass hurrying past him with a large bundle of blankets. Bright gold ringlets and a face as pale as the grave were all he saw of Penelope.

Sir Edwin and Tom burst into the hall next, followed by Dr. Bruce. They all hastened up the stairs, leaving Jack standing in the hall, wondering. "Is Miss Garfield . . . ?" He looked at the servant who had followed them in. It was Jones, the gardener who had obliged him the first day he arrived.

"Alive, m'lord. She's bad, very bad, but alive. Crawled out of the lake near Mr. Colson's house. His dogs barked and raised such a clamor he went out with a loaded shotgun, sure it was a robber. She called out, and he brought her in the house and wrapped her up. Met up with us as we were searching nearby, and told us. 'Twas I who fetched the master and told him to bring the carriage." Jones' face glowed with pleasure at having had this honor.

"Good man," Jack said, clasping him on the shoulder. "I don't doubt you'll be well rewarded."

"Didn't do it for a reward, sir. Miss Penelope and Miss Amanda be the finest young ladies around, and Sir Edwin the finest master!" Jones turned away, to hide tears, Jack thought.

The starchy butler tardily arrived on the scene just then and shooed the gardener out of the house. The news of Miss Garfield's return by no means unbent him enough to allow such an inferior man in his front hall. "Wait in the servants' dining room, if you please. Word will be sent there on her condition."

Amanda and her mother kept watch together in the girls' bedroom. Amanda had refused a sleeping draught so that she could do the one thing that was in her power to do for her sister: pray. For several hours the two women alternately knelt in prayer, read the Bible, and walked the floor. The sounds of arrivals in the hall brought them out to look anxiously down the stairway. Hearing Cass speaking reassuring words to Penny as he carried her, tears of joy ran down Amanda's cheek. *She's alive! Thank you, Lord, for answering my prayers!* Amanda and Lady Garfield hugged one another and then hurried down the stairs to meet Cass and follow him up again, peppering him with questions as they went.

Amanda never left Penny's side as she was stripped, sponged off, and dressed in a warm nightrail. Dr. Bruce then entered and listened to Penny's heart, his face grave.

"Exhaustion," he pronounced after completing his examination. "I don't like the sound of her lungs, either. As yet I see no sign of fever, though. She needs quiet, and when she can take it, a nourishing broth." He looked at the circle of anxious faces around him. "It will be a few days before we know, but she is a strong young woman. I think she will recover."

Sir Edwin's grim features relaxed a little at this prognosis. Lady Garfield hugged each of her other children in turn before putting her head on her husband's shoulder and weeping with relief. Dr. Bruce pushed them out of the room, except for Amanda, whom he studied with some concern.

"What of you, missy? Let me feel your forehead."

She tried to refuse but he persisted, then shook his head.

"As I thought from the hectic roses in your cheek. You're coming down with a fever. Best if you don't sleep with your sister tonight."

"But I want to sit up with her!" Amanda fought back tears.

Dr. Bruce shook his head. "Sit up and make yourself sick. No, indeed!" He steered her out into the hall, where she turned rosier than before at being seen in her robe and nightrail by most of the household, including Lord Maitland and Hal Bingham. The memory of Maitland's ugly accusations quickly drained the color from her cheeks. Her mouth set in a grim line, she turned her face away from him. *How could I have loved someone as arrogant and suspicious as he is?* she wondered, quite sure that her feelings for him had been destroyed.

Dr. Bruce issued instructions for Amanda's care in a rapid-fire voice, and Lady Garfield and the servants hastened to tend to her, leaving the men to talk over the day's events. Lord Penstock had joined them by this time, and anxiously asked after Penelope.

"Miss Garfield is barely alive," Jack said, his eyes boring into Penstock. "No thanks to you. Miss Amanda is ill, too, as a result of your perfidy."

This immediately launched a series of questions by the Garfields. With each answer wrung from Penstock, their looks turned darker. Tom growled out, "You will meet me for this. I will allow you until the day after tomorrow so that you can put your affairs in order."

Sir Edwin intervened. "You'll do no such thing, you hasty young puppy! Any duels will only serve to make Penny and Amanda the subject of gossip. With careful management, we can rub through this without scandal. Now, go to bed, all of you, and get some rest. I shall think about what we should do, tomorrow."

Penstock, his jaw working, waited to see if the others would obey. One by one they filed past him, stepping far to one side in disdain. Left standing in the hall with only a sleepy footman, he slowly walked back to his room, head down.

Chapter Twelve

~

When Penstock offered for Penelope the next day, he became the second suitor for one of his daughters that Sir Edwin had turned down flat that morning. The baronet shook his finger at the gloomy young man. "She wouldn't have you, even if I approved, which I don't. Nasty thing, underhanded thing, what you did. Wouldn't give my daughter to a man who could stoop so low. Still, I have convinced my boys to leave you in possession of your skin, for their sisters' sake, not for yours. The same with Lord Maitland. He has promised to take no action if you keep what happened to yourself. He did suggest you might like to take the grand tour, however."

Penstock scowled, but did not quibble. "I am aware that I have behaved very badly, Sir Edwin. I will not compound my folly by telling tales. As for leaving England, I had already taken the resolution to do so if you refused me. Though you may not believe it, I love your daughter deeply, and cannot bear to remain to see her married to another."

"Particularly to Lord Maitland, eh?" Sir Edwin's disdain increased. "Not a kind of love I recognize, sir. If you'll excuse me, I would not wish to delay your departure."

Penstock's nostrils flared, but he had no right to resent such Turkish treatment, and he knew it. He bowed and left Sir Edwin to continue with his rather unpleasant reflections.

Lord Maitland had been before Penstock, offering for Amanda before Sir Edwin had even had his breakfast. He had put the question to his younger daughter immediately. Her answer, when informed that Lord Maitland had paid his addresses, was an emphatic "No!" His offer had been very proper, in Sir Edwin's opinion, but Amanda would have none of it.

"I have no interest in him," she had whispered hoarsely.
"He has behaved as a gentleman ought, and he is Penelope's suitor. Only think, Father—he risked his life to avoid
compromising me. How could anyone think that I would
marry him under such circumstances?"

The child has a point, Sir Edwin acknowledged to himself. It would be painful for any young woman to be pressured into marriage with a man who so obviously wanted
another woman, and her sister at that! So Sir Edwin had
allowed her to refuse, but not without misgivings.

If it had been Penny marooned with Lord Maitland, she
would have been fine, even if she didn't marry the man.
Her beauty would weigh more than the scandal and gain
her a husband eventually, whether it be Hal Bingham or
some as yet undiscovered swain. But it had been Amanda
who had been alone with Maitland. While by no means as
despairing about her prospects as his wife, Sir Edwin knew
finding plain, unprepossessing Amanda a good husband
would have been difficult under any circumstances. Would
last night's adventure make it impossible?

Sir Edwin scolded himself for feeling so blue-deviled.
*Last night I thought I had lost both of my daughters, and
this morning one is very ill but has good hopes of a full
recovery, and the other has nothing worse than a slight cold,
according to Dr. Bruce, and a certain depression of spirits.*

Depression of spirits? Understandable! It was difficult to
put Maitland's dangerous swim in a favorable light as far as
Amanda was concerned. Sir Edwin tapped the letter opener
against his desk. *I don't really blame her for refusing him,*
he thought. Still, as he tried to see into her future, he felt
less than sure of the correctness of his decision. He knew
Maitland hadn't seduced her last night. Amanda knew it.
Her brothers and sisters knew it. Hal and Lord Penstock,
whatever their private opinions, would say nothing. Sir
Edwin wondered whether he could rely on Mr. Tittlecue.
His behavior last night when he learned where Amanda had
been, and with whom, had left much to be desired. He had
torn his hair and gnashed his teeth in fury, declaring her
to be ruined. Fortunately, he did so while speaking privately with Sir Edwin. It was clear he wouldn't wish to
marry her now, but surely he wouldn't spread gossip
about her?

As for the two young ladies who had been their guests, and who, given the illness of their friends, were packing to return to their homes, Kathryn and Barbara had volunteered the assurance that they would say nothing that would harm Penelope and Amanda. *If there were none but our guests to worry about, we might rub through without difficulty.*

But Sir Edwin's foreboding increased when he thought about all the other people who might say something harmful about Amanda, whether out of spite or simply because of the all-too-human love of a good story. For instance, the servants. He doubted his own servants would say anything to denigrate their mistress's honor, of course. But no matter how solemnly Lord Penstock swore himself to silence, his servants would gossip, as would those of Kathryn Majors and Barbara Satterfield. Then there were Hal's servants, Mr. Tittlecue's servants, and Lord Maitland's servants, to say nothing of the tenants and neighbors who had joined in last night's search.

Given all of these potential scandal-mongers, Sir Edwin's usual optimism failed him. He shook his head gloomily. The thought that Lord Maitland surely loved his older daughter and would offer for her when she was well, cheered him somewhat, but he still felt considerable anxiety about the outcome for Amanda.

Later that day, when Hal and Jack offered to leave rather than be a burden to a household with two sick daughters, Sir Edwin urged them to stay on. "If the hunting party breaks up now, that would only fan the flames of gossip and speculation. The young ladies are leaving because their hostesses are ill. Penstock's leaving might be passed over, and Tittlecue's will cause little comment since he lives nearby, but if all four men leave instantly, the wrong conclusions will surely be drawn."

Jack readily agreed, and Hal was nothing loath to remain near his goddess. He had no hope of winning her, he knew, with Jack in the race, but just to be near her was happiness of a sort.

Amanda's cold was mild; she left her bed the next day, and by the third was taking up the reins of the household, which permitted Lady Garfield to attend Penny. For the first few days it seemed that she would develop a pneumonia, but the crisis passed. In defiance of everyone's anxiety about her, Penny made a rapid recovery, and within the week wished to be anywhere but lying in her room upstairs. Keeping the fretful young lady quiet and in her bed until she fully recovered became quite a challenge, and it seemed her mother was the only one capable of being as firm with her as was needed.

During Penny's recuperation period, Amanda made sure no opportunity presented itself for private speech with Jack, and when in his company she treated him with politeness of a sort that held him very much at arm's length. He found this bothered him far more than the lack of Penny's company. Contrasting his feelings with Hal's despondency, which he relieved by writing page after page of poetry, Jack knew that his feelings for Penny had been very shallow, and felt a certain shame in realizing how much they had depended upon his rivalry with Penstock.

Amanda had somehow managed to shield him from her family's anger. *Very likely,* he thought, *she made me out a hero, rather than the bastard I was that night.* He also realized that everyone, from Amanda to Hal, expected him to court Penny when she recovered. It was a devilish awkward situation, considering that he wasn't at all sure he wanted to.

Amanda's determination not to marry Jack increased tenfold with her sister's reactions once she had recovered enough that they could talk frankly. Penny had seemed sad and pensive, and avoided the entire subject of the incident on the lake, which she and everyone else now referred to as *that day.* When Amanda, thinking to cheer her, said, "I have refused Jack's offer, you know. I won't marry him. If you want him, I am quite content that you should have him."

Penny had shaken her head and looked at Amanda with large, sad eyes. "No, sister. He doesn't love me. He as good as told me so that day."

Amanda had smiled at this. "Was that before or after he kissed your hands in front of everyone?"

"Before," Penny had answered with a touch of her old verve. "He had just been reading me a scold for patronizing you! Shortly thereafter, he chose to go off with you, instead of spending the afternoon with me."

"Pooh! It was an act of kindness." At Penny's reproachful look, Amanda admitted, "I do believe he enjoys my company, and he has a genuine interest in botany, as I do. But as for romantic feelings, nothing could be further than the truth!"

Penny brightened somewhat at this. She lay quiet for a long time, a pleased smile on her face. Gradually it faded into a thoughtful frown. "And how about your feelings, Mandy-love? For I have sometimes wondered . . ."

Amanda looked away. "Having seen how desperate he was to avoid matrimony with me, I can only say any slight infatuation I had for him has quite drowned!"

"I wonder if you are telling me everything?" Penny cocked her head to one side. "Amanda, *do* I patronize you? Or manage you? Or . . ."

"Don't be silly. Of course you don't patronize me. You are the best of all sisters. As for managing me, well, you manage everyone, but as Cass always says, you are a benevolent dictator. Now, stop fretting and get some rest. I will read to you."

"I am flattered to think he tried to swim ashore for my sake, but I don't want to see you be hurt."

Amanda twisted uncomfortably in her chair. *Should I tell her about his suspicions? Is it wrong to let her think him better than he is?* She tried to imagine Penelope married to Jack. *I wish she would not. With his temper, his excitability, and his suspicious nature, I fear he will make her an uncomfortable husband. I would be a much better wife for a man of Jack's temperament.*

That last, most unwelcome thought told Amanda that her opinion about Jack might not be based on a sincere concern for Penelope's best interests. So she held her tongue about his accusations, and left it up to Penny to decide on his worthiness.

"I shan't be hurt, unless it be by you, passing up a match you may want out of some misplaced feelings of concern for me."

Penny smiled. "I shan't, then, I promise."

After this conversation Amanda believed that when her sister left off being an invalid, she would welcome Jack's courtship once again. She had no doubt that he would renew it.

*   *   *

When it became clear that Penny was out of danger, Sir
Edwin decided it was time to resume their normal activities.
He invited the gentry of the area to join him once more in
the fields, where the season to hunt his plentiful supply of
grouse had arrived with October's chilly winds. The invitees
assembled before Garfield Manor the next day, and a
merry, noisy lot they were, with mules braying, horses rear-
ing, servants scolding them, and masters calling out
instructions.

Mr. Tittlecue stood at the top of the steps with Sir Edwin
and three other local gentlemen, listening politely to an
account of the young ladies' rapid recovery, when Jack
joined them, riding whip in hand. The second Tittlecue saw
Jack, he drew himself up to his imposing height, his pink
cheeks flushed red.

"You astound me, Sir Edwin, to be still allowing
houseroom to this seducer of young women!"

Jack's scowl was nothing compared to his host's. Sir
Edwin hissed, "Lower your voice, man. Everyone is listening. And let me tell you . . ."

Far from lowering his voice, Tittlecue fairly shouted, "I
understand perfectly that you hope to pretend all is well,
for it is as clear as day that this scoundrel has not offered
his name to Miss Amanda, though he has ruined her reputation. He should take himself off, so that decent folks do
not have to meet him."

Below them on the stairs and the carriageway, everyone,
servant and man, within sound of that strident voice
stopped stock-still, all eyes on the men at the top of the
steps.

Sir Edwin raised his voice, too. "Lord Maitland behaved
as the perfect gentleman in a situation not of his making,
and yet had the condescension to offer for Miss Amanda.
She assured me there was no need, and she is a truthful
young lady. We treasure Lord Maitland's friendship, so I
will not hear you speak against him again, sir."

"Hah! As usual, you sacrifice Amanda for her sister. You
still hope he will marry Penelope. Take care he does not
ruin her as well. As for me, I heartily do pity Miss Amanda,
for no respectable man would consider marrying . . ."

His words were cut off by Jack's hand at his throat. "Shut

your vicious mouth, sir, or I'll cut your tongue out of your head," he snarled. Sir Edwin and Cass, who had just joined them, pulled the two apart. Tittlecue, choking violently, ran down the stairs and called for his mule. Once mounted, he opened his mouth to speak, but the sight of Jack, Amanda's father, and both of her brothers glaring murderously at him made him think better of it, so he turned his mule's head and put his spurs in the animal's flanks, thereby assuring himself of a departure more speedy than dignified.

Sir Edwin's other guests crowded around, letting him and Jack know that they did not credit Tittlecue's rantings at all. Grateful, but knowing full well the damage that had been done, Sir Edwin still acted the hearty host, urging them to forget the unpleasantness and enjoy their sport.

That evening Jack approached Sir Edwin again, and they agreed that scandal would be harder than ever to avert. "Let me speak to Amanda," Jack urged him. "Perhaps I can convince her to marry me."

Sir Edwin knew his youngest daughter better than to suppose it would be easy. Once she had made up her mind, she was difficult to budge. Still, he gave his permission, and Amanda found herself summoned to the library after dinner that evening, to be alone with Jack for the first time since the day they were marooned.

Before Jack could so much as get out a word, Amanda rushed into speech. "I heard what happened today, Lord Maitland, and it makes no difference to me. Do you suppose I regret losing Mr. Tittlecue as a suitor?" She laughed. "Far from it. I am grateful not to have to be kind to him anymore, for he is the sort of man who mistakes kindness for favor."

"Amanda, I'm sure your father already told you that half the county heard what that wretched man said. And their servants! That is the worst of it. Through no fault of yours, or mine, you have been ruined. Tittlecue spoke truly: no respectable man will wish to marry you now."

Amanda avoided his effort to take her hands in his. She had encased her heart in ice since that fatal evening when he had insulted her and her family, and risked death rather than marry her. She would take no chance of allowing Jack's touch to thaw her. Only in this frozen state could she bear the pain of that rejection.

"I told you before that I doubted I would marry, and that I did not plan to repine for lack of a husband. I took this resolution long before you came into my life, so please stop worrying about me."

"I can't!" He followed her as she retreated, capturing her upper arms to prevent further escape. "Listen, dear heart, I . . ."

"Don't call me dear heart. Nothing could be more inappropriate." She jerked out of his arms and crossed the room, taking a defensive posture behind a chair. "You do not love me. I promised you I would never allow you to be forced into marriage with me, and I meant it!"

"But you seem to think I regard it as a fate worse than death. I don't, I assure you. I have a great fondness for you. We deal well together. You will make me an admirable wife, a wonderful countess one day. Or, more likely, a wonderful mother of the future earl, as my father is a vigorous man who may well outlive us all."

"And what of Penny?"

"She will make me a wonderful sister-in-law."

Amanda shook her head. "Never. Never!"

"If you think I still suspect you, or any of your relatives, of scheming to entrap me, you are wrong. I behaved like a gudgeon that day. Please forgive me, and accept my proposal."

"I will not marry you. As for forgiveness—I might be able to, if I understood why. Will you explain one thing to me, and then we will consider how to outface those who would accuse you of dishonorable behavior."

He growled at her: "Amanda, I won't take no . . ."

"You will have to. Father won't force me, and it is not in your power to do so. Now, please tell me why it is that from the first few moments of our acquaintance, you harbored that unfounded suspicion? Is the sort of scheme you suspected attempted against you frequently?"

If I explain, perhaps she will change her mind, Jack thought. But to tell anyone what his father had done would be excruciatingly embarrassing. He released her and walked to a window that looked out over the park. The lake that had brought them to this moment gleamed in the moonlight in the middle distance.

"The one person I should be able to trust to have my

best interest at heart enlisted a young woman I have known
and respected since infancy, in a conspiracy to trick me into
compromising her." He turned to look at Amanda. Though
her eyebrows arched to their highest, and her eyes were
wide, there was nothing amused or amusing about her appearance. Instead, she looked astonished and pained at the
same time.

"I mean, of course, my father."

Amanda inhaled sharply. "No. Surely not!"

"My father and Victoria, the daughter of his friend and
our neighbor, Lord Ridgewell. They had often hinted at a
match between us, but she and I were united in laughing
such a notion down. At least I thought we were."

He rubbed his finger down the bridge of his nose. "I
suppose I must tell you all. When Napoleon left Elba, I
wanted to volunteer my services to the army. With so many
of his best troops still in America, Wellington would need
all the help he could get. But when I told my father of my
plan, he harshly forbade me to do so. He said that my duty
to the family name came first." He banged his fist against
the window. "I did not see it! There have been Stanwells
fighting for the crown since the Conqueror. We began as a
warrior class, and I do not think time, wealth, and privilege
have freed us of our obligation to fight. To the contrary,
we are the natural leaders. Why should we retain so many
of the privileges of our ancestors if we refuse to accept the
responsibilities?"

His eyes searched Amanda's face. As expected, he saw
understanding and sympathy there. "In the end I told him
I would volunteer, even if it meant defying him. I thought
he had accepted my decision. I was in London, outfitting
myself for the army, when Victoria lured me to a private
salon in her friend's home during a ball. She needed my
advice, she said. When I entered, she cast herself into my
arms and began crying. I comforted her, and while I begged
her to tell me what was the matter, my father, her father,
our hostess, and her daughter all burst into the room. Instead of pulling away, Victoria pressed herself closer. My
father's face—I shall never forget how triumphant it was."

"Abominable!"

"He has been after me to marry since I was barely out
of short pants. The succession! It is all he could think

about. Doubt not—to him I am breeding stock, and nothing else."

"Oh, Jack." The bitterness in his voice wrung Amanda's heart. The icy coat around it cracked. She longed to go to him, to put her arms around him and comfort him.

"I was furious! I told them that if they pretended to believe her compromised, and spoke of it to anyone else, any bad consequences she suffered would be upon their heads."

Silence descended as the two wrestled with their own complex emotions.

Jack turned back to the window. "When I was wounded, my father came to Belgium to take care of me. Such touching concern! His version of looking after me was to try to convince me to have my leg amputated. He said, "If you had already sired a son, you might do as you wish with your life, but until then, you owe me to preserve it at all costs. If gangrene sets in, you will perish. Amputate that leg immediately. Then you shall at least survive to begat an heir."

Amanda felt tears coursing down her cheeks. She dug her fingernails into her palms to keep herself from going to Jack and embracing him, giving him some of that tenderness he had needed and sorely lacked when he was injured.

"With Haskins' help, I resisted him. Instead of getting the peace and quiet, and the kind of love that you and your siblings would receive from your parents in a similar situation, my father tortured me with his demands to marry, from the moment he came to Belgium, until I was well enough to get away from him. In fact, I made the move far too soon for my health's sake, but I feared I might commit patricide did I not get away, so my valet helped me escape and hide in lodgings in London. I owe him the fact that I still have my sanity, as well as two legs."

Amanda could no longer resist; she touched Jack gently on his shoulder, and when he turned, embraced him in a comforting hug.

For a long moment he rocked her back and forth as she murmured her sympathy to him. Then he shifted his posture. Bringing his right hand up to cup her chin, he tilted her head back. "Amanda, sweet Amanda. To suspect you, to punish you for my father's sins was despicable." He lowered his head and gently kissed her on the lips.

To Amanda, the feel of his mouth against hers was an entire novelty. She had never been kissed as Penelope had. Her bolder, more experienced sister had attempted to describe the sensation, but nothing she said had prepared Amanda for the subtle thrill, the pulse of warmth that ran through her. Instinctively she lifted her head and pressed her mouth against his, seeking to prolong the contact.

Jack pulled her deeper into his embrace and intensified the kiss. Her naive yet eager response aroused him as no experienced courtesan had ever done. Still, he ended the kiss rather than give in to the temptation to plunder her mouth with his tongue—that would not do at all. Decent young woman that she was, she would likely be scandalized by such an intimacy.

He whispered against her cheek as he held her close, "You see, Amanda? We shall deal very well together indeed. Now, let us have no more roundaboutation. Marry me!"

Amanda pulled away, a dazzled expression in her eyes. She touched her fingertips to her lips. But she shook her head, tentatively at first, and then emphatically. "I cannot. I won't. You don't love me, or . . . or I, you. If we found that kiss pleasant, it still doesn't change the facts. We cannot found a marriage on scandal and lust."

He reached for her again, thinking that actions might carry more weight than words, but she ducked away. "We shall be friends, my lord. Friends, and perhaps, who can say, in-laws. As for the opinions of society, I shall adopt the motto of the knights of the garter: *'honi soit qui mal y pense.'* The shame rests with those who see wickedness where there is none."

She smiled at him as she opened the door. "Let us rejoin the others. You will be glad to know that Penelope has been given permission to come downstairs for a few minutes after dinner."

Chapter Thirteen

~

Penny was as bad a patient as Jack had ever thought
about being. The first evening she was allowed downstairs, she begged to extend her allotted time until the tea
tray was brought, and pouted mightily when this request
was denied. Over the next week she fussed and fumed at
not being allowed to resume normal activities, making all
around her almost as miserable as she was. Jack took his
turn reading to her and playing chess with her. She and
Mandy played him and Hal at innumerable games of whist,
piquet, and silver loo. He admired the calming influence
Amanda had on her sister, and the endless patience Hal
showed toward her foibles. He himself was no better at
cosseting than at being cosseted, so he found himself dreading evenings after dinner.

Fortunately for her and for those who tried to interest
her in passive entertainments, she healed with all the rapid-
ity of a healthy young animal, and soon returned to her
active life.

The Garfields regarded Jack as Penny's suitor, which
made him increasingly uncomfortable. With the rivalry between himself and Lord Penstock ended, his interest in
courting The Beauty continued to wane. It was not that he
disliked her, just that he had no wish to do more than
admire her beauty as he might admire a magnificent jewel
or painting. Never once had he felt desire for her in the
way he had for Amanda. Moreover, the loss of interest
seemed to be mutual: When he made halfhearted attempts
to flirt with her, it seemed to him that she did not flirt
back. He counseled himself to be patient. *Perhaps she is
just not feeling the thing yet. Once she is her old vibrant self
again, I will once again be attracted to her.*

On the other hand, he longed for the camaraderie that

he had known with Amanda while exploring the flora of Xanadu and exchanging drawings, but she seemed determined not to be alone with him, and even in company had little to say to him. His confession to her may have made her hate him less, but it did not return them to their previous footing.

In an attempt to reclaim her friendship, he rowed back to Xanadu and retrieved the remnants of their sketch pads. Wet and then dried several times, the drawings therein were not in very good shape. He asked Amanda to redo the series of mushroom sketches for him, hoping this would rekindle their rapport. He had the satisfaction of seeing a slight flush mount her cheeks, which he took as an indication of her pleasure at the request. She did as he asked, but sidestepped his invitation to explore the environs of the home woods for interesting flora with him, reminding him that it would make Penny too unhappy to be left behind.

He still enjoyed going hunting with the men, and in other circumstances would have looked forward to the fox hunts planned in November. But the evenings became more and more awkward and difficult for him to endure.

When he ripped the seat of a pair of trousers while riding one day, his valet unwittingly provided him with the excuse to leave that he had been seeking. "My lord, the Garfields' cook has accomplished what your London cook could not," Haskins observed as he repaired the seam.

"He's put some meat on my bones, hmmm?" Jack recalled his finicky appetite after Waterloo. Like his nightmares, it was gone. Cass had been right in thinking immersing himself in this family would chase away the miasmas of memory, though not in just the way anyone would have planned.

Jack turned about while looking in a standing mirror in his dressing room. "Yes, I do seem to have gained weight. I only hope I may not become fat."

Haskins smiled. "You have quite a ways to go before that happens. Still, you will require a new wardrobe before long."

To Haskins' surprise, Jack yelped out, "Yes! That is the very thing."

"Did I not know how tedious you find it to be measured by a tailor, I might suppose you meant to employ one on the instant. I am told that Highton has one competent tailor, if one is merely ordering clothes suitable for country pursuits. Shall I send word for him to call here?"

"I shall need dress clothes, too, for the hunt ball if nothing else. Begin packing immediately. I will inform my host this evening that we plan an excursion to London for just that purpose."

Haskins put aside the pants. "A strategic retreat, m'lord?"

"Something of that sort. Now, what is that sour look about?"

"Everyone is in hourly expectation that you will offer for Miss Garfield."

"The best reason I can imagine for said retreat."

"Wise, perhaps, but is it kind?"

"Do you think her affections are engaged? I would swear she shows more interest in Hal than in me." Jack rested his hand on his chin and stared into the fire. Returning health had brought back Penny's old sparkle, but his interest in her did not revive. As for The Beauty, her attitude toward him remained friendly, but entirely lacking in coquetry. "Still, I suppose I must put some sort of period to matters, rather than leave them unresolved," Jack conceded. "That way, if I decide not to return . . ."

"If, my lord?" Haskins smiled and exited before his master's volatile temper erupted in flying hairbrushes.

Jack decided that plain speaking was the most honorable path, even if it caused Penny momentary pain. To that end he invited her to play a game of chess with him. He was surprised that she acquiesced so readily, for now that she felt better, she preferred more active entertainments such as charades or glees. She had only played chess during the first few days of her convalescence, when her family insisted that she be entirely quiet.

Chess was the only activity he could think of that would give him the opportunity for private speech with her. As was her habit, she sent away all observers, declaring that they gave her the fidgets when she tried to concentrate. *Quite as if she hadn't been born with the fidgets,* he thought, smiling as she restlessly fingered the pieces while he studied his first move.

After they had played for several moves, and the other

occupants of the drawing room were paying them no attention, he spoke to her softly as he held his hand above one
of his rooks.

"Penny, I apologize for foisting a chess game on you,
but . . ."

"But you wished to speak to me privately," she responded saucily, her vivid blue eyes laughing at him.

"Yes. You see, I am in something of a quandary." He
had rehearsed in his mind several different versions of this
speech, but now none of them seemed right. He had a
sudden image of himself as a very large, very clumsy bull
in the Garfields' china closet. *I've insulted one sister terribly,
and am about to do so with the other.*

As Penny watched him struggle for words, the amusement died out of her eyes. "Never say you are going to
offer for me!"

At the note of alarm in her voice, Jack's tense expression
sagged into one of relief. "I can see that is not precisely
your heart's desire, so rest easy. This is not a proposal. I
didn't *think* you had a tendre for me, but . . ."

"But everyone else thinks so. You have been placed in
a most difficult position. Your heroic efforts to avoid compromising Amanda convinced everyone you were mad to
marry me. After our brief contretemps that afternoon, I
seriously doubted it. But that leaves the question open: why
attempt that swim?"

Jack moved his rook without any clear concept of the
effect it would have on his position. He avoided Penny's
intelligent gaze.

"Did you dislike so much the thought of marrying
Amanda? No wonder she refused you so emphatically.
Oh!" She broke off her interrogation to take his rook with
her knight, chortling gleefully.

Jack smiled. "I shall have to concentrate more. I do not
dislike the thought of marrying Amanda, as I have tried to
convince her. That night I behaved rashly, foolishly. But I
would like to make amends. Are you aware she has refused
me twice?"

"But you didn't offer out of love." Penny shook her finger at him. "I would not want you under those circumstances, and Amanda is quite as proud as I."

And I hurt her pride terribly. So much so she hasn't even

confided the truth about that evening to her twin. Jack sighed. "It's all very lowering. I used to think myself a tolerable marriage prospect." He smiled ruefully.

"And I used to think you a tolerable chess player," Penny crowed.

Jack looked from her to the board and back again. "So did I." He tipped his king in recognition of her checkmate, but did not seek a rematch. "I spoke to you this evening because I find I must go to London to bespeak a new wardrobe. Your father's much-beloved French chef has helped make my clothes obsolete."

Penny looked at him sapiently. "You wished to be sure you weren't leaving a lovesick young woman behind to pine over you."

"Well, I . . ."

She tossed her head. "Your conscience may rest easy. I daresay we each regarded the other as highly eligible when first we met, but have discovered we will not suit." She stood. "If you come back for foxhunting, you will be welcome, but no expectations will embarrass you. You have made friends here, Jack. Friends for a lifetime, if you will have us."

Jack stood and looked into her eyes. Her gaze was warm and candid. "I am glad of it!"

On his first evening in London, Jack found Gerrard Linderhill and Richard Dremel dining in White's. They hailed him eagerly, and exchanged affectionate insults in the way of young men everywhere. Something very particular in their manner put him on his guard, but they contented themselves with sharing the latest *on-dits*, and asking his opinion on the fortunes, or rather misfortunes, of the iron duke, who found restoring the French monarchy more difficult than defeating the French army.

Confessing he had not kept up with developments in France, Jack changed the subject. "Have you still the Morris in your keeping?" he asked Gerrard. "Such a beauty. If you had not snatched her up when Sir William dropped her, I would have!"

"We hear you have been sporting in loftier pastures than mere opera dancers," Linderhill retorted. "Miss Garfield is a stunning beauty, and a well-connected one. We've been in hourly expectation of an announcement of your engagement. I collect that is why you are in London, to arrange settlements and the like?"

Inwardly Jack cringed. Why was everyone pushing him on Miss Garfield? Outwardly he assumed a devil-may-care attitude. "How much did you wager on it, Gerry?"

"Oh, a monkey is all."

"You wagered five hundred pounds that I would wed Miss Garfield? What a gudgeon you are! Sorry, but you have lost your wager. Or perhaps not, if you stated that I won her over Penstock, for he withdrew from the field, and I told you I did not mean to be legshackled for some time yet."

Gerrard and Dick exchanged astonished looks. "Can't think how you managed to avoid offering for her and lived to tell the tale," Gerrard protested. "Though you haven't, of course. I mean, well, you've lived, but you didn't tell the tale. Heard it from that pathetic country squire you won her from."

Dick chimed in, "Yes, do tell us why you are not to marry the chit. Beautiful as she can stare—how can you turn her down? I would have thought Caspian and Tom Garfield would have had something to say about it, after you marooned yourself with The Beauty on an island for days? Underhanded, I say. Not like you. That should cancel our bet, Gerry."

Gerrard began to sputter out a denial, but Jack put both hands on the table and half stood, glaring at both men. "Not another word, Ger, Dick. There is no truth in what you are saying. I wasn't marooned with Miss Garfield, and I've not 'sported' with either of the Garfield sisters. Who told you so?"

"Told you it was a take in," Dick crowed. "You owe me ten crowns for that one, Ger. And that pink-faced creature Tattlecup was never engaged to Miss Garfield, was he, Jack?" Dick rubbed his hands gleefully. "You may as well hand over your quarter's allowance, Ger. My superior reasoning ability won out. Diamond of the first water, she is. Penstock dangling after her, Hal Bingham, too. Can't ever have preferred Tattlecur to either of those two."

"Tittlecue!" Jack's voice thickened with loathing. "So he's the one! He'll answer to me for this!"

"You know the bloke? So, was he engaged to The Beauty, then?" Gerrard looked anxiously at Jack.

"Certainly not." Jack sat back down. "Delusions, that's what it was. And it was the younger sister he referred to, not Miss Garfield."

"But what a tale he made up! Said Penstock had been driven from the country in disgrace. That part true? He's gone, that's for sure. Came through London as fast as a scalded cat, and wouldn't answer any of our questions. Which side did I take in that bet, Dick?"

Jack dropped his head into his hands. *How am I to put a stop to this? At this rate, both girls will be ruined.* He looked through spread fingers at his two bickering friends. "Listen, you two. Stop this nonsense and let me tell you what really happened."

When he finally had their attention, he gave an abbreviated account of the incident. "An unexpected storm blew up while we were on the lake. Penstock, the cowhanded clunch, ran aground on some rocks. The Beauty was in his boat and nearly drowned as a result of his carelessness. Fortunately, she is a strong swimmer . . ."

"That perfect model of femininity a strong swimmer? Jack, Jack, your story is more unlikely than Trebble-comb's." Dick pulled Jack's hands away from his face. "Now, confess, you made that up."

"I did not! Penelope, for all her beauty, is as delicate as a bullock! The younger daughter, Amanda and I, were briefly stranded on a small island, but . . ."

"Amanda? The dab of a girl with all those nasty black springs on her head? No wonder you didn't offer marriage." Dick pulled out a small notebook from an inner pocket of his jacket. "Now, let's see. The odds on your marrying her were . . . oh, astronomical."

"Springs on her head?" Gerrard asked.

"Curls. First girl I ever saw with curls as stiff as carriage springs. Wears 'em all over her face. I never quite understood how she could see to walk around."

"Never met her, but she sounds a quiz. Of course you wouldn't marry her, Jack. Now, don't tell me I took that bet, Dick, because I didn't."

"You did too!"

"Stop it, you two. Two young ladies' reputations depend

upon your getting the story straight, and spreading it quite as assiduously as I gather you've been spreading the other one. How many people do you have wagers with on this?"

"Do us a wrong," Dick said, highly offended. "Private wagers entirely! Not to say others won't have put some money on the outcome, with Tumblecarp bruiting his version of events all over London. But I would have thought Tom and Cass would expect you to marry the chit, if you were marooned with her. Pretty or not, she's still their sister."

"As a matter of fact, I did offer for her, but she refused me. There wasn't the least need, she said, and she was right. I tell you, nothing happened! Of course her brothers would have my hide otherwise, as you say."

Both Dick and Gerrard looked skeptical. "Why'd Turtlecarp break off his engagement, then? Why was he in Manton's, practicing his marksmanship, saying to all who would listen that he meant to avenge himself?"

Jack groaned. "There never was an engagement. He hoped to marry Amanda, but . . ."

"Uh-oh!" Both of his friends looked alarmed and half rose as if poised for flight. "Don't turn around, Jack. Maybe he hasn't seen you."

"Let me guess. My father. It wanted only that." Jack unconsciously straightened his shoulders. "What the deuce is he doing in town? He always hunts Melton Mowbray at this time of year."

"I'd say he is hunting, all right. Alas for you, for I think you are the fox. Must have heard the tales. High stickler, your father. He'll be furious. Should we go?"

"Stay, if you please. It might keep him from making a scene here. If he is going to comb my hair with a stool, I would prefer it to be in private." Jack braced himself for his father's fury. The earl detested scandal of any sort. Like so many of his generation, he concerned himself more with the appearance of correct behavior than its practice.

"Won't make you marry her, though, will he?" Gerrard inquired in concern. "Not the drab one!"

"My father is so eager to see me marry and produce an heir, he'll likely insist that I marry the girl, no matter how fusby-faced. But . . ."

Jack intended to say he did not find Amanda unattractive, but he was forestalled by a hard hand gripping his shoulder. "My boy! Did not expect to see you here. Thought you were fixed in Yorkshire."

"Merely renewing my wardrobe, sir," Jack said, rising.

"Oh, sit down, sit down. Don't mean to break up your party. I'm meeting some friends." To Jack's surprise, his father was entirely affable. "I'll join you for just a moment, if I may."

"Surprised to see you in London at this season, sir."

"Arrived not two hours ago. I have some pressing business to attend to. I'll be off tomorrow. Will you be joining us at Melton Mowbray?"

"Ah . . . no, sir. I came only to visit my tailor, as I've outgrown almost everything I own. Mean to depart tomorrow, so I can hunt with the Garfields."

"You must give me the name of your tailor. Mine is nothing like so prompt," the earl countered wryly.

"I'll have them sent on to Yorkshire when they are finished, of course. Haskins can make any adjustments that are required."

"Ah, yes. The redoubtable Haskins. We have much to thank him for, do we not?" His father's eyes were almost caressing as they scanned Jack. "You look robust, m'boy. Glad to see it. A repairing lease has been good for you. The leg?"

"Almost entirely healed, sir."

"Good. Good. Your gamble paid off, then. Well, I expect you for the holidays." Momentarily a deep tension could be glimpsed on the earl's still-handsome face.

Jack knew that an olive branch had been extended. He took it, but knew that once his father heard about the scandal now brewing, the truce would be at an end. "Yes, sir. That is my plan. I hope I may bring a guest or two?"

"Of course! Of course!" The Earl of Chalwicke nodded his head vigorously. "As many as you like. Well, I must be off. Gentlemen." He bowed cordially to Richard and Gerrard and departed.

His two friends looked at Jack with awe once the earl had gone. "You rubbed through that one! Hasn't heard yet," Dick exclaimed.

"Luckiest man I ever knew," Gerrard agreed.

"No, he hasn't heard yet, but he will, and I don't want

to be in London when it happens. Good job I went straight to my tailor. Gentlemen, I bid you good evening. I'll be setting out at first light tomorrow."

"France," Dick said knowingly.

"Ten guineas says he'll head for Scotland."

"No, Yorkshire, to claim my bride. I would appreciate it if you two would not make her the subject of vulgar wagers."

"But wait! Do you mean to marry the plain one?" Dick asked.

"Of course he doesn't, you clunch," Gerrard exclaimed. "Can you see Jack standing up with a female with such hair as you have described?"

"I am marrying Amanda Garfield, for whom I have a very high regard. As for those curls, fear not, old friends. I mean to banish them as soon as I can!"

Chapter Fourteen

～

Jack's worst nightmare had come to pass, not because of gossiping servants, but because of that idiot, Tittlecue. All the way back to Yorkshire he alternated planning revenge on the man with worrying about how he would convince Amanda to marry him, and her parents to allow him to take her to Scotland for a swift wedding. For even though he had told his friends that his father would insist he marry Amanda, he wasn't entirely sure. It would be disastrous if the earl showed up at Garfield Manor, raging as only he could, forbidding his son to unite himself to mere country gentry. He knew that Amanda's pride, her family's pride, would prevent them from countenancing a marriage of which his father disapproved.

Amanda, sweet little Amanda, what will become of you if I don't marry you? You'd be shunned and gossiped about, and doubtless always remain a spinster, and you wouldn't like that as well as you think. You were made to have a husband, a home, and children of your own. It was a matter of honor to marry her, but more than that, Jack had grown to like the younger daughter too well to wish such a fate on her. He liked the Garfields, too, better than his own family. And some small, vindictive corner of his mind whispered that marrying a girl his father would think beneath him would serve to pay the old man out almost as well as not marrying!

Tired, his leg aching from so many miles of jostling about in his curricle, Jack turned onto the drive leading to Garfield Manor, to be hailed cheerily by the two sisters. He pulled his horses up and watched them approach. Amanda was mounted on her pretty little mule, while Penelope rode a fine Arabian mare. He smiled to himself. *Mandy still pre-*

tends she prefers to ride Hippolyta for her father's sake. When once we are married, I shall see that she has a beautiful little mare. And riding habits that flatter her. He suppressed a shudder at the effect the purple riding habits both girls wore had on Amanda's coloring.

"You came back," Penelope said, smiling welcomingly.

"Not that we are not glad, Lord Maitland, but we had not expected you—ah—so soon," Amanda added. She smiled, too, but it was a wary smile that did not bode well for his purposes.

"Something came up. Something urgent. I must speak to your father at once. Is he at home?"

"No," Penelope said, wrinkling her brow at Jack's peremptory manner. "He and the boys have gone to shoot grouse on Dr. Bruce's farm."

Drawing a deep breath to stem the urge to swear, Jack nodded. "I feared as much. I need to speak to him right away. I wonder if I might borrow a mount? These horses are exhausted."

The girls exchanged glances. "Of course," Amanda replied. "We'll ride with you to the stables."

Sensing that something extraordinary was afoot, the young women let him go ahead a bit so they could talk. "There is scandal," Penny supposed. "He has come to renew his proposal to you."

"No, he has realized how much he loves you, and has returned to ask for Father's permission to address you," Amanda declared. She wondered if Penny would accept him. She had shown no sign of repining while he was away. Rather, she had spent many happy hours with Hal, who read poetry to her—his own and others'.

Penny considered Amanda's comment, her head on one side. "Would you say his greeting was that of a lover? Jack hasn't courted me since Lord Penstock decamped, and well you know it. I do believe his interest in me stemmed from a long-standing rivalry between them, which is a lowering thought. At any rate, I don't want to marry him."

Amanda studied her sister's profile. "Penny! Is that the truth? You aren't pretending, are you, thinking that he will offer for me again? For I assure you I will not marry him."

"If you must know, my affections are otherwise engaged.

So if he has come back on my account, he has wasted a trip."

"Hal, then?"

Penny nodded, eyes shining. "I have loved him ever since he sent up that ode to me while I was recovering from the pneumonia. I know you do not think him good husband material, Mandy, but he will suit me very well. I don't love Jack, and I would never marry him knowing that my sister does."

Amanda almost dropped her reins. "Penny! Why would you think . . . Oh, no, dearest. You mustn't turn down a wonderful man like Jack because of such a ridiculous notion."

"You haven't confided in me," Penny said, an offended note in her voice. She turned to spear her sister with her vivid blue gaze. "For the first time in our lives, you have been keeping things from me. But how did you think you could? I know you too well."

"I tell you, I don't!" Amanda tried to meet Penny's intent stare, but had to look away. "Well, I don't," she insisted, but in a small voice.

Penny reached across the distance to squeeze her sister's hand. "Foolish Amanda! Be honest, at least with yourself, if not with me. Now, we must think what to do to prevent him from proposing out of a sense of duty, yet keep him here so he can fall in love with you."

"It is hopeless," Amanda said. She squeezed Penny's hand in return before releasing it. "You can't suppose someone like Jack will fall in and out of love like a boy. He is a man grown. He loved you before that day. I think he only left off courting you because he felt that he had compromised me and it would be too awkward."

"That isn't true, Amanda. I didn't tell you before, but we had a frank discussion before he left, and agreed we would not suit. I said nothing to you then because I wasn't sure he would return and didn't want to give you false hope. I think he likes you very well, and that liking could turn to love if given the proper conditions."

Amanda shook her head. "Don't say any more, Penny. I have excellent reasons for knowing that Lord Maitland would never marry me for any reason except his strong sense of honor, and I swore to him that I wouldn't allow him to throw himself away like that. I meant it, too! Do you think I would have a husband who so emphatically did not want me? Who might be in love with my sister? So for heaven's sake don't discourage his suit on my account."

"I tell you he required no discouragement, but even if he did, I don't love him, and that's the end of it. We shouldn't deal well together. We both have too much temper. And he has no sensibility, whereas Hal, dear Hal, will feel as I do on everything. Think! I shall be the wife and the inspiration of a great poet!" Penny's face shone at this pleasing prospect.

Amanda shook her head. She did not dislike Hal, but he seemed so bland, so quiet, and so utterly unworldly. *I hope that Father will devise a settlement to protect Penny from her prospective husband's impractical nature.* Then her thoughts turned, with sincere pity, upon Jack, so worthy and so soon to be disappointed, for she discounted her sister's story, thinking Penny had misread Jack's feelings. *He has hastened back from London in a pelter, intent on offering for her, and she will turn him down.* The thought of his pain brought a lump to her throat.

Amanda, Lady Garfield, Tom, and Cass were all astonished when Sir Edwin, after closeting himself with Jack for a long time after dinner, sent Bennington to invite Amanda to the library. Penny laughed softly in triumph, and Hal gave a long, low sigh of relief.

"Bennington! Have you mispoken?" Lady Garfield's hand clutched her throat. Amanda's mother had been in alt on learning of Lord Maitland's return, absolutely sure that he had come to renew his suit for Penny's hand. She had ransacked their wardrobes, seeking exactly the right dress to best set off Penny's beauty. Of course, both girls must wear the same dress, which was unfortunate for Amanda, for the chosen garment was an ivory satin, cut with a low V-neck and draped close to the bodice, outlining all of Penny's considerable charms.

I look like an underfed waif in this dress, Amanda had thought while dressing for dinner. *And ivory makes my skin look yellow.* But she said nothing, lacking the courage, as usual, to challenge her mother. *What does it matter anyway, what I wear?* she thought, submitting to the curling iron.

He won't notice; he'll be too busy devouring Penny with his eyes.

So when the butler summoned her to join Jack and her father, she shrank back into her chair, echoing her mother's question. "Are you sure he asked for me?" It would be utterly humiliating to go to the library as if she were expecting a proposal meant for her sister.

"Very sure, miss, for he repeated it to me."

Amanda entered the library hesitantly. "Was it I you sent for, Papa?" She glanced sideways at Jack. "Bennington insisted . . ."

"Yes, my love. Please have a seat." He indicated a chair between himself, seated at his desk, and Jack, sitting nervously on the edge of an Egyptian throne chair. "Lord Maitland has learned something quite disturbing during his brief sojourn in London." He explained what had happened, ending with, "So, my dear, although I felt at the time that we might brush through without scandal if we were extremely lucky, now that Tittlecue has behaved so foolishly, I feel I must insist that you accept Lord Maitland's proposal."

"Insist, Papa?" Amanda frowned, her eyes searching her father's face. He was the mildest, the kindest of fathers. Surely he would not force her to marry.

"Darling girl, you are ruined if you do not. I cannot bear the thought of people bandying your name about. And it would be most uncomfortable for the rest of the family, too."

Amanda looked sideways at Jack, who regarded her with a worried expression. "I swore to Lord Maitland that I would not allow our accidental stay on the island to force him into marriage to me, which he made very clear he would not like at all."

"It was not you, but the situation I objected to, Mandy. I have explained it to you, you know. I thought you promised to forgive me for my hasty judgment."

She shook her head. "I have forgiven you, but it makes no difference. Papa, I can't marry under these circumstances. It isn't fair to either of us. I shall go away somewhere, so as to avoid embarrassing you."

Sir Edwin sputtered indignantly. "As if we would turn

our backs on you! You will always be our beloved daughter, no matter what . . ."

Jack interrupted. "May I speak with Amanda alone for a few moments, sir?"

Amanda protested, but her father nodded and removed himself. Jack pivoted in his chair and leaned toward her. He had considered at length what might cause her to change her mind. Her weak point, for his purpose, lay in her love of family and concern for the feelings of others, including, he hoped, himself.

"Mandy, I am surprised to see that you put your pride above everything, even the pain this scandal could cause for your family."

Amanda stiffened. She hadn't thought of that before. He held up his hand to prevent her rushing into speech. "In addition to that, you should consider what it may do to me. I enjoy a good reputation just now, but what will be said of me if people believe I debauched and abandoned the daughter of a respectable gentleman? What will my father say? I shouldn't be surprised if he were to disinherit me!"

Amanda laughed. "Doing it too brown, Lord Maitland. He may be vexed at the scandal, but surely not enough to take such drastic action. If he should, though, I will speak to him. Once he hears the truth from me, he will not be so upset."

"Hah! He will be even more disgusted with me, for he will learn that I offended you so much you cannot forgive me even in the face of social ruin."

"I will never allow him to think that. I will simply tell him that I have always intended to be a spinster, a well-loved maiden aunt. I would far rather be that than an unwanted wife. If you hasten to woo her, you might even still win Penny from Hal, and then your father could not fail to be pleased, and to know that the reports were untrue, for what father would give one daughter in marriage to a man who had ruined the other?"

"Apparently Penny has not confided in you, Amanda, but we spoke frankly about this before I left. I don't wish to marry her. She is lovely, and sweet, and I will welcome her as my sister-in-law, but I don't believe we would suit and she assured me she feels the same. I much prefer you."

A dainty but unmistakable snort was Amanda's only response. *He may be right about Penny's feelings, but if he thinks I will believe such fustian as to his feelings for me, he is a want wit!*

Desperate, Jack rose and closed the distance between them. He pulled her out of the chair and into his arms. "I care for you, Amanda. I may not claim to have the grand romantic passion that so many young females today seem to require, but I do care for you, and I will be a fond husband to you. You will be a wonderful wife and mother. Please, sweetheart!" He turned her averted face to his and pressed a gentle but insistent kiss on her lips.

"Jack, I . . . oh, Jack, don't. That isn't fair."

He smiled down at her. "You will be a loving wife, too. Now, let us have no more fuss about this. Your father has given permission for us to be wed in Scotland; I would like to depart tomorrow. We can honeymoon at my hunting box."

Jack's kiss had almost weakened her resolve, but alarm bells began to ring at this plan. "Scotland? Why? And why the haste?"

"Having made up my mind to do it, and having talked you into it, I wish to waste no time."

She pushed against his chest, leaning as far away from him as his arm encircling her waist would permit. She studied his face closely. "No! That is not it. You don't think your father would countenance the marriage, do you? You wish to be wed before he has a chance to forbid it."

"Not true. I . . ." Jack found that he could not just blatantly lie to her. "I am not sure what he may say, but I am a man, and of age to choose my own wife."

"I won't marry you if he disapproves! What am I saying! I won't marry you anyway! This is all silly. If my family stands beside me, no one else's opinion matters to me." She struggled frantically, and Jack finally let her go.

"Mandy, I am going to send your father in and see if he can talk some sense into you. If he can't, I suppose I shall just have to throw you over my saddle and carry you off!" He sent Bennington after Sir Edwin, and climbed the stairs to his room, disheartened to think that Amanda distrusted him so much. *You brought it on yourself,* he reminded himself as he wearily undressed. *You were brutal with her that night.*

Chapter Fifteen

After Jack went upstairs, a family conference took place. Sir Edwin, failing to convince his daughter to marry Lord Maitland, called in reinforcements. Tom agreed with him; Caspian and Penny took her part. Her mother was the most vehement supporter of the proposal. In alt to think that her youngest daughter, for whom she had despaired of finding a husband at all, might marry so well, she was furious with Mandy for refusing him.

But Amanda, as Jack had perceived the first time he met her, was a force to be reckoned with. She stood out against her parents and Tom, refusing even to discuss the matter.

In passionate tones Penny represented to their parents and older brother how painful it would be for Amanda to marry a man who didn't want to marry her, particularly since she loved him unselfishly and didn't want to be the means of making him unhappy. "If Papa sends you away, I shall marry Hal on the instant, and you shall live with us," Penny declared. This led to another uproar, as Sir Edwin and Lady Garfield found out how far advanced had become Penny's interest in the young man they found so boring.

Finally Sir Edwin, regretting inviting so much advice, silenced them all. "We shall leave it for tonight, and think upon the matter. Tomorrow may bring with it another perspective for all of us." With varying degrees of dissatisfaction, the family could not but obey, and so went upstairs to their beds.

After Jack, missing Haskins sorely, had done what he could for his boots, he began undressing himself. When he heard a scratch at the door, he opened it to admit Hal.

"Maitland, you gave me quite a scare today," Hal

groused as he took a seat before the coal fire in Jack's
sitting room.

"Thought I'd come to propose to The Beauty, didn't
you?" Jack grinned. "She'd have had me, too, I think." He
could not resist needling his friend.

"She would not have done any such thing," Hal asserted
fiercely. "But I feared her parents might kick up a dust and
try to force her."

"So it is April and May with you two?"

Hal nodded, beaming beatifically. "Her illness was the
best thing that ever happened to me. Never much good
talking to females, but I can put my feelings into poetry all
day long. It is my good fortune that she has sensibility and
good taste."

"Your maunderings won her over, hmmm?" Jack stirred
up the fire. "Well, I wish you will tell me how to win
Amanda over."

"Do you want to, though? I mean, I've come to admire
her more as I've become acquainted with her, but wouldn't
think such an ordinary little miss would do for you. You
have always had a diamond of the first water on your arm."

"I do want to." Jack lifted his eyes to Hal's. "Truly. I
liked her from the first moment I met her, you know. She
is a fine young woman, and though not a beauty, she is
very appealing."

"Except for that hair! Poor thing, why *will* she try to
imitate Penelope?"

Jack grinned. "I don't dare say anything about those
stiffly pomaded curls yet, but once we are safely riveted
you may be sure they will disappear, along with all her
clothing designed for Penelope's figure and coloring."

He then filled Hal in on what was being said in London.
"Mean to call Tittlecue to book over it in time." He chuckled maliciously. "They called him Tattlecur—an apt version
of his name. I cannot wait to so address him to his face!"

"Practicing shooting at Manton's! As if a few hours of
target practice would help that cawker's aim!" Hal sniffed
derisively. "In the field he never takes down a bird, but
has filled two gundogs with shot!"

"I know." Jack shook his head wonderingly. "He kept
trying to lay claim to my birds the last time we stood side
by side."

Both men laughed heartily. Then Jack added, soberly, "But I don't plan to duel him. My purpose is to save Amanda from scandal, not to make her name a byword. No, I shall try for some subtler form of revenge."

The two young men talked long into the night, for which Jack was grateful. He did not expect to sleep much, for worrying about how to find a way to convince Amanda to marry him.

The next morning Amanda rose early, breakfasted, and was in the stable at first light. She rode out on Hippolyta, with no particular destination in mind, but determined to avoid her family for as long as possible, simply to keep them from urging on her any more the course she had determined not to take. A night of tossing and turning had not changed her mind: she would not marry Jack. His entreaties, she knew, arose from his sense of honor; it was up to her to protect him from himself.

She returned shortly before noon and skirted the house to enter unobserved through the stillroom door that gave onto the herb garden. Loud masculine voices coming from the direction of the rose garden attracted her curiosity, so she peeped around the tall hedge that separated the two gardens. She saw Jack talking to an older man, a little shorter than he, but with a commanding presence. That and his pronounced resemblance to Jack announced him to be the Earl of Chalwicke. Curiosity overcame breeding, and she listened in on their acrimonious conversation.

". . . avoided the gentle and loving trap I set for you to see you married to a member of your own class, only to fall into a trap laid by another."

"It was not a trap, sir. It was a misunderstanding that resulted in our being marooned together. And far from trying to force me to marry her, she has thrice refused, though she faces ruin."

"Indeed she does, and your family faces great shame if you do not marry this chit."

After a short but pregnant silence Jack exclaimed, "You want me to marry her?"

"No, I do not, but you must. I would much prefer that you wed Victoria, but at least this way you will be married and will present me with an heir in due time."

Amanda could just imagine Jack's fury; his father still regarded him mainly as a breeder. *How glad I am that I refused him,* she thought. *This would make him resent me even more.*

Jack took his time in responding. Finally the earl prodded him impatiently. "Well? That *is* why you dashed back here, isn't it? To propose to her."

"It is. Unfortunately, she won't have me."

In a voice laced with scorn, the earl responded, "You seem to expect me to believe that the plain younger daughter of a country squire will not have you. I am not so easily gulled, my boy!"

"I tell you the truth. She, unlike Victoria, has a conscience. She feels that it is unfair to me, and she thinks because I have not touched her, the incident has not harmed her. She is innocent of the world, alas."

"Well, you will just have to convince her! Make love to her, for heavens' sake. You were so determined to be a soldier—plan to take her like an enemy castle. Lay siege to her heart."

"I'd catch cold at that! We have been too honest with each other already. She would reject any such efforts as Spanish coin."

"You young idiot. I don't doubt you asked for her hand disdainfully, hurting her pride. Shower her with some of that famous charm of yours."

"She is a very intelligent young girl, who knows me all too well. She would see through any such attempt in a minute, even if I would stoop to a dishonest courtship, which I won't."

"Ah! So much more noble than your father, in love as well as war, eh? Well, you had better win her over. If you do not, I shall disown you!"

Amanda clamped her hand over her mouth to keep from screaming a protest at Jack's tyrannical father.

Such a long silence followed this pronouncement that Amanda risked another peek around the hedge. The two antagonists stood staring at one another, both breathing hard as if they had been exchanging blows instead of words. Finally Jack growled, "Do you mean that, sir?"

"I do. Stap me if I don't! I'll petition the crown to name your cousin Crawford my heir." The earl's fists were

clenched, his head thrust forward aggressively. "Even if I
don't succeed in changing the succession, I can leave
enough of my wealth away from you to make the title
meaningless."

"I don't think I deserve that," Jack said, the words coming slowly and laden with pain. "I offered for her, did my
best to convince her, and will try again, not for your sake
or the sake of the earldom, but because it is the right thing
to do. But it is really not in my hands."

"Make it your business to succeed, or I no longer have
a son!" The earl turned and walked away, leaving a stunned
young man standing in the rose garden.

Amanda listened, and when no sound indicated movement on Jack's part, came out of hiding. He stood frozen
in much the same position she had last seen him, hands
clenched, body rigid. "Do you think he means it?" she
asked.

He started and turned toward her. "You heard?"

"Yes. But surely . . ."

"I don't know." The earl's desperation to see him legshackled had Jack perplexed. But as he looked down into
Amanda's concerned countenance, he knew that his father
had handed him the means to convince her to marry him.
"I think he does. My father's pride in his heritage is very
strong. To have his son debauching and then abandoning
respectable young women would be a black mark upon the
family's escutcheon." He rubbed his brow like one with a
terrible headache. "I don't suppose there is any chance of
your having changed your mind, Amanda?" Jack did his
best to look forlorn.

For answer, Amanda pressed the fingers of both hands
to her lips, her eyes fixed on the ground.

"Mandy? I know you don't love me, but . . . No, I don't
have the right to ask it of you. It would be taking unfair
advantage of your good nature."

Amanda's stubborn rejection of marriage to Jack grew
partly out of pride, for she had no wish to be an unwanted
wife. But the stronger motive was her love for him, which,
though only half acknowledged, made her determined not
to ensnare and betray him the way his father had tried
to do. The thought of Jack losing his inheritance tugged
irresistibly at her heartstrings. As he looked down at her

so sadly, her love for him joined forces with her deep attraction to him. *He really seems worried. And judging from the earl's tone of voice, he seems capable of disowning Jack.*

Another of Amanda's reasons for so firmly rejecting marriage to Jack was the conviction that he would regret it sooner or later, making them both unhappy. *Perhaps his father's threat would keep him from hating or resenting me if I marry him. We might have a chance at a decent marriage after all.*

"Do you truly think he might disown you? What a cruel man! I couldn't bear it if you lost so much because of this situation."

Jack pressed his advantage. "Then say yes!" He took her hands in his, stripped off her riding gloves, and kissed her fingers. "You have a good heart, Amanda. I know you won't allow my father to disown me. You will never regret it, I swear to you, and neither will I. I'll marry you with a grateful heart!"

"Well, then . . . if you truly wish it . . ."

"I truly do." He slid his hands along her arms and drew her into a firm embrace. She nestled there, feeling warm and protected.

At least for one of us it is a love match, Jack, she thought. When he tilted up her chin for a kiss, she received it willingly, and soon found herself returning it with fervor. It was thus that Penny and Hal found them.

"Oh! What are you doing?"

Penny's indignant voice ended the kiss. Jack refused to let Amanda pull away from him, though, only tightening his hold on her as her sister complained.

"Amanda Garfield! Don't let that wretched man kiss you. Do you know that he has just defied his father and refused to marry you, in spite of pretending he wishes to do so."

"I thought you wanted to marry her," Hal chimed in. "I know you are still angry with your father, but why compromise Amanda yet again because of it? Let her go! I've a notion to call you out!"

Jack's shoulders began to shake with laughter. "You going to hie yourself to Manton's like Tittlecue, Hal? For you, too, lack precision with a pistol, you know."

"Jack Stanwell! You are an incorrigible tease," Amanda

struggled free of his grasp and scolded him, hands on hips. "Penny, Hal, you have just witnessed our betrothal kiss."

"But the earl said . . ."

"He doesn't know yet. I just this minute decided to accept."

Penny rushed forward, crushing Amanda in an exuberant embrace. "That is of all things wonderful!"

"I thought you did not want me to accept him?"

"Oh! No, I don't. That is, I didn't. I . . ." Penny looked as confused as her speech. "Why *did* you change your mind, Amanda?"

Amanda did not wish the earl's threat known, as it might embarrass them all in the future. "I will explain later," she temporized. "Let us go and tell the earl and our parents. I think they will be vastly relieved."

When they tracked down Amanda's parents at the entryway to Garfield Manor, they found the earl on the verge of departing. Jack swore and ran down the steps, grabbing the door of the carriage just as the footman started closing it. The Garfields heard Chalwicke call out angrily, "Drive on," and watched in some anxiety as Jack forced himself into the moving carriage. It proceeded several feet down the drive before coming to a halt, and then Jack emerged, closely followed by his father. The older man, a broad smile on his face, threw his arm around his son as they walked back to the waiting group.

His smile slid a little when first presented to Amanda. He looked from her to Penelope and back again before pasting a too-bright grin on his face and holding out his hand to her. Amanda felt her cheeks flush with chagrin, and began to regret her decision. *No doubt all of Jack's friends and acquaintances will react the same way. They will feel sorry for him for marrying such a plain girl. How will I bear to face them?*

Jack's sense of grievance toward his father increased with the earl's reaction to Amanda. He realized that at some point he had stopped noticing Amanda's ridiculously stiff curls and unattractive clothing. Because his father placed an inordinate value on physical beauty, it had been Jack's intention to get her legshackled and then take her to London for a new wardrobe and hairdo before presenting her to him.

But that rebellious, vindictive impulse that had led him to refuse to marry at his father's behest reasserted itself. He was almost glad his father had seen her before her transformation. *Let him stew about her lack of looks,* Jack thought. *Once we are wed, I will pursue my original program.*

This change of plans made Jack's life much simpler, for he knew that Mandy was sensitive about her looks. He had dreaded raising the issue with her, fearing it might further sap her self-confidence. What magic words could he have uttered that would have convinced her that he found her attractive, and yet urged her to let him change her before she met his family? *Now I shall have plenty of time to gently, subtly guide her into more suitable styles.*

Amanda's embarrassment was quickly swallowed up in her parents' joy at news of the betrothal. Tom was less demonstrative than they, but he shook Jack's hand and welcomed him to the family. Penelope pronounced herself to be pleased if Amanda was. Cass stood back, watching the scene, a frown on his face. Finally, as the earl and Sir Edwin began to discuss settlements, and Lady Garfield, Amanda, and Penny turned their thoughts to bride clothes, Jack sought Cass out. "Aren't you going to wish us happy?"

Cass grimaced. "Of course. But I wonder what the chances are? I wish I could protect her from people like your father. And you—you are doing the honorable by Mandy, but very likely you think yourself poorly matched. The heir to an earldom, and a handsome devil, too—I've no doubt you expected to marry a beauty from the cream of the ton. What kind of husband will you be to a plain wife? I regret having brought you here! She would be happier living with her siblings, than constantly being made to feel the defects in her appearance. I have to tell you that I mean to make a push to get her to cry off."

Caspian was not the only resident of Garfield Manor who hoped to see the engagement ended. Indeed, in the next few hours Jack began to wonder if he would have to steal Amanda away against her will and elope with her to Gretna Green after all.

First his father came to him while he was dressing for

dinner. "I have come to beg your pardon, my boy," he began, startling Jack and Haskins so much that the valet dropped the tiepin he held and Jack crushed the cravat he had very nearly succeeded in tying in an elaborate *en cascade*.

"Father, are you in good health? For I must tell you that you are behaving in a most uncharacteristic fashion these days. First you threaten to disown me, something you didn't do when I disobeyed you to join the army, nor when I refused to fall into the trap you laid for me with Victoria. Now you beg my pardon. I do not know for what, but I never thought to hear those words out of your mouth."

"Don't be impertinent, you young jackanapes! Haskins, that will do. If he can torture a cravat to that extent, he can certainly manage to put a tiepin in it by himself."

Haskins looked to Jack for confirmation of his dismissal, and received a curt nod.

"Now. Explain yourself, sire, for I am all aquiver."

"You did not tell me the chit was such a dab of a creature. I had heard her described as plain, but . . ."

"I do not find Amanda plain. She is not an animated Greek statue, it is true, but in her own way she is quite appealing."

"Huh! To each his own. But what concerns me more is her stature, or lack of it, and her delicate build. I thought Lucinda Garfield's children would have her same height and build. Unfortunately, while that is true for the pretty one, this child is not up to your weight, my boy! Nor up to the rigors of childbearing, neither."

"I should have known." Jack's mouth curled in a grim parody of a smile. "Bad breeding stock, you think. Well, we are not horses, so give over!"

"You pretended to have concern for her today. Like it or not, you will get children on her. Don't you care that it might kill her?"

What a horrible thought! Jack turned away from his father and looked into the mirror, seeing not his own reflection, but Amanda. Did his father have a legitimate concern? Then his mind's eye conjured her as she had looked dripping wet that evening on the island.

"No, Father, I don't. She is shorter than Penelope, and small of bosom, but she has a womanly figure, and is a most robust young lady. Were she not, I would be dead by now." He told his father how Amanda had made her way down the line of buoys and tossed him the racket, then helped pull him out of the current.

His father listened quietly, solemnly, to this tale. When it was finished, he said, "Grateful to her. Game to the core. Still, pity it wasn't the beautiful twin."

"It wasn't, and won't be. Penelope and I don't suit one another, whereas Amanda and I deal extremely well together. Shall we go down for dinner?" Jack did not wait for a reply, but left the room without a backward glance.

The earl did not exert himself to charm his host family. He did justice to Sir Edwin's chef, but made no remark upon the cuisine, opened no topics of conversation, and answered in monosyllables to all questions. Mostly he sat and brooded, his eyes running back and forth between Amanda and Penny.

In the drawing room afterward, Penny and Hal entertained them with a reading of some of Hal's poetry. Jack listened in astonishment. *I had no idea quiet, dull old Hal could express himself so beautifully, so passionately!* Even if he had been utterly besotted, Jack would have been embarrassed to utter such sentiments in private to the woman he loved, much less to a drawing room full of people. He wondered if Amanda felt cheated not to have such an ardent and expressive lover.

After the reading and performances by the musically inclined among them, time hung heavy on their hands until the tea tray arrived. Afterward the ladies decided to retire early. Sir Edwin and the earl began to discuss settlements, so the four young men repaired to the billiard room, where Jack suddenly found himself besieged by Hal and Amanda's brothers.

"My thought," Tom began as he racked up the balls, "is that you can announce your engagement, be seen together in London next Season. Help her to make friends there, and then end the engagement."

"Thought you were in favor of our marrying," Jack responded, perplexed.

"I was. Hadn't thought how it would be for her with a husband who doesn't love her and in-laws who look down on her and her family. My poor Mandy. She doesn't de-

serve that. The scandal will die down once she is seen to
be a well-behaved, respectable girl. And if not, Cass and I
agree: She can make her home with any of us, or remain
here with our parents. Better than being with those who
don't appreciate her."

"Just so," said Cass. "And don't tell me again that you
are fond of her. Too tepid by half."

Hal chimed in, "You should hold out for love, Jack.
Never realized how important it is until I found it. If all of
us pull together, get Dick and Gerry in on it, we can bring
her into fashion, see that she finds someone who'll care
for her. Leave you free to follow your heart." Hal's brow
wrinkled, and he hastily added, "Just so it doesn't lead you
to Penelope, that is."

"Now listen, one and all," Jack growled, unconsciously
taking the stance of an animal at bay. "I do care about
Amanda. I admire her, I find her attractive, I don't doubt
that I will love her in time. I won't abandon her to the
tender mercies of my father, you may be sure. We are marrying, and that is an end to it!"

He stalked from the room and went upstairs, where he
found his valet waiting for him, prepared to be impertinent.
"Sir," Haskins began, "the servants say she only accepted
you because the earl threatened to disown you."

"I see there were spies in the rose garden." Jack sat
down heavily in a chair by the fire and poured himself
some brandy.

"I hear that he shouted so loud it could be heard all over
the estate. At any rate, I don't think you should go through
with it."

"*Et tu Brute?* I don't suppose there is any way to prevent
you telling me your reason."

"I think the poor child loves you."

Jack turned at that. "What?"

"I've thought so for some time. She looks at you so. And
wouldn't agree to marry you until she thought you'd suffer
for it if she didn't."

Jack knew Haskins for a keen observer of human behavior. This news raised his spirits immeasurably. "Then she
will be pleased to have me as a husband."

Haskins looked doubtful.

"No? Why not?"

"You will fire me, no doubt, but I must speak plainly.
You will find it tedious to be loved by a woman you do
not love. You will not be able to help but show it. And
she will be miserable."

Jack's elation turned to indignation. "It is comforting to
know that my character is so universally understood," he
snarled. "For your information I would be in the altitudes
to learn that Amanda loves me. I will tell you what I told
the others: I intend to marry her. Don't bring up the subject again."

Haskins studied his employer's face carefully before bowing. To Jack's surprise he smiled enigmatically as he responded, "As you wish, sir."

Sir Edwin was not bound by Jack's command. The next
morning he summoned the engaged couple to his study.
Lady Garfield also was present, and her visage reflected an
uneasy, tearful night.

"I wish the two of you to reconsider your engagement,"
Sir Edwin said without preamble.

Jack stiffened. Had his father said something to offend
the baronet?

"Papa!" Amanda looked truly startled.

"It is not too late," Lady Garfield threw in. "You have
not sent in an announcement yet, have you, Maitland?"

Jack was sorely tempted to lie. "I have not," he admitted.

"Well, then, none know except those in this household,
so no explanations will be needed."

"May I ask, Sir Edwin, Lady Garfield, why you have
changed your mind since yesterday?"

"Until I met your father, it had not quite been borne in
upon me how unequal a match it is." Sir Edwin looked out
the window of his study gloomily.

"I do not find it so. My father is a man of irascible temperament, Sir Edwin. And lately he has been inconsistent,
as well. But the nub of the matter is that Amanda's good
name has been ruined; it is my fault; only marriage will
save us all from scandal."

"I don't care for that," Amanda snapped.

"No, but you do care that I will be disinherited. Aren't
you going to stand buff, my dear?" Jack's conscience didn't
tweak him in the least for pretending that his father's inter-

dict still stood. *The way the old man is acting, he might veer back around by the time we call it off, and then matters could never be put to right.*

"Mother, do you agree with Father?"

"Yes, Amanda, I do. I bitterly regret that I ever encouraged you to accept. Nothing could be as humiliating as the cool treatment we all received from the earl. I believe our ancestry is as good as the Stanwells', and our manners superior, but your father was made to feel as if he offered the earl a tavern wench for a daughter-in-law."

Amanda looked at Jack, mutely inquiring why this should be. To his chagrin, he had to admit, "I cannot find any way to excuse or explain my father's behavior. If it is of any comfort to you, I quite agree with Lady Garfield. My family's manners are vastly inferior to yours, and I perceive no great inequality of bloodlines, setting the title aside, nor do I care if there were."

Unappeased, Sir Edwin grumbled, "His demeanor and his demands for an astonishing dowry make me believe that he meant to make us withdraw from the engagement."

Lady Garfield nodded her head. "Well, he succeeded." Seeing that her daughter meant to object, she sternly called her to order. "Amanda! In your own way you are as proud a young miss as I ever saw. How could you bear it? Such a disagreeable connection it would be for us all, with the earl so lacking in civility to us. And as for you, Lord Maitland, I am sorry to speak so bluntly, but I have found your temperament most unamiable on occasion. I fear you will become more like your father with each passing day, and more unlikely to seek my daughter's happiness."

Amanda turned a stricken face to Jack. "He took me in dislike at first sight, Jack. I think if you spoke to him, he might change his mind about disowning you."

"Oh, never mind!" Jack stood abruptly. "I shall return to my regiment. I did not find war a pleasant occupation, but it will allow me to earn my bread. Father may have my cousin for his heir with my good wishes, rather than take a reluctant bride!"

Chapter Sixteen

〜

The bleakness on Jack's face, the despair in those golden-brown eyes as he looked down at her, wrung Amanda's heart. She held out her hand in supplication.

"I cannot bear to see you disowned, Jack! But I had the feeling that the earl's wish for the match died when he laid eyes on me. Suppose we asked your father to join us for a frank discussion. Perhaps he will no longer insist upon your marrying me?"

Amanda's deep concern for his well-being, which made her dismiss the danger to herself, made Jack grind his teeth. It infuriated him that his father's disdain for her and her family had been so obvious. *What have I brought her or them but hurt?* he wondered, and renewed his determination to undo as much of the damage he had done as lay in his power. To do that, he must revive their engagement if at all possible.

"I do not know if he would change his mind, but he has been strangely inconsistent lately, so even if he did so, I would fear that he would change it back yet again. At any rate, I want to marry you." He took Amanda's hands in his, in spite of her half-voiced protest. "I know you don't believe it, but I truly want you for my wife. I only wait for you to tell me that you are willing, before departing for London to obtain a special license."

The look in his eyes almost convinced Amanda. Her heart cried out to accept him, though her mind still with-held approval.

He looked past her to where Sir Edwin and his wife stood. "I hope to marry her with your blessing, Sir Edwin, Lady Garfield. I promise you that I will cherish her as I ought. My father's behavior makes me ashamed. I intend to object strenuously, and in the end, the settlements will be all they ought to be, I assure you."

"It is not a question of money . . ."

"No, sir, I know it is not, with you. Nor is it with me. But I won't expose Amanda to hardship because of my father's vagaries. I shall see that our future income is secured!"

When he saw that neither of Amanda's parents intended to repeat their objections, though they continued to look anxious, he turned his attention back to the young woman who stood in front of him. "Amanda?"

"Very well, Jack. If you are still of a mind to marry me after speaking again with your father, I am willing. But I don't think a special license is necessary. There is no need to rush matters."

Jack expected this objection from her family and his, and intended to ignore them all. Too many starts and stops had confused the issue already. "I want it settled and done. You will enjoy my place in Scotland, but it can get devilish uncomfortable there in the middle of the winter. I plan to take you there immediately, for our honeymoon trip. Then we will return to England to visit my family over the holidays. I hope your family will join us at Chalk Hill from Christmas through Twelfth Night." He turned to Amanda's parents. "Then you will see that you and your daughter are treated with the respect that you deserve."

He lifted Amanda's chin with his knuckle. "While I am in London, will you complete arrangements for a quiet family wedding here? No need for an elaborate trousseau—it will be my pleasure to provide you with the latest fashions for the coming Season." When she did not respond, he lowered his head and pressed a gentle kiss to her lips, whispering against them, "Say yes, Amanda."

"Yes." Amanda still had doubts, but the touch of his lips on hers completed the conquest of love over judgment. Her eyelids fluttered; she smiled dreamily. "Yes."

Jack looked at her parents. Taking their silence as acquiescence, he went in search of his father.

Jack found the earl in the stables, admiring Sir Edwin's mammoth Spanish jack. He made quick work of informing his sire that plans for a wedding were going ahead and stating his requirements for a settlement succinctly. "Since you have threatened to disown me, I realize that I must not rely upon your continued goodwill once I take on the responsibilities of a family. Either make Crawford your heir without further ado, so that I will know how I stand, or settle a competence on me so that I can support my wife and children no matter what your future opinion of me may be."

"You are a stiff-necked creature, Jack. Marched off to war in spite of my disapproval, and now intend to marry against . . ."

"Intend to marry the woman you threatened yesterday to disown me if I did not marry."

"But I am trying to undo my rash act. I spent several uncomfortable hours creating the conditions in which she might cry off. It sounds to me as if you have defeated my efforts."

"You had best hope that I have. For I tell you this: if my marriage to Amanda Garfield falls through, for any reason whatsoever, I will not marry. You may indeed look to Crawford for the continuation of your line."

The earl drew back as if struck. "Surely you don't mean that!"

"I do. If I cannot be an honorable man and be the earl, I will not be the earl. Just as joining Wellington to administer the coup de grâce to Napoleon was the honorable thing for a nobleman to do, the honorable thing in this situation is to marry her, and so I now consider myself married to her, whether the marriage is solemnized or not."

The Earl of Chalwicke snarled at his son, "Unnatural cub!" He swore and ranted and threatened, but Jack stood his ground. In the end his father capitulated.

When he learned that Jack intended to go to London for a special license, he said, "Very well. Send our solicitor to me here. I don't fancy another flying trip to London, when I would only have to return here for the nuptials. In the meantime, I will hunt with Sir Edwin; may give these mules of his a trial."

"If they will permit it. You have some fences to mend with the Garfields," Jack warned him.

The earl had the grace to look conscious at this. "Meant it for the best. I shall make myself agreeable henceforth."

They shook hands on it, and Jack, though road-weary, departed for London before the day was out. Thus he was unaware of an exchange between the earl and his fiancée that threatened to undo all of his efforts.

After luncheon Amanda announced her intention of inventorying the linens, her charge for the month being the upstairs housekeeping. To her surprise, she had scarcely begun when the earl appeared at her side.

"I am extremely pleased to find you alone," he began.

Amanda looked apologetically at the young housemaid she had appointed to assist her. "Begin by separating those linens that need mending, if you will, Mary."

She turned to the earl, smoothing her hands on the apron she had donned. A metallic taste in her mouth made her slightly nauseous. She realized she was afraid, though she didn't know which she feared most—that the earl would encourage her to marry his son, or that he would forbid it! "Would you care to visit the picture gallery, Lord Chalwicke?" she inquired politely.

He bowed and motioned her to precede him. When they had descended to the long gallery, he rushed into speech. "My son tells me I have blotted my copybook, Miss Amanda. I have come to beg your pardon. I was out of sorts yesterday—the vicissitudes of travel wore on me, I suppose."

Amanda eyed him consideringly. *This is a time for plain speaking,* she thought, gathering her courage. "Please, Lord Chalwicke, let us be frank. I know very well that your enthusiasm for the match died when you laid eyes upon me. I do not blame you for it, sir. I have a mirror, you see. I know I am far from the diamond you might have expected Jack to wed."

"No, no, no. Absurd little creature." He smiled down at her, a smile that did not quite reach his eyes.

"Not absurd, sir. Realistic."

The earl sighed. "Frankness would be best, I suppose, else you will think me shallow as well as ill-mannered. You see, I felt when I saw you that you were . . . ah, too small for my Jack."

"Small?"

"It is perhaps indelicate to speak of such to an innocent

maiden, but you are country bred, after all. You surely know what may happen if a plow horse covers a Shetland pony?"

Anger chased away fear. "Jack was right," she exclaimed indignantly. "You do think of him as breeding stock. You have a wonderful, courageous, honorable son, and all your interest in him lies in his potential as a stud. Now you extend the same treatment to me. It is outside of enough! I'll have you know, sir, that I am not a pony, I am a woman, and . . ."

"And a small woman, at that. Have a care for your own life, my dear."

Amanda gnawed at her lip as she tried to think of something sufficiently withering to say to him. But her ire died as she observed the look of genuine concern on the earl's face.

"As for me, Lord Chalwicke, I am of a size with my grandmother on my father's side, and she bore her husband six healthy children. Never lost a one of them, and outlived Sir Vincent by ten years."

"But doubtless Sir Vincent was of the same type as your father, my dear, and . . ."

"Grandfather Garfield was a giant of a man. My father and I take our stature from my grandmother. Oh! Why am I letting you manipulate me into such a discussion? It is highly improper, and does no justice to your fine son, who is not an animal, sir, but a man. A very good man, of whom you should be proud."

"I am proud of him. I cannot tell you how my heart swelled with pride upon learning how he had comported himself when he joined Sir Hussey's line during that last charge of Napoleon's elite cavalry at Waterloo. And I know he is doing the right thing by you, too, and without any prompting from me."

Amanda wryly noted this outrageous lie. But at that moment her attention was focused on the earl's relationship with his son, which she knew troubled Jack very much. "Have you told him so, sir? Or have you merely alluded to his merits and demerits as a potential sire? For I can tell you, your behavior in that regard has caused him a great deal of pain."

"He has told you of . . ."

"The attempt to force him to wed Lord Ridgewell's daughter? He has."

The earl turned away, a dull red suffusing his face. In a strangled voice he said, "It was wrong of me. Never have I felt so ashamed of myself as on that day. But hang it all, the boy shouldn't have gone off for a soldier with the succession unsecured. A disloyal son, that is what he is. Still, I regret that trick."

"You regret attempting to entrap him. Don't you think you will regret forcing him to marry me?"

"Forcing? Hang it all, he does tell you everything, doesn't he?"

"Yes, he does. I think you might regain some of his lost regard, and eventually be much more pleased with his selection of a wife, if you released him from that terrible threat to disown him. I can tell you, sir, I dislike intensely being forced upon him in this way."

The earl turned back around and looked at her, his eyes hard. "Oh, indeed. A match such as this is a dream come true for . . ." He brought himself up short.

"For a plain little nobody like me? Yes, Lord Chalwicke, it would be, if it were a love match. As it is, I dislike it intensely."

"Then why accept?"

Amanda shook her head. "I care for him, sir. I don't think your threat was fair, but I couldn't bear to think of his losing his inheritance."

"You accepted only because of the threat?"

"Yes." She lifted her chin and glared at him. "But now we both know that threat is moot, isn't it? Since you have admitted that you don't particularly want me for a daughter-in-law, why don't you make both Jack and me very happy? Rescind your threat, follow your son to London, and repair your relationship with him, Lord Chalwicke, and allow my family to return to our obscure but formerly happy existence!"

A few hours earlier, this request would quickly have been granted. Almost too late, the earl realized that he had endangered the engagement his son had sworn to keep or never marry.

He realized, too, that Amanda was a fine young woman, not a schemer who had entrapped his son. Her willingness to release Jack from their engagement would have pleased him before his last confrontation with his son. But now it sounded the death knell to his dynasty. Panic lent urgency to his denial.

"I will not! However concerned I might be about your well-being, my son must marry you. I won't have it said that he ruined a perfectly respectable young woman."

"But . . ."

"Particularly now that I see what a fine person you are." His smile was genuine now, which mellowed his harsh features so that he looked even more like an older version of his son. "In fact, you remind me of my Caroline. She was the anchor of our family, the calm in the midst of all storms. Jack is fortunate to have found another such a one. As for his happiness, you may rest easy on that score. He assured me, just before he left, that he is devoted to you. He censured me sternly for being impolite to you and your family, whom he also holds in high regard."

Amanda had thought she saw the way to escape. "But, Lord Chalwicke . . ." she cried out in dismay.

"No! Absolutely not. Amanda Garfield, you must wed my son or see him disinherited. I am pleased that he wishes to do so without my threat, but if the marriage does not occur, I will carry it out." Clamping his jaw shut on this lie, the earl gave her a stiff bow and stalked away.

Chapter Seventeen

"I take it very ill that you will have Caspian Garfield as your best man, when I've known you all of my life!" Gerrard Linderhill turned away from Jack, the line of his jaw and stiffness of his posture underscoring his words.

"It is because we do not plan on a large wedding. Family only. I doubt my sisters will even be there, though they have been invited. They will say it is too far to come on such short notice."

"Humph! Richard and I are almost like family. You have often said we were brothers. I collect you have forgotten all about that, though!"

"I still feel that way. I just thought it would be imposing on you to drag you into Yorkshire at this time of year. In fact, I felt sure you would have departed to the country by now, to terrorize the foxes."

"Couldn't, until we heard the outcome of your perplexing situation."

"Until you knew who had won the various wagers you have laid thereon!" Jack tried to look angry, but laughter at his friends' predictable behavior bubbled up. Gerrard did not join in the laugh, but continued to look affronted.

Jack realized he would have to invite Gerrard and Richard in spite of his request for a small wedding. He counted on them and one or two other good friends to help him establish Amanda in the ton. He knew that the hasty marriage he planned would seem like a confession of wrongdoing in many circles. He couldn't bear the thought of her being snubbed. One way to prevent that was to create a loyal circle of friends around her from the first, a circle composed of men and women of excellent *ton*.

"I've already asked Cass to be my best man, so I can't take it back without offending him. But if you are willing to make the trip, I would be greatly relieved to have you and Dick with me."

Mollified, Gerrard entered enthusiastically into his plans to turn Amanda into a fashionable young lady. When Richard Dremel joined them later in the evening, he was drawn into the plot.

Getting the special license took longer than Jack expected; he was given to understand by the archbishop's staff that it would have taken longer still, had he been any less a personage than the heir to the Earl of Chalwicke. In spite of this advantage, it was a full week before he was able to depart for Yorkshire. This delay gave him time to do some shopping for wedding presents and improvements to his own wardrobe. The much-put-upon Haskins, whom he had met en route to the Garfields' and had brought back to London with him, had quite a few of his new garments in hand, but nothing suitable to be married in.

He heard nothing from Yorkshire during this time, so it was with uneasiness that he once again entered the great hall of Garfield Manor, Gerrard and Richard in tow.

He had sent word ahead, so he was not surprised to see Amanda descending the stairs as they entered the hall. He *was* surprised at the surge of pleasure he felt as he saw her coming toward him. The now-familiar sense of ebullience in her company suffused him, and he embraced her.

Amanda smiled shyly at him when he released her. Cheeks pink, she greeted his two friends. She graciously brushed aside his apologies for bringing someone who was not immediate family. When Gerrard declaimed at length about the long-ago-forged bonds among the three of them, she nodded her head.

"I do understand entirely. I was unable to enforce the family-only rule, too, for I found I could not be wed without the presence of my two very good friends, Kathryn Majors and Barbara Satterfield. And Mama declared she would be forever ostracized in the county if she did not invite our close friends among the local gentry. You don't mind, do you, Jack? They won't all be present for the actual ceremony, but Mama has invited them to a wedding breakfast afterward."

He hastened to reassure her, and they followed her into the Isis drawing room, where she instructed Bennington to serve them tea. When he had left, Jack asked how their parents had dealt with one another.

"Oh, they are bosom beaus now. They have had several days of excellent shooting together, and the earl rides one of Father's mules. He bids fair to become one of the mule enthusiasts. You and your friends will have to take care you do not find yourselves drafted into the effort to bring into fashion the notion of hunting on mules, hitching them to your curricles, and riding them in Hyde Park."

He could have chosen no better way to ingratiate himself with Sir Edwin, Jack thought. *Perhaps he still has his wits about him after all.* He grinned happily as Amanda and his friends laughed over this notion. *She is delightful! I wonder if I am falling in love with her?* He entirely overlooked the tightly curled hair that tumbled over her forehead and half hid her cheeks. He scarcely remarked her less than flattering dress. He leaned forward in his chair. "Amanda, love, enough about mules. Is everything in readiness for our wedding?"

Amanda's heart did a little flutter dance at the caressing tone in Jack's voice. "Everything but the precise day. The vicar had two mornings open this week, today and Thursday, so after I received your note, I set it for Thursday. But if you think it too soon . . ."

"Too late! I had not thought to wait two more days." He did not notice the astonishment Gerrard and Richard displayed as they listened to this conversation.

When the men returned from their hunting that evening, Jack got a chance to see how well the earl had succeeded in ingratiating himself with the Garfield men, and how little he had succeeded with the women. Lady Garfield treated him with frosty civility, Penny with ill-disguised hostility, and Amanda with wary courtesy. They made a stiff company when they gathered just before dinner. Jack's attempts to converse with Lady Garfield met with heavy weather also, so he almost welcomed the disturbance at the drawing room door. Bennington lost the battle to deny the entrance into the room of a large man, his face a deep rose with emotion and exertion.

"Where is he?" he demanded, eyes glaring around the room. "Where is the coward who has ruined my darling Amanda?"

"Mr. Tittlecue!" Sir Edwin identified the caller in tones of deepest loathing. "You are not welcome here, sir."

"Hide behind the complacent father and pandering brothers if you may, Lord Maitland," Tittlecue shouted as the two Garfield brothers moved to evict him. "But I will have satisfaction for this."

"A moment, Cass, Tom," Jack called, intercepting the three. "I would have speech with this gentleman."

Amanda felt queasy at the deadly look in her intended's eyes, and took an involuntary step toward them before her mother restrained her with a hand on her arm and a sharp admonition.

Her brothers loosed their hold on their father's erstwhile friend, whose face went from deep rose to the palest pink as he perceived that menacing look on his opponent's face.

For a few seconds they formed a frozen tableau. Then Jack felt within his vest pocket and withdrew a quizzing glass, an object Amanda had never before observed him to use. He put it to one eye and looked Tittlecue over slowly from head to toe.

"Ah, yes. Tattlecur. It is indeed the man who bandied my fiancée's name all over London, is it not, Dick? Gerrard?"

These two worthies stepped up beside Jack and repeated the insulting survey. "The very one, Jack. Mr. Tattlecur. Heard him myself in Manton's."

"Tittlecue," their victim snapped. "My name is . . ."

"Just as I said. Tattlecur. Aptly named chap," Gerrard chimed in. "Never forget that name, so suited to a man who casts aspersions on a decent woman's honor."

"M-my name is Tittlecue, as *this* so-called gentleman well knows." He faced Jack squarely. "You, sir, are a bounder and a . . . What did you say?"

"Tattlecur."

"No, I mean . . . did you say 'fiancée'? Have you then made an honorable offer for Miss Amanda?"

"I have, as you well know. I am happy to report that the third time I offered, she accepted my humble petition for her hand, Mr. Tattlecur."

"I'll thank you to call me by my right name, sir!" Tittlecue drew a deep breath and turned toward his unwilling host. "Well, Sir Edwin. My congratulations. Miss Amanda." He essayed a bow, difficult to accomplish while he contin-

ued to eye Jack the way one might eye a snake within
striking distance. "I congratulate myself that my announced
intention to call this rogue to book has resulted in his doing
the proper . . ."

Jack's hand snaked out to grasp Tittlecue's tie and pull
him so that they faced one another nose to nose. "I shall
not call you out over my fiancée, sir, for that would be to
dignify your slurs on her honor. Nor shall I call you out
for insinuating I offered for her out of fear of you. But I
feel compelled to tell you that if you do not henceforth
answer to the name of Tattlecur in my presence, you will
meet me."

He flung the perspiring pink man away.

"You . . . that is abominable. Insulting. Sir Edwin, I call
upon you to . . ."

"I shall stand your second, Lord Maitland," Sir Edwin
declared.

Four other male voices chorused a similar message. Tittlecue looked from one to the other in horror.

"Indeed, Mr. Tattlecur," Sir Edwin said, "henceforth you
shall have that name, both here in your home county, and
in London, and anywhere else in England that I, my sons,
or my son-in-law happen to be."

"Please add your prospective father-in-law to that list,"
the earl said, coming to stand beside Jack. "I know my son
well enough to know that he would never force himself
upon a woman, and have come to know my new daughter
as a young woman who would never submit to improper
advances. That you have blackened their reputations sits
very ill with me."

Tittlecue's eyes very nearly bulged from his head. One
quick survey of the united group of men, and he fled in as
much haste as he had arrived, followed by a roar of male
laughter and its echo in higher tones as one of the young
ladies joined in. Penny's high-pitched giggle pursued Tittlecue from the room. Amanda's innate kindness warred
with her sense of outrage at what her former suitor's med-
dling had caused, so she stood silent.

Lady Garfield did not even admonish Penny for such
hoydenish behavior. Her lips were pinched together in a
grim smile, and when Jack and the earl came to her side,
she treated them as cordially as they could wish.

*   *   *

That evening when Amanda and Penelope stood before the dressing table mirror, brushing their hair, Penny looked curiously at Amanda's downcast expression. "What is the matter, Mandy-love?"

Amanda awoke from her stupor. "What? Oh, nothing. Just thinking."

"About what?" When her twin did not answer, Penny resumed her brushing. "Why did you not laugh, or thank Jack for putting Mr. Tittle—I mean Tattlecur—in his place?"

"Why should I thank him? He did it out of anger that he has to marry me because of Basil's interference."

"Why, Mandy! I don't believe that."

"Think on it, Penny. He had accepted my refusal and left us. When he heard of Basil's inept efforts on my behalf, he posted back here to try to stop the scandal."

Penny put her brush down. "I wish you would not marry him until you feel more secure in his affections. I think you will regret it if you marry now."

"I would wait a long time! No, Penny, I must go through with it. The earl will disown him if I do not." Mandy tried to smile. "Ridiculous as he is, in a way I feel sorry for Basil Tittlecue. He was only trying to protect my honor."

Penny shook her head. "I cannot pity him. His bluster has the look of a man trying to regain his self-respect, for he could plainly see that you preferred Jack's company to his. Too, he fled in fear before the storm, knowing that you were missing. As for Jack, I think you underestimate his feelings for you. I have seen how he looks at you. He cares for you, Mandy-love. I know he does."

"Do you truly think so?" Mandy's expression became more hopeful. "He says he does, but I can scarce credit it. Well, I shall strive to be a good wife to him."

Their wedding day proved to be more like summer than mid-November. Lady Garfield expressed her gratitude to the Almighty for this boon, for it allowed her to set up trestles on the carriageway's grassy oval, around the fountain. There she directed the servants to set out the large feast she had planned. In lieu of a large wedding, she and Sir Edwin had invited all of their friends and neighbors, as

well as the Garfields' tenants, to a wedding breakfast after
the service, and she had been in somewhat of a state of
panic at the thought of such a large, ill-assorted mob inside
her home.

Attending the actual exchange of vows were the Garfields, Barbara and Kathryn, Jack's sister Sarah and her
new husband, the earl, Hal, Richard, and Gerrard. The
earl's complacency could not have been greater. *If he is
simulating friendship with Sir Edwin, he is doing a very
convincing job of it,* Jack thought.

The beautiful Sarah had given him a bad turn when she
arrived the day before. Upon being introduced to Amanda
for the first time, she had positively looked down her nose
at his bride-to-be. Since she had at least six inches on
Amanda, this was not hard for her to do. Sarah had pronounced herself "charmed" in a faint voice after the two
young women had been introduced, then joined Penelope
with happy exclamations over the opportunity to renew
their friendship, for they had been acquainted during the
recent Season in London.

A pity Mary could not have been here, Jack thought,
knowing she would have been much more cordial to
Amanda than Sarah, who valued beauty in others as much
as it had always been valued in her.

After Amanda and Jack said their vows, the estate servants serenaded them on the front steps of the manor with
several local folk songs. Then everyone descended upon
the feast as if they had not eaten in days, rather than hours.

Jack kept Amanda by his side, gazing at her fondly as
toasts and newlywed jokes kept her blushing and giggling.
He knew she did not understand some of the allusions
these jokes included. *She will know more tonight,* he
thought. He had every intention of consummating their
marriage that very evening, and anticipation made his
blood heat as he looked into her eyes after one such
naughty toast. Her quizzical eyebrows arched high as she
looked questioningly up at him, a hesitant smile on her
face.

In that moment Jack knew the answer to the question
he had asked himself two days before: yes, he was falling
in love with her. *In fact, I may have loved her from the first
and simply did not recognize the unfamiliar emotion,* he

thought. He kissed her more passionately than propriety might have dictated, but loud cheering and applause told him the wedding guests heartily approved.

Ever since the day I met her, I have had this feeling of lightness, almost of effervescence, in her presence. I thought it was our shared sense of humor, but now I know it was love bubbling up. I can't wait to tell her, though I daresay she won't believe it at first.

"Why don't you go in and change into your traveling clothes, love?" he whispered in her ear. "If we are to spend the night in Darlington, we need to be on our way."

Amanda's blush deepened at the mention of spending the night together. *It has really happened,* she thought, astonishment and joy warring in her. *We are married, and he looks at me so fondly that I can no longer doubt that he truly wishes it.* She looked forward to her wedding night, yet felt the dread that goes with uncertainty, too. Her mother had educated her on the process, and cautioned her that there would be some pain. "You will bear it very well, I know, and I urge you to reassure your husband and help him to take his pleasure, though you may feel none. This is, I believe, one of the keys to a successful marriage."

When Amanda had attempted to pursue the subject of whether she might feel pleasure, too, her mother had grown suddenly reticent. "As to that, some women do, and some do not, my dear. But whichever group you fall into, remember that husbands are less likely to stray when their wives are accommodating."

"Do you, Mother?" Amanda had asked. "Take pleasure in it, I mean?"

"This is very personal, Mandy." Lady Garfield had turned her head away for a moment or two. When she turned back her face was pink, but she smiled. "Yes, love, I do. Your father is a skillful, thoughtful lover. I pray that your husband may be so, too."

"Amanda? Not woolgathering at this critical moment, are you?" Jack's amused voice broke into her memories of the night before. "Why don't you find your mother and sister, to help you change? I will order the carriage."

"Not just yet, Jack. I want to say good-bye to my friends first. That way when I am dressed we may leave immediately." Jack nodded, so Amanda left her husband and family, and when she had exchanged a few words with Kathryn and Barbara, she managed to slip away through the rose garden, into the herb garden, and by that route, to the stable block where one of her very best friends, Hippolyta, stood in her stall.

While Amanda made her way to Hippolyta, Penny waylaid Jack by the punch bowl. "Amanda asked me to look after Hippy last night, Jack."

"Ah. I trust you agreed?"

"Of course, but I wonder why you do not have her sent to Rosebriar? Won't Amanda need a mount there?"

"She will, of course. You must pledge yourself to secrecy now, little sister, if you wish to know my plan."

Intrigued, Penny promised.

"I have bought her a horse. The prettiest little mare you ever saw, with a light chestnut coat—a pale gold, in fact. An Arabian . . ."

"Pooh!" Penelope scowled at him. "You could buy her twenty mares, and they would not compensate her for Hippolyta. Don't you realize she loves that creature? Amanda has made a great pet of her. She will cry her eyes out if you don't allow her to take Hippy along!"

Jack recognized that Penny had taken up one of her indignant postures, championing her sister perhaps beyond what was needful. He doubted that any woman could resist such a beautiful wedding present as the mare he had for Amanda. Still, he didn't want to risk upsetting his new wife. "Then I will ask your father if I might purchase her. One of my grooms can bring her along slowly, after we have left."

Penny smiled blissfully. "There. I knew you would not be cruel to her! You do care for her, don't you, Jack?" Her blue eyes pleaded for reassurance.

"Very much so. I am in love with your sister, and I hope soon to convince her of it."

"Then you are the best of all brothers to me!"

Slipping into Hippolyta's stall, Amanda hugged the mule about the neck without regard for the delicate lawn of her wedding dress. "Well, old friend, it seems we must part. I know my husband will wish me to ride a horse. He is entirely too fashionable to be seen with a wife mounted on a mule, however charming." She fought back tears. *You are being very silly, Amanda! You know you will enjoy riding a horse.* Still, she found it difficult to say good-bye to the animal she had raised from a foal and trained herself. She rubbed Hippolyta's forehead, and then offered her a sugar lump she had snagged from the kitchen on her way through.

"Oh, Hippy! I am so happy—frightened a bit, but happy. Wish me well, girl." Hippy snorted and nudged Amanda with her head, hoping to coax another sugar lump out of her.

"Oh, you! As long as you get your sugar lumps every day you won't even miss me. Well, Penny has promised to take care of that, so good-bye!" She let herself out of the stall and hastened back by the same route she had come.

Thus it was that she chanced to be walking along the hedge that separated the rose garden from the herb garden when she heard her name pronounced, followed by a short burst of laughter.

Chapter Eighteen

"I had my blunt on Jack, and Dick had his on Penstock." Amanda recognized Gerrard Linderhill's voice.

"To marry Amanda? No, you shan't cozen me that way." A female voice laughed raucously. It was Sarah Stratford, Jack's beautiful sister. "Even as mad as you two are for wagering, you needn't tell me either of you placed money on the likelihood that my brother would marry Amanda Garfield. Nothing could be less likely than that my handsome and eligible brother would have done so, except in these circumstances, which you can hardly have foreseen. Now, if it had been a wager about Penelope, I might be convinced."

Amanda knew she should not stay to hear herself abused, but a sort of horrified fascination held her motionless.

"Originally, we wagered about whether Jack or Winston would succeed in marrying Penelope Garfield, of course. But since neither married her, that bet is moot. No, we are trying to decide another wager altogether. And I tell you, Dick, I have taken the trick!"

"I do not see how we can decide," Richard Dremel drawled. "Miss Amanda is not unpleasant to look at. When Jack said, 'no matter how fubsy-faced,' I was misled."

Amanda stiffened. *Fubsy-faced? He called me fubsy-faced?* Pain lanced through her.

"I agree," Gerrard answered. "She is not so plain as all that. But with those nasty stiff curls, like big black springs glued around her face, you must admit that her hair looks a quiz. No wonder Jack pronounced a sentence of banishment! So I say I win."

"Banishment!" Sarah crowed with delight. "Now, that is just the thing. Let him take her to Rosebriar and leave there! For I do not know how I am to face London society with such as her as my sister-in-law."

"Sarah, do stop interrupting," Gerrard said irritably. "This is man's business. Now, whether Amanda is fubsy-faced or not, his father *did* threaten to disinherit him to get him to marry her, just as he expected, so I say the bet is on, and I win."

"And I say . . ."

Amanda lingered to hear no more. Cheeks flaming, eyes stinging with tears, she ran back to the stables and into Hippolyta's box stall, where she threw herself onto the hay-stack in the corner and wept. *Fubsy-faced! Oh, how could he tell me he thought me pretty when he spoke so of me behind my back! And my hair! Well, I know it is not attractive, but to say he would banish me because of it!* Not only did this cut her deeply, it frightened her. Recollecting how she had made clear to him that she preferred to remain in the bosom of her family, unwed, rather than marry a man who had no affection for her, she realized Jack was not merely dishonest, he was cruel. *He convinced me to marry him, against my better judgment, when all along he planned to consign me to lonely exile at this distant estate in Scotland, knowing full well how much I should dislike it.*

"Lord Maitland?" Ben Smith, Jack's coachman, stood respectfully at his side, seeking his attention as he exchanged pleasantries with one of the Garfields' tenants.

Jack smiled down at his servant, expecting to hear his congratulations. But instead, Smith looked disturbed, and asked him to step aside for a moment.

"What is it, my man?" Jack tried to keep the impatient note out of his voice. Penny and Lady Garfield still circulated among his guests, which meant that though half an hour had passed, Amanda still had not gone up to change clothes. He was eager to be away.

"It's Miss Amanda, sir. That is, Lady Maitland."

"What of her?" Jack demanded, alarmed by the man's uneasy manner and nervous tone.

"You see, m'lord, I went to check on the horses, make sure all was ready for your departure." Smith waited for a word of praise.

"Excellent man. But what of my wife?"

"Thought you might be wishful of knowing, my lord. She's in the stable, cryin' her eyes out. With that mule of hers, she is."

"What?" Jack's irritation gave away to alarm. "Crying? With Hippolyta? Why? Never mind, I'll go see for myself." With difficulty Jack extricated himself from his many well-wishers and made his way to the stable. As he hurried to Amanda's side, he realized that for once Penny had not exaggerated: parting from Hippolyta was breaking her heart. *She is indeed very fond of that creature. I should have known without having to have Penny spell it out for me.* A wave of tenderness swept through him at the thought of her crying over her pet.

But why did she say nothing to me about it? Never mind. I shall turn those tears to smiles on the instant, for I will speak to Sir Edwin and have the mule brought to Scotland as soon as may be. He felt a pang at the realization that Amanda might not like the pretty mare he had purchased for her while cooling his heels waiting for a special license.

By the time Jack let himself into Hippolyta's stall, Amanda's sobs had died down to sniffles, and she had begun to think how she could extricate herself from her marriage of one hour's duration. At the sight of her husband, she scrambled to her feet and stood stiffly, hands clenched at her sides.

"Amanda, sweetheart, what is the matter? If you want to take Hippolyta with you, I . . ."

"Don't call me sweetheart! I have heard enough of your lies."

Nonplussed, Jack stared at her. "Lies? But I never said I wouldn't take her. It was just that . . ."

"Oh, I know what you thought. You couldn't bear the scandal, could you? Couldn't bear the thought of being censured by the ton, not to speak of your father."

Jack would have laughed if Amanda had not been so serious. He replied with as much dignity as he could muster, "I think I could survive the scandal of having a wife who rides a mule."

Hippolyta stepped between them, snorting nervously at their raised voices. Amanda put a calming hand on her neck and stepped around her.

"Of course you could, for you mean to see that my mule

riding is done far, far away from society! What I think is the cruelest of all is for you to banish me to Rosebriar. You misled me, and now instead of living with my family, I must spend most of my life alone."

Jack's eyebrows knit together. "Alone? Just because the mule won't be there?" Considerably offended, he asked her, "Don't I count? You know very well I am going to Scotland with you, and that we only plan to stay a month. What maggot have you gotten in your brain, love?"

"Don't you dare try to pull the wool over my eyes with your sophistry! You meant me to think you cared, so I would give you an heir before I found out your intentions. But I won't! Not ever! I demand an annulment."

"Annulment!" Jack's mind reeled. He had thought Amanda one of the sane Garfields on the subject of mules. "Of course I care, Amanda. To prove it, I will reunite you with this long-eared lovely as soon as possible. One of my grooms will bring her to Rosebriar right behind us, if your father agrees to part with her." He put his hand on the mule's neck. Once more she stepped between them, ears back, and nudged her mistress.

"Beast! Odious creature. You won't turn me up sweet with that charming smile this time! Look at Hippy's ears. She sees through you, too. You tried to make me fall in love with you, and very nearly succeeded. But now I know what a lying hypocrite you are, so don't attempt to sway me. My mind is quite made up. It must be an annulment. We've only been married an hour. Surely it would be a simple matter to end it now."

Jack ducked under the mule's neck so he could glare down at his new wife. "I will certainly not agree to an annulment over so small a thing! Even if I would, I promise the Ecclesiastical courts would not!" He chuckled and reached for her. "This must be bride's nerves, my love."

To his surprise, she dodged him and slapped at his hands, colliding with Hippolyta in the process. "Don't touch me."

The mule threw her head up and bared her teeth. "Look out, Jack," Amanda warned him. "You'd better leave. She thinks you are trying to hurt me."

"I won't leave without you. Why don't you go back to the house and let me send your mother and Penelope up to your room? They will know how to calm you." He

opened the stall door and reached for her, intending to
escort her through it. Just as she dodged to avoid his touch,
Jack felt a strong force closing down on his left arm just
below the shoulder.

"Ow! Let go, damn you! Amanda, get this beast off me
or I'll send her to the knacker instead of to Scotland!"
He managed to jerk his arm loose, ripping his jacket in
the process.

"Serves you right! I tried to warn you!" Amanda caught
at Hippy's halter and began to croon soothingly to her as
she turned the mule's head away.

"Oh, fine. Sympathize with the mule, when she tried to
take my arm off." Jack snarled.

"She didn't really try to hurt you, or you would have a
broken arm," Amanda retorted. "That was just a warning
nip. Please leave the stall, and once I've got her calmed
down, I will follow."

"I don't want to leave you with that vicious brute," he
retorted, but under her withering glare decided to retreat
to allow all three of them to gain control of their temper.
A watchful eye on the mule, he slipped past her and let
himself out of the box stall to await his wife.

In a few moments Amanda let herself out of Hippolyta's
stall to confront her husband, who was rubbing his arm and
grimacing. "It feels crushed. And just look at my coat!"

Amanda narrowed her eyes, determined not to be softened by the pain on his face. "Serves you right. She was
only protecting me. And I thank God you do *not* own her,
for to send her to the knacker is just what a cruel, heartless
man like you would do!" With that, she turned on her heel
and ran away.

Jack followed her as she ran into the house through the
kitchen. When she headed upstairs, he decided to seek out
Penelope or Lady Garfield to send to her. *My sweet, calm
Amanda's nerves have been completely overset,* he thought,
his concern for her warring with the pain in his arm. *Would
that I had made myself better acquainted with her preferences before buying that mare.*

The party had entered the champagne-fueled stage of
lively interaction of all the social classes by the time Jack
returned. His jacket was much the worse for Hippolyta's
teeth, and he was unable to mask the pain he felt in his

arm, so he found himself surrounded by concerned friends wanting to know what had happened. Dr. Bruce joined the crowd as the fact that Hippolyta had bitten him swept through the wedding party. Those who could not see his face found it a subject of merriment. Those who could knew by his pinched mouth and tense demeanor that it was far from a laughing matter.

"You poor man," Penny cried out. "I've never known Hippy to bite, but I can imagine how it must hurt. How did it happen? Where is Amanda?"

He smiled ruefully, trying unsuccessfully to pass it off as a good joke. "I don't know for sure. I think the mule thought I was attacking her mistress when I tried to kiss her. Amanda probably has gone upstairs to change, for in separating me from Hippolyta's teeth, she soiled her dress. She . . . she was most upset by the mule's attack. I hope you will go up to her and calm her."

Penelope put her hand to her mouth. "Oh, my. Of course she is upset. How terrible for you both. Dr. Bruce, you must see to him!" She started to go to her sister, but her mother forestalled her. She whispered in Penny's ear, "You act as hostess in my stead, Penny. There is something smoky about this business." While Penny reluctantly did her bidding, Lady Garfield hastened upstairs in search of her younger daughter. She found Amanda pacing the floor, wringing her hands and muttering to herself like one possessed.

"There, there, child. Do not take on so. I am sure he has not taken any permanent hurt from it."

"I hope he may have done. Despicable man! Do you know that he wants to send Hippy to the knacker? You won't let him, will you, Papa?" For Sir Edwin had followed his wife upstairs. He, too, sensed that something was wrong, for he would have expected Amanda to be seeing to Jack's injury, rather than running upstairs to nurse her own sensibilities. He felt considerable perturbation at the thought that Jack might have attempted far more than a kiss in the stable. *Foolish man, I hope he isn't the sort to rush his fences. Amanda deserves gentle handling.*

"That depends upon the facts of the case. I certainly don't want a vicious animal on my hands. Tell me what happened."

At this question she dropped her head in her hands and began weeping. Between sobs she choked out, "He called me fubsy-faced. He hates my hair!"

"Well!" Lady Garfield's cheeks bloomed with angry color. "I don't see why he would insult your looks, just because your mule bit him!"

"Fubsy-faced? Surely not, Mandy." Sir Edwin put an end to her agitated pacing by pulling her down onto a sofa next to him. "Such a fuss over a mule!"

"And he described my hair in such a nasty way! You will think me foolish for letting it hurt me so. I know I am plain, Father, but don't you see? He lied to me, for he told me several times that he thought me pretty. But that is not the worst of it. He plans to banish me. I am to stay at Rosebriar, so he won't have to look at me, or be embarrassed by me in front of his friends. I don't want to have to live somewhere far away from my family, with no husband to keep me company. Oh, Papa. We have to get an annulment!"

Sir Edwin looked unconvinced. "He will not do it, though. Daresay he was in a pet over the mule biting him. Looked as if he were in a devilish bit of pain a few minutes ago."

"You are as bad as he is! Hippy has nothing to do with it. She only bit him because she thought he was attacking me. Besides, it was just a nip. He is exaggerating."

Sir Edwin offered hopefully, "Ah, I see. He tried to kiss you, and she misunderstood?"

"No, Papa. He tried to grab me because I said I wanted an annulment."

"That is when he said you were fubsy-faced?"

"No, that was earlier." Amanda broke into fresh tears.

Her parents exchanged puzzled looks. "I can scarce believe it," Amanda's mother exclaimed. "He has looked quite besotted with you all morning."

"He is the greatest hypocrite alive, Mother." Amanda proceeded to recount the conversation she had overheard.

Sir Edwin scowled. "If he said that of you, I believe he must indeed be a hypocrite and a liar, for he gave me to understand he had formed an attachment to you. But an annulment . . ."

"I won't go with him. I won't!" Amanda had never felt so utterly hopeless and furious at the same time.

Her parents exchanged looks of utter consternation. "You try to calm her, Lucy," Sir Edwin said. "I am going to talk to him. And for goodness' sake, change clothes, Amanda. People will think you've been ravished in a haystack." He turned back at the door. "You weren't, were you?"

Amanda lifted her tearstained face. "What?"

"Ravished in a haystack?"

"No, Papa. It wasn't that. Indeed, I doubt he has enough interest in me for anything like that."

Sir Edwin met Jack on the stairs. His blue morning coat had been slit up the left sleeve, and his arm was in a sling. "Is it broken?" He had good reason for apprehension. A mule's bite could well have crushed his son-in-law's arm.

"No, thank goodness. Merely bruised, and perhaps some tearing of the muscle, according to Dr. Bruce. Hurts like the devil, though. About that mule, sir . . ."

"What about her?" Sir Edwin asked in a hostile, wary tone.

"I didn't realize how attached to it Amanda is. I hope you will sell the creature to me."

"I would gladly make a present of her to my daughter, of course, but . . ."

"You're not worried about that remark I made about the knacker? You may rest assured that I spoke in anger. I would never do such a thing, especially seeing how attached my wife is to the beast."

"I'm afraid the situation is more complicated than that." Sir Edwin sucked on his lower lip, not at all sure how he was to deal with this.

"It wasn't just the mule, was it? I thought not. I have always heard of bride's nerves, but never imagined so calm and self-possessed a young woman as Amanda would be so completely overcome. Did you know she asked for an annulment over it?"

"As to that, Lord Maitland . . ."

"Surely you can call me Jack, now that we are related by marriage?" Jack looked hopefully at his usually affable father-in-law. The worried, almost angry look on Sir Edwin's face alarmed him. *What if he, too, thinks forgetting her mule a matter for an annulment? It would never succeed, of course, but even attempting such a thing would be an embarrassment. We would be the laughingstock of the ton.*

Sir Edwin confirmed his worst fears by his reply. "There is some question as to whether we will be so related."

"Now, that is carrying mule-madness too far!" Jack exploded, then struggled to keep from saying a good deal more. He looked around, wishing for Cass to assist him, for he seemed the least affected of all the Garfields by this mania.

"It is not mule-madness, as you so kindly put it," Sir Edwin snapped, seriously affronted. "It is your insult to my daughter, sir, and your plans to banish her."

"Insult? Banish? Over a mule bite? I beg leave to tell you, sir, that you are being ridiculous." Jack put his free hand to his temple and massaged it briefly. "No, wait! This is quite a puzzle, for she said something about banishment, too, even before the mule bit me. I want to speak to Amanda, see if I cannot get to the bottom of this."

"Not just yet. She is too upset. Will you join me in my study, my lord?" Sir Edwin brushed past him and started down the stairs.

"Not before I've reassured her about that blamed mule!"

Sir Edwin turned around. "Again I say: It isn't about a mule, sir, it is about a young nobleman who, whether for honor or to safeguard his inheritance, felt compelled to marry my daughter, yet was so dishonorable as to pretend to admire her and feel affection for her in order to convince her and her family to agree to the marriage, while at the same time he ridiculed her to his friends."

Jack stomped down the stairs after his father-in-law. "I mean to have a full explanation for that, sir!"

"Then we both have some explaining to do."

When Sir Edwin told him what Amanda had overheard, Jack's indignation knew no bounds. "That pair of wager-mad halflings. This is connected to some sort of a bet they have made. I did not call Amanda fubsy-faced. I recall the conversation very well. They started laying out a wager as to whether my father would be in favor of my marrying Amanda or against it. I did not like having her made the object of their betting. To forestall them I jokingly said that my father would try to force me to wed any female, no matter how fubsy-faced, who seemed capable of giving him a grandson to inherit the title. I certainly was not referring to Amanda."

"Ah!" Sir Edwin considered this for a moment. "And you did not say you meant to banish her after you were wed?"

Jack frowned and pinched his nose, trying to remember what he had said to give that impression. Then he began to laugh. "I said I meant to banish her curls. Well, begging your pardon, sir, but they do not suit her. I plan to put her in the hands of a skilled hairdresser when once we return to London. Truly, sir, I adore Amanda, and think she is very pretty. She will only require a bit of polish to bring general admiration, I am sure."

Sir Edwin studied Jack's features, eyebrows knit. "If you don't mean what you are saying, I swear I am taken in completely."

"I am telling the truth. And I'll tell you another truth, which I meant to tell Amanda as soon as we were alone: while we were saying our vows, I realized that I love her with all my heart!"

Sir Edwin was once again all smiles. "That settles it, then! Come, we must contrive to calm her enough to bid a dignified farewell to our guests, then I leave it to you to convince her of the truth of those words."

The two men found Tom, Cass, and Penny lying in wait when they opened the door of Sir Edwin's study. "What is wrong with Mandy?" Tom demanded.

"Yes, Dr. Bruce has gone up to her, and Mother would not admit me. Did Hippolyta hurt her, too?" Penny looked near hysterics herself.

"I'll shoot that long-eared monster if she has," Cass growled.

"Dr. Bruce?" Jack thrust his way through Amanda's family and mounted the steps two at a time. Sir Edwin stayed to reassure her siblings that Amanda was only a bit overset.

"Bride's nerves," he said, smiling. "Happens all the time."

"Amanda? That isn't like her," Cass said, and Tom nodded agreement.

"Well, as if she isn't allowed to have the vapors occasionally like any other young woman!" Penny, ever ready to do battle, leapt to her sister's defense, but stopped when her father held up his hand.

"Now, no more argufying. We have a plethora of guests, and as near as I can see, not one member of the family is out there playing host and hostess. We don't want gossip beginning, do we? Let us all go out and mingle, and make a great joke of a jealous mule trying to rescue her mistress from Jack's kiss." Reluctantly, uneasily, with many a backward glance, Penny and her brothers did as their father bid them.

While the Garfields put this plan in effect below, Jack discovered to his dismay that Dr. Bruce had put it out of his power to explain matters to Amanda by giving her a cordial with a strong sedative effect.

"Laudanum," he growled, furious. "Not good for her. Knocking her out on her wedding day—what were you thinking? How is she to say good-bye to our guests?"

Dr. Bruce glared at him. "The cordial contains syrup of poppies, among other things, yes. I have never seen Amanda in such a taking. She grew more hysterical by the moment. You don't want her taking a brain fever, do you?"

Jack looked to Lady Garfield for confirmation. She nodded, her expression freezing him to the bone. "I think you will have to postpone your trip for a day or two at least, my lord."

"The devil you say! And before you decide to slit my throat, I suggest you talk with your husband!" He pushed past the two and went into Amanda's bedroom. She wasn't entirely asleep; her head rolled toward him on the pillow as he spoke her name, but what she said was incoherent.

"Perhaps it is for the best," he said, leaning forward to kiss her forehead. "When you are yourself again, we will be alone, and I can explain all to you. Then we will have a good laugh together!"

She put her hand out, but he wasn't sure if she intended for him to hold it, or if she was trying to push him away. He chose to believe she wanted him to hold it.

Dr. Bruce stood in the doorway. "It was a misunderstanding?" he asked.

"I gather you heard what a monster I am? Yes, it was a

misunderstanding. Oh, don't look at me that way. Send for her maid to help her change. We need to reach Darlington before nightfall."

"I'm not sure if that is a good idea," Dr. Bruce objected.

"It is what is going to happen, though. She is my wife, now, Doctor. And Sir Edwin knows everything; he will not attempt to prevent me from claiming her."

What explanation Sir Edwin offered to his guests for Amanda's condition, Jack did not know, for he looked neither to the right nor to the left as he carried her downstairs, ignoring the pain in his arm. She mumbled vaguely as he handed her into the carriage. His father, nonplussed by the sight of Jack carrying off an unconscious bride, entered right behind them and demanded an explanation.

"Dr. Bruce gave her something to calm her, because she was so overset by the mule attack. But he must have miscalculated the dose. I don't intend to let it delay me, though. She will come to in an hour or so, none the worse for the experience. Good-bye, sir. We will see you at Christmas." His steady gaze and determined manner left the earl with no choice but to shake his outstretched hand and withdraw from the coach.

If Jack thought his troubles would be over when Amanda awakened from her long doze, he was very much mistaken. As she began to awaken, she became nauseous, necessitating a sudden carriage stop and several unpleasant moments spent holding her while she retched beside the road.

Back in the carriage, she gradually regained consciousness, and with it, memory. She pulled away from the curve of his arm and scooted to the opposite side of the seat, burrowing deep into the cushions as if she could somehow escape his presence.

When he began his explanation, she turned her head away. He persisted, though he had the impression that she had suddenly become deaf. Abruptly she turned and speared him with a baleful glare. "Did you describe my hair as like black springs stuck to my forehead?"

Jack rubbed his forefinger up and down his nose. "No, I did not." *Richard, you addlepate, I would thrash you if I could lay hands on you now!*

"And I suppose that you also did not say that you would banish me as soon as possible after we were married?"

"Definitely not!"

Voice dripping with sarcasm, Amanda observed, "Your friends certainly take liberties when quoting you, then."

Though he hated to explain, because it would show her what unkind things had been said of her, he knew only the truth would convince her. "Someone else said the bit about black springs, in jest. But I did say that the hair had to go. I said I would banish your curls, not you. I don't know what your mother has been thinking of, with her excellent taste, to let you imitate Penny's hairstyle. What suits her quite overpowers your more delicate features."

"Oh! Oh! That makes me so angry! Just because you don't like it, that doesn't mean it is in bad taste! For your information, we paid one of London's most expensive hairdressers to style our hair and . . ." Amanda paused, wondering why she was defending the hairstyle she disliked so much. "Mother was very well pleased," she finished lamely.

"I don't care who designed it, or who was pleased by it. You are no longer under your mother's thumb. The hairstyle goes!"

"Ah, I see how it is. Now I am under *your* thumb. Well, my lord husband, I shall wear my hair as I see fit!" Amanda turned her head away from him.

Jack gentled his voice. "No, Amanda. I shan't force you to change your hair. But I hope you will do so."

Although this conciliating speech relieved her mind somewhat, Amanda was far from ready to make peace. She pushed her lower lip out. "You will find that will make little difference in my appearance, my lord and master! My hair is very difficult to style. In its natural state it is utterly straight. Unlike Penny's, which curls naturally, it has to be pomaded and . . ."

"I know. Practically burned with the curling iron. I have fancied more than once that I smelt burned hair about you."

That was the wrong thing to say. Humiliation only fueled her anger. "Then you should have kept your distance! We would both have been much happier if you had never returned from London." She turned her back on him again. When he attempted to turn her around to face him, she jerked away, saying, "I don't believe a word you have told me. Why should I trust you? I want an annulment."

Jack's arm was throbbing, and he had a headache. He could feel his temper rising. "That, my girl, you shall not have."

"Why not? Why would you want to stay married to a fubsy-faced girl with ugly hair?"

"Because I love you," he shouted. *Not exactly a romantic declaration,* he realized, annoyed at himself.

She jumped at his loud voice, and glanced fearfully over her shoulder. Seeing his furious expression, she decided not to provoke him anymore. Still, the only thing she felt at his shouted declaration of love was disgust at his hypocrisy.

"Did you hear what I said?" Jack's voice softened. "I love you, Amanda. I realized it today as we were saying our vows. I think I have been falling in love with you gradually, from the first time I met you."

Amanda did not, could not believe this. *He is such a volatile man.* She remembered her mother's cautioning words to her just before Dr. Bruce administered his calming draught: "Don't make him too angry, dearest. An annulment may not be possible, and a husband has so much power over his wife."

Would he beat me in such a fit of temper? Amanda fought to hold her tongue, though longing to give voice to sharp words of skepticism. She continued to eye him uneasily, her eyes wide with apprehension.

The thought that she feared him hurt Jack more than the mule's bite. "It is obvious that you don't love me, though, or you would believe me and not look at me as if I am like to have you for dinner."

"So let me go. Clearly I do not deserve your 'love.'" She pronounced the word with a sneer, then regretted not keeping to her resolution to remain silent, for Jack in a full-blown temper was an awesome and alarming sight.

His jaw worked; his fist clenched and unclenched. Abruptly he pounded on the roof of the carriage. "Stop!" he called out when the coachman looked down through the peephole. "Stop the carriage. I am going to ride on top."

Without a backward glance at Amanda, he did just that.

Chapter Nineteen

❦

The Green Lion Inn at Darlington bustled with activity, as mail coaches, post chaises, and private carriages arrived and departed in a bewildering chaos of shouting grooms and neighing horses. Jack's head and arm both ached with a white-hot intensity, and the busy inn did not have a settling influence on him. But he held himself firmly in check, retreating into remote aristocratic hauteur as he assisted his equally cold wife from the carriage, identified himself to the innkeeper, and climbed the stairs to the suite of rooms he had sent a footman ahead to reserve for them.

Amanda looked around herself uneasily. *Only one bedroom and a tiny dressing room,* she thought, feeling hysteria rise in her at the thought of sleeping with the remote man who stood beside her.

"I have also reserved a private parlor," he informed her. Correctly interpreting her wide-eyed, worried expression, he continued, "I will not ask for another bedroom. It would not be available on such short notice in any case, but I don't choose to advertise our quarrel. However, I will not force myself upon you, Amanda. We shall sleep together, but quite platonically, I assure you."

She nodded and turned away, warring emotions in her breast. *At least he does not look ready to beat me,* she thought. During her lonely carriage ride, she had talked herself into believing that he might well do such a thing, but the chilly reserve with which he now treated her was almost too painful to bear. She believed that it far more accurately reflected his feelings toward her than his pretense of admiration. *I love you, Amanda.* She had wept over those patently false words, which would have pleased her so much if true, until her tears had all been shed, or so she believed.

Planning for a cozy honeymoon, they had not brought either maid or valet. The redoubtable Haskins had been given a vacation and told to report to him in London in December. Amanda and Penny had shared a maid, so Jack had asked Haskins to hire an experienced dresser for her by the time they reached London. He had arranged for George Clintick, one of his footmen, to act as his valet when needed on their trip, and planned to engage one of the inn's staff for Amanda. Once they reached Rosebriar, Mrs. McGregor, the housekeeper there, could assist Amanda when needed.

"I'll summon a maid to help you change," Jack said. "If you won't mind too much, I shan't change for dinner myself. The donning and removal of jackets promises to be agony on my arm." For the first time since he became an adult, he hoped that an injury would elicit some sympathy toward him. But he was doomed to disappointment.

"I would prefer a tray here in the room if you don't mind." She tilted her small nose up and walked to the window, which overlooked a charming garden leading down to a brisk stream.

"Not at all. Under the circumstances my mutton will taste much better taken in solitude." He bowed to her and turned on his heel.

Sadness and anger warred in Amanda's mind. By the time she had nibbled at a delicious repast for which she had no appetite, anger had begun to take the upper hand. It was directed as much at herself as at Jack.

"Fool!" she accused her reflection. "You know what you look like. How could you allow yourself to think 'Irresistible' Maitland would admire you? And you've only exposed your folly the more by raising such a fuss." Her eyes drifted upward to her hair, and suddenly all of her anger and despair focused on those curls, which she had hated from the minute they were first layered around her face, but which she had lacked the fortitude to refuse. She had thought of herself as being considerate of her mother; but in her present mood it seemed to her that she had merely been a coward.

The maid scratched at the door just then. She was followed in by a serving girl, who began clearing the table.

"Ma'am, shall I bring you bathwater?" Mary Fitzgerald

looked somewhat apprehensively at the grim-faced young woman she had been hired to serve for the evening.

"Yes," Amanda replied. "And bring an extra jug to rinse my hair. I plan to wash it. And . . ." Amanda drew a deep, composing breath. She turned to face the rosy-cheeked woman. ". . . and bring me a pair of scissors. Large ones."

No accounting for the quality, the maid told herself for the thousandth time. *Fancy washing your hair on your wedding night. And such hair! Well, if my fine lady expects me to repair those curls afterward, she will be disappointed.*

The maid carried out her commission, however. When she followed the burly servant carrying the water buckets into the room, Mary asked, "Shall I assist you at your bath, my lady?"

"No, thank you. Help me undo the tapes on my dress and then come back in—oh, an hour, if you will."

"Very good, my lady." Mary curtsied and withdrew, wondering at the steely glint in the newlywed's eyes.

Alone at last, Amanda locked the door, then marched to the dressing table, scissors in hand. Contemplating her stiff locks, her anger surged anew. *Nasty black springs.* Whether or not Jack had said that of them, the description was too close to the truth to be in the least bit humorous. She lifted the center curl and slashed at it. *That, for having hair as straight as a board.* She progressed to the next: *That, for having hair of no particular color.* And the next: *That, for being short. That, for having a snub nose.* Her pace quickened: *And for eyes the color of lichen! And for preferring mules to horses. And for falling under the sway of a handsome man. And for letting him convince you to marry him. And . . . and . . .* She hesitated. The curls around the front of her face were gone.

"Courage," she whispered, loosing the pins that held her long, thick braid in place around the crown of her head. *And that, for falling in love with a deceiving rogue who never, ever, will love you!*

She winced at the sound of the scissors chewing their way through her braid. When she had finished severing it, she threw it angrily across the room.

"I won't look, I won't look," she repeated, turning away from the mirror's disturbing image, but too late to avoid seeing that her hair stood up in spikes around her face where the curls had been. *I look like a hedgehog! I should leave it that way, so that his-high-and-mightiness can see what his cruel comments have brought.*

Instead, she stepped into the hip bath and ladled water over herself, top to bottom, then vigorously soaped and scrubbed her hair.

If Amanda had hoped her shampoo would improve the appearance of her hair, she knew only disappointment when, after toweling it dry, she looked into the mirror. As expected, the short, straight hair lay flat against her head. It no longer resembled a hedgehog. *I look like one of those unfortunate French ladies on their way to the guillotine.* The sight of it produced a profound depression. *It makes me look all eyes, like some hungry waif,* she thought, turning away. All her furious defiance escaped her like the heat from her bathwater, and she sat on the edge of her bed, head in her hands, and gave way to tears.

"My lady. My lady?" There was a slight note of panic to Mary's voice when Amanda did not open the door immediately. *What if that unhappy little creature has done herself in with the very scissors I brought her?* Her relief at hearing the door open gave way to astonishment when she faced her temporary mistress, now dressed in a long robe and shorn of her hair.

In a wobbly voice, Amanda asked the maid to clear away the cut hair and send a man up for the bathwater.

That cold, toplofty gentleman in his private parlor has a shock coming to him, Mary Fitzgerald thought as she hastened to do her bidding. *She is a brave wee thing to risk angering such a man.* Shaking her head once more at the ways of the quality, Mary efficiently removed the scattering of curls that had fallen around the dresser.

Once dressed for bed, Amanda risked one more look at her decapitated locks. *Banished indeed,* she thought, smiling grimly. *Almost, I am tempted to leave off my nightcap.* But further confrontation with Jack this evening did not appeal to her. It seemed that cutting her hair had taken the last shred of her energy. Wearily she mounted the bed, hoping that she would be sound asleep before he joined her.

His silent repast, washed down by liberal doses of wine, restored Jack to some semblance of good humor. A generous snifter of brandy made him almost mellow. In this mood he looked back over the events of the day. As he reviewed the confrontation in Hippolyta's stall, he found himself chuckling. *I thought she was that upset over my forgetting her mule. And her father must have thought me mad, we misunderstood one another so thoroughly.* The person he wished he could share the joke with, however, had been hurt by the mix-up instead of amused. *She thought I had ridiculed her and was making light of her feelings.* Oh, what a sad little comedy of errors.

He climbed the stairs full of dread, knowing Amanda would still be upset. *Not the wedding night I had planned!* He flexed his left arm tentatively, and bit back a moan. *Just as well, I suppose. This injury would certainly complicate lovemaking.*

He entered the room quietly. A soft glow from the coal fire in the grate provided the room's only illumination, but he could see that Amanda was in bed. Only her head could be seen, and it was covered with a lacy nightcap. She didn't move, so he thought she must be asleep.

He lit a candle and walked over to the bed for a closer look. The way her eyes scrunched slightly told him she only feigned sleep. As he looked down at her, so obviously pretending, that effervescent feeling welled up in him again. And with it that same odd sense of amusement over their misunderstanding of the morning. *Would she, could she see the humor in it?* Thinking he could hardly stand in worse odor with her, he sat on the edge of the bed and gently shook her.

"Amanda, I know you are awake. I wish to have a word with you."

Amanda had, in fact, dozed off, but the sounds Jack made as he moved about the room had awakened her. She opened one eye. "I am very tired, Jack."

"As am I. But there is something I am not sure was made clear to you today."

"A great deal became clear to me today," she sniffed, squeezing her eye closed again.

"When you accused me of lying, and of not being able to face the censure of the *ton*, I thought you were talking about riding Hippolyta."

"Hmpfff."

"I was insulted when you said you'd be alone at Rosebriar. I thought you valued the mule's company more than mine."

"There have been times today when that is exactly how I felt."

"Yes, you made that very clear! And when you said that you wanted an annulment, I still thought it was over the mule." He waited, watching her face closely. "And I said the courts would never give you an annulment because I forgot your mule."

"That was ridiculous." She rolled over abruptly, her back to him.

"So I thought. I remember thinking you must be as mule-mad as your father, to think of going to such extremes."

"You didn't really think that was what I meant." She lifted her head just till she could see him out of the corner of her eye.

"I did. You see, Penny had just read me a jaw-me-dead about how much you loved Hippolyta, and . . ."

In a defiant tone, Amanda exclaimed, "Well, I do! She is much more to me than just a means of getting about. If you understood me in the least, you would have known that."

"I did know it," Jack replied somewhat mendaciously. "I just hadn't supposed you'd want an annulment because of such an oversight." When she continued to glare at him but made no reply, he thought he had failed. *I've only made matters worse.*

She turned her head away again, and after a moment he heard a tiny sniff.

"I'm a beast. I've made you cry again!"

Her shoulders began to shake. He leaned across to turn her toward. "Amanda, I am sorry. Please, I shouldn't have . . ."

When her face came into view, his world suddenly turned right side up again, for she was laughing silently, eyes half shut, merry little mouth tucked in until every dimple showed.

"Y-y-you r-really thought I'd want to end our marriage over H-h-hippolyta?"

"For a few mad moments, yes. And then later, when I met your father on the stairs, everything he said seemed to confirm it. I thought I had landed in Bedlam!"

She could contain herself no longer, but burst out in peals of laughter, which he joined, relief surging through him. When at last they both sobered, Jack stroked her forehead gently. "Ah, Amanda, I am sorry that your feelings were hurt, even by misunderstandings."

She caught his hand and cradled it to her cheek. "I fear I have been sadly unreasonable."

He smiled and flicked her tipped-up nose. "We shall come about, shan't we, Amanda?" When she didn't answer he bent to press a kiss on her forehead. "Go to sleep, dearest. Tomorrow we'll have a better day."

He picked up the candlestick and carried it into the dressing room. As he began to undress, he felt the lack of Haskins acutely. Before departing from the Garfields' that afternoon he had changed into a fresh suit coat, since Hippolyta's teeth had ripped the previous one. The perfectly fitted garments always required a bit of assistance to remove. Tonight his arm deeply resented the movements he had to go through to try to extract himself. *My arm must have swollen since I put this on,* he realized. *I should have had George come up with me instead of sending him to his bed.* He couldn't suppress a moan as he tugged again. "Oh! Damnation!" he exclaimed as he tried to work himself free.

"Do you need some help?"

He turned. In the door to the dressing room stood Amanda, hardly more of her visible than when she lay in bed, for her cap was pulled down low on her forehead and she wore a long-sleeved, floor-length robe. Her eyes were wary but concerned.

"I do, indeed. I don't want to cut this off if I can help it."

Overwhelmingly aware of her husband, Amanda stepped to his side. Gently, patiently, she helped him work the coat sleeve off his arm.

"Ahhhh. Thank you. If you will just get the shirt started?" She repeated the procedure on his shirtsleeve.

He turned his back to her while pulling the shirt over his head. When he turned toward her, he stood bare-chested, ruefully exploring the swelling in his left arm with his right hand. In deep blue-black splendor was a perfect imprint of Hippolyta's teeth, one row on the outside of his upper arm, one on the inside.

Amanda's shock at the swollen, purpling bruise overcame any shyness she felt in the presence of a half-dressed man. "Oh, Jack," she wailed. "I had no idea!"

"Nasty, isn't it," he agreed. "Wish I had some of Haskins' liniment here. Tonight I shouldn't even mind the odor!"

"I shall make you some of mine." She turned and headed for the hall door.

"Amanda, I don't think it is a good idea for you to go wandering about this busy coaching inn in your nightclothes."

She stopped, the door half open. "I forgot I wasn't in my home. I shall ring for assistance."

"Thank you, love, but I will be quite all right. Dr. Bruce gave me some of his infernal powders to take. Swore there was no laudanum in them."

Amanda closed the door and turned back toward him. At that moment she took in his muscular bare chest, heavily fleeced in golden-brown hair that arrowed downward into his pantaloons. She felt her mouth go dry and looked away, confused at the hot flush that ran through her.

He smiled at her embarrassment. "Go back to bed, love. I'll be with you shortly." He watched her flee to the bed, clambering in and pulling the covers up to her chin, and once again regretted the condition of his arm. *Few would blame me if I were to send that mule to the knackers for wrecking our wedding night,* he thought. Of course, he would not do such a thing in any case, but especially now that he knew how much Amanda loved the animal.

This reminded him of the mare he had sent to Rosebriar for his new wife. *I told her I knew how she felt about the mule, that leaving her behind was an oversight. Once she sees Aurelia, she will realize just how far I have perjured myself.* Somehow he would have to get the mare out of the way before Amanda saw her. Their relationship was on far too shaky a ground to risk upsetting her any further in the near future.

After slipping into his long nightshirt, he padded to the door to be sure it was locked. As he did so, he saw something in the corner of the room, something dark brown and hairy. He approached it with caution, thinking there might be a rat in the room. But the object didn't move, and when he bent to look closer, he saw that it was a long brown braid of hair. He picked it up and studied it.

"Amanda!" He walked toward the bed, swinging it in his fingers. His wife had turned over on her side, her back to him. "Amanda, look at me."

Chapter Twenty

〜

Amanda turned cautiously, knowing from the ominou
tone of his voice that his mood had changed. Sh
gasped when she saw what he was holding.

"It appears that you have already dealt with the hai
problem." He eyed her sardonically before putting th
braid on the nightstand. He slipped into the left side o
the bed and rolled over on his right shoulder. "Turn over
Mandy," he commanded, his voice gentle but firm.

Hesitantly, she faced him. "I . . . think it would be bette
if we get some sleep, Jack. I really do."

He smiled. "We will. But I could never sleep wonderin
what you have done to yourself. Now, I am somewha
handicapped, so perhaps you will be so good . . ." H
looked meaningfully at the nightcap pulled down so firml
on her brow.

With a sigh, Amanda nodded. "Before I do, let me ex
plain something."

"Very well." His eyes glittered in the lamplight.

"I have always hated that hairstyle."

He lifted his brows in surprise.

"Mother feels that long hair is a badge of woman's femi
ninity. She never would let Penny or me cut ours, but when
it was time for our come-out, Pen fussed and fumed unti
she agreed to allow us to consult a fashionable hairdresse
He persuaded her to allow us to cut the front so that i
could be arranged more à la mode, for the fashion, he said
was for curls to frame the face. Mother succumbed to hi
enthusiasm, and loved the results. The style becomes Penn
very much, as you no doubt noticed."

"I did." He began to look grim. *I might have known tha
as usual her relatives noticed only Penelope's looks.*

"But Penny's hair curls naturally. And then, our heads re shaped somewhat differently, don't you think?"

"To put it mildly."

"I did not like the way it made me look. I felt that the urls falling down onto my forehead overpowered my face, nd of course, my hair is so straight and fine that it had to e absolutely soaked in pomade to curl. But once it had een cut, it was too short to permit me to pull it back as efore. Besides, our dresser sided with the hairdresser. She aid curls were all the rage, and that pulling my hair back nly emphasized my eyes, which are much too large."

Jack snorted. "Your eyes are magnificent."

Amanda ignored this. "But Mama insisted that I wear ay hair as the hairdresser had suggested, just like Penny's, or, she said, she wouldn't have people thinking she didn't o as much for me as she did for the beauty in the family."

Jack swore softly. "Your family's admiration for Penny as often led them into hurtful behavior toward you. A ity you didn't tell your sister how much you disliked the tyle. I'm sure she would have insisted they change it."

"That's partly why I didn't. Why make Penny unhappy, vhen until my hair grew out there was little to be done vith it, no matter how much she harried Mother? Penny oves a cause, as you may have noticed, and I am her avorite."

"Yes, I have noticed that rebellious streak in her. In hampioning you, she has not always understood what is in our best interests, though."

Amanda considered this. "No, I suppose not. But when he is so good, and so loving and devoted, how could I tell er so? And besides, I did not like to have a great fuss nade. And Mother did what she thought was for the best or me. You may think her cold, but she feels things very leeply."

"So you pretended to be reconciled to those curls, hough they did not become you, to keep the peace."

"I suppose you think me dreadfully fainthearted."

"I think you dreadfully kindhearted, and since I know hat I shall be the beneficiary of that kindness many times n my life, I cannot dislike it in you." He leaned forward nd kissed her on the nose. "But I hope you will tell me

if you are doing something for me only out of kindness
don't wish to impose on your good nature."

Jack's kiss on her nose stunned Amanda. *To think
being kissed there. And what a shameful creature I am,
feel that wicked warmth in me from such a platonic kiss.* S
closed her eyes and turned her face away so he couldn't s
how much his kiss had affected her.

"Amanda?" Jack touched her cheek, ignoring the d
comfort the movement caused in his arm. "Have I do.
something wrong again? You aren't afraid I am going
force myself on you? I gave my word . . ."

She put her finger on his lips and hastened to reassu
him. "No, Jack. I am not at all afraid." *Only sorry y*
aren't going to break your word on this.

"Don't think you have succeeded in distracting me fro
my purpose." He looked at the cap meaningfully again.

"Oh, very well. But it looks awful. I will have to purcha
a wig before we leave Darlington tomorrow." She slow
pulled the cap off.

Jack stared at her for a long time, his face at first solem
but gradually a smile crept into his eyes. It was not a moc
ing smile, but a smile of pleasure. He sat up in bed an
motioned for her to do the same. Relieved that he had n
flown into a rage, Amanda sat quietly as he considere
her. He stroked her head with his right hand, fluffing an
examining her hair in the candlelight.

"So soft," he murmured. "And lighter in color by sever
shades, without all that pomade. It makes you look eve
more like a little woodland sprite. I like it."

"Doing it too brown," she said, shaking her head at hi
and trying not to believe his words, for to believe the
might be to invite more pain.

"I do, though. Have you ever seen Lady Caroli
Lamb?"

"Well, of course I have." Amanda cringed. Caro ha
been widely ridiculed for her excesses, including her boyi
hairdo. "I promise you I don't intend to begin dressing li
a page!"

"Thank God for that. But your features are somewha
similar. In spite of her reprehensible behavior, I found th.
gamine look very appealing. On you it is perfect." H

turned her head from side to side. "All it needs is to be evened up a bit and shortened in back."

"Shortened!" After having cut off so much hair, never had she expected to be told that it should be shorter.

"Yes, at the nape of the neck, I think. I should be able to do it tomorrow morning."

She searched his face for signs of insincerity and saw none. "Oh, Jack. You truly don't hate me for it? You don't think I have mutilated myself?"

"Indeed, no. I dread the day you tire of it and decide to grow it long again."

"In that case I never shall," she breathed fervently, taking his caressing hand from her cheek and kissing it.

"Amanda!" He leaned forward and kissed her forehead. "Precious girl."

She lifted her head, he lowered his; their lips met. His pressure on her mouth was soft and caressing until he moved his hand behind her head. Then he deepened the kiss, urging her for the first time to open her mouth to him. Confused but excited, she did, and melted with the heat that seared her at the meeting of their tongues.

He bore her back onto the pillows, following her down and trailing kisses down her jawline. Nuzzling aside the neck of her gown, he kissed her shoulder. Desire led him to attempt to push it aside with his left hand, whereupon a jab of pain reminded him of his injury.

"Drat!" He sat back up.

"What is it?"

"My arm."

"Oh. Your poor arm. We can't . . . ?"

"We could, but it would require a great deal more cooperation on your part than would be fair to ask of an innocent young woman."

Amanda looked at him solemnly. Curiosity and fear both had been driven out by desire. She felt a restless need in herself, and with it a certain wantonness.

As her husband gazed back at her, something about his tender, yearning expression emboldened her. "Jack," she whispered, "I can be very cooperative."

Jack's nostrils flared. He wrapped his right arm around her and pulled her to him.

*   *   *

The next morning Amanda felt extremely shy; she tried
to slip out of bed without waking Jack, so that she could
resume the nightrail he had removed, before facing him in
the light of day.

Her husband, however, woke the instant she stirred. He
opened his eyes and smiled dreamily at her. "Wife," he
said in a husky morning voice, "your cooperation last night
was indeed exemplary! Do you suppose . . . ?"

"In the daytime?" She pulled the covers up to her chin.
Color flooded her cheeks, and she looked anywhere but
into his tawny, passionate eyes. "I . . . I am very hungry,
Jack. I ate but little last night. W-would you please go down
and order our breakfast?"

He tilted her chin up. "Look at me, Amanda."

She lifted her gaze reluctantly.

"Oh, very well," he said, seeing how embarrassed she
was. "I shall indeed order our breakfast. But don't be shy,
love. What passed between us last night was not only wonderful, it was just what man and wife were created for.
There is no need for shame or guilt."

"I d-don't feel guilty, but . . ." She put her hands to her
cheeks. "I must look a fright, and . . ." Amanda feared
that her lack of feminine charms would be all too obvious
to her handsome husband in the harsh light of day.

He chuckled. "You look adorable to me." But he took
pity on her confusion and eased from beneath the covers.
He found his discarded nightshirt and draped it casually
across his shoulder, then handed her nightrail to her.
"Shall I ring for George, or will you act as my valet
this morning?"

Amanda's modesty warred with her fascination with his
masculine figure. Pique at his obvious enjoyment of her
predicament made her voice sharpen. "I shall, but please
put on your small clothes first."

He bowed. "As you wish, madam." Then he treated her
to an unobstructed rear view as he walked into the dressing room.

Amanda scrambled into her nightrail and entered the
dressing room when he called. Once again his bruise ap-
palled her. By this time his entire upper arm had turned
several interesting shades of purple. "No wonder you
wanted to send her to the knackers," she remarked as her

fingers lightly traced the darker spots that marked the points of contact with the mule's teeth. "I wonder if she will do such a thing again."

"I doubt it. As you said, she thought she was protecting you. Rest easy, love. Your mule is safe. In fact, I intend to send a note to your father before we leave here, reminding him to have her brought to Rosebriar."

"I mean to make a liniment for that arm before we go, sir!" She put her hands on her hips as if prepared for an argument.

"I doubt not your ministrations will be infinitely more enjoyable than Haskins'." He grinned at her. "I hope you remain quick to blush, for I love to see it."

"Here! Put this shirt on, you looby." She held out a clean shirt for him. "We'll have breakfast here so you won't have to put on a coat."

It seemed to Jack that he had almost succeeded in healing all of the pain and misunderstanding between them. Their trip into Scotland became a true honeymoon. They dawdled on the way, stopping wherever a beautiful view appeared or the guidebook told of an interesting ruin or old church. They spent an entire day at Hadrian's Wall. Originally Jack had intended to arrive at his hunting box within two days, but that stretched into four, the happiest four days and most passionate nights of his life.

In one way, though, he knew he had failed. Amanda was still insecure about her appearance. At night she was all that a man could expect from a lover, but she would not hear of making love by light of day.

For Amanda, too, the days were enjoyable. The nights very nearly overwhelmed her. What had begun as curiosity and a vague longing exploded into passionate responses that made her blush to think of them in the light of day. At times her self-doubts reasserted themselves, and she cautioned herself not to grow accustomed to this sublime experience or love him too much, or she would be destroyed when he lost interest in her. But most of the time, she allowed herself to believe he loved her, and her love for him deepened with each passing day.

At last their carriage bore them up a bumpy, hilly road to Rosebriar, Jack's "hunting box," a commodious cottage nestled among trees and looking out over a magnificent mountain view. A middle-aged couple came to the door to greet them.

Jack presented his young wife proudly to the dignified pair. "Mrs. Molly MacGregor keeps house for me here, and her husband, Dan, is my gamekeeper and overseer." He led her into the rustic but well-kept cottage and turned her over to Mrs. MacGregor, who kept her surprise well hidden when Amanda removed her bonnet to reveal her short hair, which Jack had trimmed so that it conformed to the shape of her head.

He turned his steps to the stables, to which his groom had brought Triton in easy stages a few days ahead of them. "How did he stand the trip?" Jack asked Angus McLean.

"Very well, my lord. He has made an excellent recovery, which I never thought to see."

"Nor I." Jack patted the animal's sleek rump approvingly. "Tough stock, eh?" He proffered a sugar lump.

"I believe his journey was much sweetened by the little lady here." McLean nodded toward the next stall, where a horse with a pale gold coat and mane peered out. Her dished-in forehead and enormous dark eyes revealed her Arabian descent.

"I don't doubt it. Aurelia's a beauty, eh, Angus?" He held out a lump for the mare. "A great pity her mistress won't have her."

"Eh?" McLean scratched at his head.

"She prefers her mule. She should be here in a few days. Once Aurelia has rested, I plan to send her to Chalk Hill. My sisters will enjoy riding her when they visit."

"So Mistress Aurelia must go, eh?" McLean shook his head. "A pity it is indeed. Such a beauty as she is."

"Ah, well. You and I may think her rival plain, but beauty is in the eye of the beholder, they say." The two men chuckled over the old saying.

Jack had carefully pondered Amanda's possible reaction if she knew he had sought to replace her beloved Hippolyta. Certainly the mare would not be a treasured gift as he had hoped. He felt chagrin at how little he had succeeded in understanding Amanda. The horse's presence would reveal not only his lack of sensitivity to his new, and still very insecure, wife. It would also reveal his dishonesty.

You told her you did understand, that it was a mere over-sight. Cowardly though he felt it to be, Jack hoped to conceal the truth from Amanda, at least until she had gained more self-confidence.

"I wish to keep her out of Lady Maitland's sight, McLean. It would be best if she never knew Aurelia was here."

"Aye, my lord?" McLean sounded puzzled. "How might that be done?" He looked meaningfully around the small, crowded stable.

"Take her over to Tait Hall. They're good neighbors. They'll keep my secret. See to it at once."

He turned back to Triton and began examining the large bay's legs again. Both he and McLean had their backs to the stable door, and did not see Amanda standing there, white with shock at what she had just heard.

Chapter Twenty-one

$\mathscr{\sim}$

A manda stood frozen in the doorway, her mind whirling around the words she had overheard as she approached the open stable door. *Mistress Aurelia must go. A beauty. Her plain rival. It would be best if she never knew Aurelia was here. They'll keep my secret.*

Oh, heavens. What does it mean? Amanda backed out of the stable and started walking, little heeding where she was going. That she had plunged into the thickly wooded area north of Rosebriar she knew not, nor cared. *He has kept a mistress here. A beautiful one. She must be a servant, else he could not just order her about like a possession, could he?* To Amanda, the corruption of a young servant made his keeping a mistress even more reprehensible. And these neighbors of his? *The inhabitants of Tait Hall must be as libertine as my husband! I suppose he'll visit her there while we are at Rosebriar.* The thought of Jack going from her bed to that of the beautiful unknown devastated her.

I've married a liar and a libertine. "Beauty is in the eye of the beholder" indeed. The tears started as Amanda remembered the tender, overwhelming moment last night when he had called her his beautiful wife.

Vaguely aware that she was climbing, Amanda plunged farther into the woods, pondering why Jack had insisted on doing the honorable thing in marrying her, if his character was as stained as these actions suggested.

And to laugh and make fun of me with his friends was bad enough, but to discuss me, to compare me to his mistress, with a servant—why, it is the ultimate humiliation! As her tears blinded her, Amanda stumbled and began falling down a steep, rocky slope. She rolled over and over for what seemed like forever, before she grasped at a stunted bit of furze and broke her fall. Just ahead of her lay a drop-off, she dared not guess how steep, and evening had already laid its shroud on the opposite hill.

Her predicament drove all other thought from Amanda's mind. Without releasing her hold on the shrub, she tested the rocky surface with her feet to see if she could climb back up. The rocks rolled beneath her feet, denying her purchase, and she could hear the little avalanche she had started, as it bounced down the incline and then—nothing. *It's far enough down that I can't hear them when they land,* she realized, shuddering.

She wound her hands in the foliage of the little evergreen that had saved her life, and managed to maneuver herself so that her body lay across the shrub. The chill in the air began to permeate her, for she had donned only a scarf, and it had been torn from her hand in the fall.

Carefully she loosened her grip, to ease the cramping in her hands, but she kept one wrapped loosely in the spiny branches, in case she should begin to slide again. *At least I had my gloves on,* she thought, though tiny prickles of discomfort told her the thin leather had been penetrated.

In the diminishing light she studied the bit of greenery her life now depended on. Though it had little in the way of top growth, the base was thick and gnarled, the sign of an old plant struggling for life in an inhospitable location. How long would those roots hold her in such thin soil?

She would have to lie still and wait for rescue. Her hope lay in a husband who did not love her, who even now was perhaps taking leave of his mistress instead of seeking out his wife.

That was such a lowering thought, it propelled Amanda to new efforts. She could not bear the thought of owing her life to Jack. She looked around her, noticing for the first time that the incline on which she lay was dotted with numerous other clumps of furze and some sort of tough grass, and that here and there slabs of rocks protruded that seemed to promise support for feet or hands.

Just above her, the scarf dangled, caught on another such furze bush. Hungry for its warmth, she cautiously reached for it and gave a sharp tug. It didn't budge, which suggested another use for it. Moving slowly and deliberately, Amanda pulled herself up, maneuvering her feet so that she stood on the woody base of the furze bush. With her left foot on the furze bush, and both hands hanging on to the scarf, she found a toehold with her right foot just above a clump of grass. Carefully she shifted her left foot to one of those rock slabs protruding just above the furze bush. It held her weight, and put her in position to work her scarf free. She used it to cast for another, higher clump of furze. *A pity I am not more skilled at casting,* she thought. *This is the most dangerous, and important, bit of fishing I ever did.*

Her efforts paid off: she entangled the fabric in another little shrub and repeated the procedure. Slowly, carefully, she worked her way up the incline and at last fell forward onto more level ground near the top.

How long it had taken her, she knew not, but the last few feet had been managed in darkness, slightly illuminated by a quarter moon. *Just a little larger than the moon that appeared when the clouds passed, that stormy night on the lake which led to this disastrous marriage,* she remembered.

I slid into marriage the way I slid down that cliff, she thought ruefully, crawling on her hands and knees several more feet away from the edge. When she thought she had gone far enough to be safe from sliding back, she tried to stand, but her legs had begun to tremble, so she sat with her back against the base of a tree while she rested.

Having seen to his cattle, and watched Angus lead the golden mare away by a back path, Jack returned to the cottage, feeling sad and a little uneasy. *I wonder if the rest of my gifts will prove just as disastrous?* He entered through the kitchen, hoping to find Mrs. MacGregor. He wanted to ask her where the goods he had sent from London were stored, intending to reconsider his gifts while Amanda rested abovestairs.

"It's glad I am ye've come back from your walk a'ready," Mrs. MacGregor said, looking up from stirring a pot. " 'Tis getting on toward dark, and . . . why, isn't the mistress with ye?"

Jack's startled look answered that question.

"Now where can she have gotten to? For she couldn't ha' missed the stables, and I warned her 'twould be danger-ous to go a'walkin' by herself, not knowin' the area at all!"

"Amanda came to the stables? When?"

"As soon as she looked around the cottage a bit. She

said she'd had enough of sitting after that long carriage ride, and preferred a walk to a lie-down. Said she would ask you to show her about a little."

Jack thrust his hand through his hair. Amanda had come to the stables? Had she seen the mare? Overheard him trying to hide the beast from her? He could well imagine her walking away in anger. *Pray God she hasn't wandered far,* Jack thought, panic rising in him as he recalled the dangers of the terrain for the unfamiliar walker. *She is somewhere nearby, composing herself,* he thought. *Or perhaps planning a scold.*

He sent Mrs. MacGregor to search the house, while he dashed out the front door and called her name loudly. The cottage was situated high on a hill, nestled well back from the rutted pathway that led to Rosebriar from the coaching road. Before it enough trees and brush had been cleared away to make a tolerable lawn, but the woods encroached at either side. Not seeing her on the lawn, he rounded the house, calling her name still, and burst into the stable. He made a hasty circuit of the boxes, and saw only Triton, the old gelding that pulled the trap for the MacGregors, and the four carriage horses. A gleam of light came from the tack room, so he turned in there. His coachman sat at a table, cleaning tack, and looked up, startled at finding his master rushing into the room, a distraught look on his face.

"Lady Maitland. Has she been here?"

Ben Smith shook his head.

"I think she's gone for a walk by herself, not realizing the dangers. I need everyone to search for her. Where is George?"

Ben rose and wiped his large hands on his leather apron. "In the kitchen, I make no doubt, makin' eyes at Molly Bridges."

"Get him. You search behind the stable, toward the Taits'. No, Angus will see her if she went in that direction. Search the woods to the west. Send George to the south, toward the hollow. I'll go north, up the hill." Jack took a lantern from the wall. "It's getting dark. Take guns, both of you, and fire twice if you find her."

He dashed back to the house to get his horse pistol, then hastened toward the north, calling Amanda's name. In the mountains, the dark seemed darker than in open country, where stars and moon could spread their light. Without the lantern he doubted even he could navigate these hills. Jack could not believe Amanda would go directly into the woods by herself, so he started up the most dangerous path, the one that led north near the ridge, calling her name as loudly as he could at every step.

Amanda strained every nerve listening for just such a sound, and heard him quite a while before he could hear her return cry. When he did, she could hear his voice coming closer, shouting in answer each time she called his name.

Finally a light appeared, and his outline behind it. "Amanda! Where . . . ?"

"Here. Watch your step. It is a long way down."

"Farther than you can imagine!" Jack started down the incline and heard the stones roll away. "You're almost over the cliff!"

"Take care! The last I heard, gravity operates on men as well as women." Angry though she was at him, she did not want to see Jack plunge down the incline to his death.

Her voice sounded quite cool and composed. Jack lifted his lantern higher. "It looks to me as if gravity has had its way with you, my love." He knelt by her, examining her scratched face and torn clothing. Glancing over his shoulder at the distance from the path to her position, he whistled softly. "You fell this far? No wonder you look so bedraggled. Good job you went no farther." He stood and held out his hands to her.

Amanda spurned his help, shakily standing on still trembling limbs. "I went a good deal farther, I'll have you know. I am cold, tired, and hungry. Please be so kind as to light my way back to the cottage."

So, she chooses frost rather than fire, Jack thought, smiling at her rigid back as she brushed past him. His joy at finding her safe was such that he welcomed whatever punishment she might mete out to him.

"A moment, Amanda." He caught at her arm. "There is something I must do first."

She turned around and saw him raise the pistol, the first time she had noticed he was armed. She flinched, fearing for just a flicker of a moment that he intended to shoot his unwanted wife. But he pointed the gun's muzzle into the air above them.

Amanda winced as he fired once, then again. "What was that for?"

"I've all the staff out searching for you. That is the signal to tell them you have been found. Now, come here." He put the gun and the lantern on the ground and held out his arms. "I need to hold you."

She lifted her chin. "No. I want to go back to the cottage."

"So unforgiving. Amanda, I have been frantic with terror. Have pity on me." He walked toward her; she retreated.

"Not half so frantic as I, nor with half so good a reason! I owe my life to a little shrub not five feet from the edge of a cliff." Amanda did not feel as calm as her composed voice seemed to indicate. The sound of rocks swishing past her and down the incline into nothingness had unnerved her; that dangerous climb back up had exhausted her. "I repeat. I am hungry, tired, and cold." She picked up the lantern and began walking away from him.

Jack sighed, collected his gun, and hastened to catch up to her. "Brave girl. How did you manage to climb back up? As I recall, it is steep and rocky there."

"Women are more resourceful than you may think, my lord," she sniffed. Suddenly a feeling of pure triumph flared in her. It was true, she realized. She had gotten herself out of a very tight spot without the least help from anyone. She found that idea profoundly liberating. *Whatever your future misdeeds, my lord husband,* she thought, *I am strong. I shall not again let your treachery overset me.*

When they reached the path, Jack took her elbow and steered her onto it. "This way," he said. "You will find it easier going and less dangerous than traipsing through the woods at night."

They met Ben on the way. "Ah, milady, it's that glad I am t'see you," he exclaimed.

Amanda smiled at him. "Thank you, Ben. I appreciate your searching for me." The coachman's broad, kind face, wreathed in smiles, broke through the icy shield she had built around herself, and she suddenly began to cry. Instantly Jack turned his gun and the lantern over to Ben,

then scooped Amanda into his arms despite her protests.
"Lead the way," he ordered the laden coachman. Amanda
struggled to be free, but he held her firmly, ignoring the
pain in his injured arm. She gave up and laid her head
against his chest, shivering and glad in spite of herself for
his warmth.

Jack did not attempt to discuss what had happened with
her. He expected that there would be some acrimony, and
did not wish to lay out their dirty linen for the servants.
My little wife has quite a temper, he thought. He did not
really mind. Ever since he met her, he had wished that
Amanda might borrow some of her sister's spirit; though
at times she could dig in and be amazingly stubborn, in
general she yielded too easily to others. He remembered
his mother saying once, by way of explanation to him after
he inadvertently observed one of her sharp setdowns of his
father, "I must stand up to him, you see, or he will turn
into a tyrant."

"You will keep me from that danger," he murmured
against Amanda's hair. "And I will keep you from becoming a termagant!"

"Wh-what?" Amanda asked, lifting her head to look into
his face. She surprised there a look of such tenderness that
she stopped pondering the scathing denunciation she meant
to give him once they were alone, and began questioning
her own conclusions.

Chapter Twenty-two

Mrs. MacGregor took charge of Amanda and soon had her snugly in bed after administering hot tea and soup for the chills. She gave Jack to understand he was not to disturb his wife until the morning. He prowled his room restlessly all evening, hardly slept at all, and rose early the next morning to return to the place he had found her the evening before. He looked over the steep incline she had tumbled down, a delayed terror gripping him as he studied the evidence of her difficult, perilous climb. The marrow of his bone froze at the sight of the half-uprooted furze that had stopped her initial fall. Tufts of her once-elegant Norwich shawl clung to various shrubs, marking her climb to safety. He marveled that she had found the nerve or the strength to attempt it.

He wondered at her taking such a risk as to walk out by herself, in an unfamiliar, mountainous area. *Surely merely learning I bought her a horse to replace her precious mule shouldn't cause her deliberately to put herself in such danger. Where has my calm, collected Amanda gone?* Fleetingly he considered whether his wife might be not entirely sane. Quickly shaking off this ugly thought, he returned to Rosebriar determined to convince her of his good intentions, and to scold her mildly for being so impetuous.

Amanda slept the sleep of emotional and physical exhaustion. She rose and dressed early, with Mrs. MacGregor's reluctant assistance. "I am persuaded you should rest abed this day, my lady," the housekeeper fussed as she fastened the tapes on Amanda's gown.

Amanda smiled at her. "Nonsense. I am fine. My arms and legs ache, to be sure, but otherwise I've taken no harm. I'm simply ravenous, too, so don't attempt to foist porridge on me!"

She felt little surprise at not finding Jack at the table. She didn't ask where he had gone, for she didn't wish to put his well-meaning and upright-seeming housekeeper to the blush, or force her to lie to protect her master's sins. It made her feel sick inside to think that he might have gone to that Aurelia woman.

Amanda opened her napkin with a determined snap. *He will give her up, if he wishes to live with me,* she thought.

Jack entered the dining room as she was finishing her morning chocolate. He eyed the remains of a considerable breakfast with approval. "You aren't ill, then?"

"Not at all. I am well and girded for battle."

"That sounds ominous." Jack smiled but found no answering smile on her face. "Right, then. Shall we adjourn to the privacy of the drawing room?"

It was a grand title for a very small salon crowded with rustic furniture. He motioned her to sit in front of the fire. She winced a little as she lowered herself into the chair.

Jack was instantly solicitous. "Did you injure yourself? Should we find a doctor? They are not thick upon the ground here, but . . ."

"Just some sore muscles, my lord. Nothing that time won't heal."

His eyebrows rose. "My lord? You are my lording me? Look, Amanda, I know you overheard Angus and me talking in the stable, and I understand that you are upset, but I think you are blowing matters out of proportion."

"I cannot decide which is more appalling—your immoral behavior, or your notion that I should take it in stride."

"Immoral! I sadly fear you have misinterpreted what you heard once again."

Oh, how she wished to believe him. She had pondered his words over and over at breakfast. But their meaning seemed so plain. "Please do not trifle with me. I know about Aurelia."

Jack studied her tense, pale face. "You do? I feared as much. Let me explain . . ."

"I would rather not hear any more about it. But we must come to an understanding about your future conduct if we are to live together as man and wife."

"Now, see here! Last night you almost perished, and today you threaten our marriage. Such a drastic response, all because of a . . ." Suddenly Jack's expression changed. If the subject had not been so serious, Amanda would have suspected the gleam in his amber eyes to be one of amusement. "You know about Aurelia?"

"I do."

"Then you know that I sent her away."

"To the neighboring estate! That is not far enough." Amanda looked down at her hands, twisting a handkerchief in her lap. She meant to speak her piece without womanish weeping or hysteria, but it was difficult with such a painful lump in her throat.

"I am not such a green girl as to be unaware that some men of our class think themselves entitled to a mistress as well as a wife. I did not think you would be such a one, but then, I don't know you very well. Last night when dark fell and I saw the moon, I realized we had known each other little more than a month."

Jack said nothing, but continued to look at her with glittering eyes and an ambiguous half smile.

"I can't keep you from such philandering, of course, but I want you to know I refuse to . . . to . . . cohabit with you if you . . . This is all so embarrassing." She looked away and swallowed hard.

"For me as well, my love. Imagine my feelings at being caught out this way. I wished to spare you pain; that is why I sent Aurelia away. Do you think Chalk Hill would be far enough?"

She turned her head back, fury in her eyes. "Only if you do not wish me to set foot there!"

"Pardon me. You mean, I collect, I must get her entirely out of my life?"

Amanda nodded.

"But I can't just turn her loose, you know. I am in some measure responsible for her. I will have to find a . . . situation for her."

"If she is as beautiful as you and Angus seem to think, that will present no problem." Amanda stood. "That is all I have to say to you."

"Well, I have a deal more to say to you, so sit down." The sharp tone in his voice made her bristle, but she did as he ordered.

"You say you do not know me. Alas, too true, nor do I

know you. I had no idea you would be the kind of woman who would be forever listening at keyholes . . ."

"That isn't fair!" Amanda clenched her fist. "I accidentally . . ."

"Three such 'accidents' in the last three weeks or so. It would not be so disturbing did you not react so strongly to what you overhear, though to be sure it served me well the first time."

"Just so. I married you to save you from being disinherited, and now I have accomplished that goal. My further involvement with you will depend upon whether you show me the respect a wife has a right to expect."

"But your second eavesdropping session was less productive, except of chaos and unhappiness. Does that not make you wary of drawing conclusions from a few chance overheard words?"

"It is true, in the case of Richard and Gerrard, what I heard is not what you said. At least, so you say. After what I overheard yesterday, I begin to wonder . . ."

Jack frowned. "Now you are doubting my veracity. I take exception to that."

"I'm sorry. I promised myself I wouldn't indulge in pointless insults. But last night I heard every word from your own lips. Heard you plotting to hide your mistress, and then laughing at my plainness with your servant! Really, Jack! I know I am no beauty, nor ever wished you to lie and tell me so, but to behave in such a way is . . . is positively bad *ton*."

"Such a thing would be the worst possible *ton*, I agree." He did not look particularly contrite, though. "But for you to act so rashly is what I cannot like. I had thought Penelope the one to overdramatize! To run out into unfamiliar woods and get yourself lost and almost fall over a cliff— God help me, Amanda, when I went back this morning and saw how close you came to dying, it made my blood freeze."

"You . . . you do care for me a little, don't you, Jack?" She bowed her head, feeling humiliated by her need to believe this.

"You know I do! I love you!"

Amanda caught her breath. Could it be possible? "And I love you, which is why I was so hurt by what I heard. It

s clear to me that you mean something quite different by
hose words than I do. But for the sake of whatever regard
you have for me, won't you promise me that you will be
faithful at least . . . at least . . ." Her voice thickened with
tears. "Until we have our nursery full," she managed to
choke out.

Jack wanted to reach for her, to enfold her in his arms,
to explain her misunderstanding, but he wondered if she
would believe him. He rubbed his nose with his index fingers as he tried to think of a way to convince her.

"Very well, Amanda. I will do as you ask. I will send
Aurelia away. It will be hard for her, as she is very young
and not, I think, vicious. I think if you got to know her,
you might agree to keep her here."

"That is outside of enough." Amanda jumped to her feet.
"Next you will be asking me to be as large-minded about
the whole thing as the Duchess of Devonshire, who apparently finds a *ménage à trois* very much to her taste. Well,
that I could never endure." She slipped past him and
walked out the front door.

"Going to plunge into the woods again?" he drawled as
he caught up to her.

"No. Yes. I don't know what I shall do. But I shan't be
here when your mistress comes. If you cannot merely send
her a message . . ."

"Ah, but she wouldn't understand, you see. The poor
creature is rather deficient in understanding."

"But very beautiful." Amanda turned her head away,
biting her lip. *Not only is she very young and a servant,
she is simpleminded. Never would I have suspected Jack of
such depravity.*

"Yes, very." Jack took her elbow. "Come, let us go to
the stables and send someone to fetch her. Perhaps when
you have seen her, spoken to her, you may be able to
suggest to me how best to provide for her."

It seemed a cruel request to Amanda, but she took herself firmly in hand. If Jack complied with her insistence to
dismiss his mistress, she had carried her point, after all.

She nodded and allowed him to steer her to the stables,
where Angus received his master's orders to fetch Aurelia
back again.

He beamed on Amanda when he heard Jack's request.

"Ah, you won't be sorry, m'lady. A proper beauty she is
And she'll do anything you ask of her, with the best spirit
in the world."

Amanda could not return his smile. "So I have heard,"
she said coldly. Then she hastily left the stable.

Jack followed close on her heels. "She is a great favorite
around here, as you will see."

"Yes," Amanda said. "A bad master makes for bad servants. I see yours are as unself-consciously corrupt as you
are. I need to be alone for a while."

"That would not be a good idea," Jack said, misliking
her pallor and the grim look about her mouth. "Instead, let
us take a walk together, as we should have done yesterday
evening. I'll show you the safe paths and general lay of
the land."

"I said I'd like to be alone. I don't intend to throw myself
off any cliffs, if that is what you fear."

Jack insisted. "It is a matter of safety, Amanda. Now, if
you turn down this path, it will take you to a mountain
stream replete with trout." Jack talked to her as they
walked along the path, but she made few responses. He saw
that she felt his supposed immoral behavior too strongly to
be able to notice any of the sights around her, which otherwise would make her yearn for her sketch pad.

The path he guided her along would eventually intersect
with the one leading to the Taits'. He wanted to meet
Angus as he brought Aurelia back, so he could end Amanda's misery as soon as possible.

To Amanda, Jack's voice seemed to come from afar. She
kept envisioning him intertwined with a surpassingly beautiful woman, as they had lain together on this honeymoon
trip, and felt that her heart might well break in two. So
abstracted was she that she hardly heard the "clop-clop"
of horses' hooves until they were almost upon her. She
looked up into the beaming face of Angus McLean.
Mounted on Jack's Triton, he was leading a lovely Arabian
mare of the lightest chestnut color she had ever seen.

"Oh!" She stopped so suddenly Jack bumped against her.
"What a magnificent animal!" she exclaimed involuntarily.
Then she looked down the path, expecting someone else to
be following.

Angus dismounted, put his reins into Jack's outstretched

hands, and led the small mare to Amanda. "I spoke true, did I not, m'lady? Fine as five pence she is. Aurelia means . . ." He furrowed his brow. "Now, don't tell me, m'lord. Need to learn it proper, for I want to be able to explain it to the other grooms."

"This! This is Aurelia!" Incredulous, Amanda held back from the mare, which had stretched her neck to take the scent of this new human being.

"Aye! Now I remember. It means 'little golden lady.' Here, m'lady. I have some sugar in my pocket." He held out a lump for Amanda, who took it automatically and held it out to the inquisitive animal. Aurelia sniffed carefully, snorted, pawed the ground a little, then stepped tentatively forward. As the soft muzzle lipped at Amanda's gloved hand, she stroked the finely sculpted forehead, scratching between the ears in a way that Aurelia seemed to find highly acceptable, for, ears forward, she stepped into the caress.

"Did I not tell ye, m'lord," Angus said. "M'lady likes her very well, I think."

Amanda looked inquiringly at the grinning Scot. "Why would I not like her?"

"That is what I said. M'lord would have it that you would be missing yon mule of yours, and upset to find he'd tried to replace her with a horse. But I'm thinking you canna' possibly want that long-eared creature when . . ."

"Thank you, Angus," Jack interrupted, looking anxiously at Amanda. Her response to Aurelia thus far had been gratifying; still, she loved Hippolyta and might yet take offense. "You may take them to the stable now; we'll look in on her again a little later."

Amanda let her hand trail down the golden coat as Aurelia was led away. When Angus and both horses were out of sight, she still stood, facing away from Jack, her head down. He took her shoulders and gently turned her around.

"No tears, sweetheart. This is a time for smiles."

"I shall never be able to look you in the eye. I thought . . ."

"You made it very clear what you thought!" Jack chuckled. "Now that it's all past us, I am almost glad, for the sin I sought to cover up was so much smaller than what you suspected, I expect you will forgive me completely before long."

"Forgive you? What have I to forgive you? She is mine, isn't she?"

"Most certainly, if you want her."

"Jack, I almost believe you and Angus have conspired to pull the wool over my eyes, for how can you have supposed I would reject such a magnificent gift?"

"More than reject it, be devastated by it. That is what your sister informed me. She said you loved Hippolyta and would not take a dozen horses for her. The way you turned to that mule when you thought I'd spoken disparagingly of you only confirmed what she said. Also, I was trying to cover up a lie."

"That I can believe."

"I refer to my telling you that leaving Hippolyta behind was merely an oversight on my part. I didn't want to confess my lack of awareness of your feelings. Partly cowardice, I know, but partly because I thought at that point our relationship was too newly repaired to put any more strain on it."

Could he possibly have thought I would be so unreasonable? Amanda bit her lower lip. *Why shouldn't he? It's not as if I have behaved perfectly rationally in the last few days.*

"I can see how you could have believed I'd be upset. It does make me a little sad to give Hippy up. But of course I understand. You would not wish to be seen with me on so unfashionable a mount."

"Rot! If you want her, she is yours. That is why I suggested sending Aurelia to Chalk Hill. My sisters and other lady visitors can ride her there."

"They may not! I warn you, I shall be quite possessive of her."

"But . . ." Jack looked perplexed.

"Mayn't I have both?"

"Of course you may. Darling girl! Ten mules, ten horses, and ten unicorns, if you wish!"

She laughed and threw herself into his arms. "I feel so utterly silly, thinking you were talking about a mistress when it was a horse you spoke of. How can you have kept a straight face?"

"Your obvious pain made the situation less than amusing

for me." He put his hand under her chin and tilted her head up. "Only promise me, love, that in future if you overhear anything, or in any other way suspect I have not done as I ought, you will come to me with it. I will not lie to you again. If I have misbehaved, I will confess my sins. But I can assure you they won't include taking a mistress."

Amanda tucked her head into his shoulder to keep him from seeing the doubt she felt. How such a handsome man, so vibrant and alive, and utterly desirable, could be content with her for all of his life seemed impossible to imagine. But for as long as she had him, she meant to treasure him and make him glad he had married her.

Jack lifted her head for a long kiss, then looked lovingly into her tear-dampened eyes. "That reminds me," he said. "Come. We are not far from that stream, and there is something there I particularly want you to see."

When they had reached the babbling water, which roiled and foamed over a rocky bottom, he directed her attention to a particular lichen-covered rock where the water sparkled as it flowed with bubble-saturated swiftness. "That is what I meant."

She frowned, puzzled.

"Your eyes."

Amanda knelt by the stream and studied the colors— blue, white, gray, green, yellow—all lightened by the bubbling water. "Yes," she whispered.

"Beautiful, don't you think?"

She laughed shakily. "On a rock in a mountain stream, at least."

He pulled her up against him. "On you, love."

After he had kissed her, she pulled away and sighed pensively. "I have been thinking that since you met me, you have been injured, forced into a marriage not of your choosing, injured again, and then today insulted most unfairly."

Jack shook his head. "When I came to Garfield Manor, my most serious wound could not be seen by human vision. My healing began when first I looked into your sparkling eyes and beheld your impish dimples. I have seen too few of those dimples lately, but I give you fair warning, I mean to see them often from now on."

She rewarded him with a tremulous smile. They walked

the paths around Rosebriar for another hour, and this time
Amanda was alive to the beauty of the place, eagerly point-
ing out fine views and questioning him about what flowers
bloomed there in the spring. They spied a few mushrooms,
and marked the spot for sketching the next day. When at
last hunger drove them back to the cottage, they had become fast friends again.

After a hearty lunch, Jack lured Amanda to go upstairs
with him. "There are some things I want to show you."

"Oh, could it wait?" Amanda's cheeks pinked. "I do so
wish to try out Aurelia this afternoon."

Jack studied her thoughtfully. Her embarrassment
showed clearly that she thought he had lovemaking in
mind, and the beautiful flags in her cheeks did indeed fill
him with the desire to pursue that blush as far as it went.
Her reluctance, he knew, sprang not from any dislike of
making love, but from her continuing inability to believe
in her own power of attraction. Though their nights had
been all a husband could hope for from his honeymoon,
she had never permitted him to make love to her in the
daytime, and it had been a continual struggle to convince
her to allow a candle.

This quirk hid a deeper problem, Jack knew. Remembering his father's long-ago recommendation to lay siege to
her heart, he realized that one last bastion of doubt remained, tucked deep inside her. The inability to believe
that she was beautiful in his eyes kept her from receiving
all the love he had to give her.

"We shall have plenty of time to ride together," he told
her, taking her hand and drawing her gently, inexorably,
up the stairs. "I am too impatient to know whether or not
you will like what I have for you."

She frowned a little, and held back, but he gently, deter-
minedly, propelled her up the stairs and into the sitting
room that their two bedrooms shared.

He directed her to sit in his armchair before the fire.
From the dressing room he carried a large box, which he
placed at her feet. "While I cooled my heels in London,
awaiting the archbishop's pleasure in the matter of our special license, I had time to do a little shopping."

"Oh, no! Jack, Aurelia is a more than sufficient wedding present."

Ignoring her, he lifted two books from the box. "I felt that when you were a married lady, you might safely expose yourself to Dr. Darwin's versification of Linnaeus."

She took the two leather-bound volumes reverently in her hands and traced the title picked out in gold: *The Botanic Garden*. "I shall feel quite the daring matron once I have read "The Loves of the Plants," she said.

"We shall read it together." Jack's eyes suddenly appeared heavy-lidded; heat spread through Amanda as she looked into their amber depths. He took one of the volumes from her and opened it.

"Here is a sample: 'In gay undress displays her rival charms,/and calls her wondering lovers to her arms.' That refers to the lychnis."

"My! No wonder Mama would not let me read it!" Pink-cheeked but laughing, Amanda took the book back from him and thumbed through it. "I wonder what the good Dr. Linnaeus would think of Erasmus Darwin's treatment of his botanical theories?"

"If you mean the way Darwin treats the plants like persons, some wanton, some modest . . . ?"

She nodded.

"Actually, there is a good deal of that in Linneaus, too. I think such subjects are rarely off men's minds, my love." He leaned forward to feather a kiss along her jawline.

Suddenly shy, Amanda pulled away. "I have a gift for you, too." She jumped up and ran into her bedroom. In a few moments she was back with a small wooden casque. When Jack opened it, he found a very fine pocket watch. "Cass said yours was damaged at Waterloo. I expect you have replaced it by now, though." She looked at him uncertainly.

"I have not. I hadn't the heart, for it was Mother's gift to me. Now I shall have one with just as much sentimental value!" He leaned over and kissed her on the cheek. "That was not all of my offerings. Sit down again, please."

When she had complied, wonderment in her eyes, he took out several lengths of cloth in a variety of colors. Saying a silent prayer that she would be pleased instead of

offended, he held them out to her. She took them and
looked up at him, puzzled.

"I chanced to be walking past a modiste's shop and saw
a dress in the window in this," he explained, holding up a
swath of periwinkle-blue muslin. "I thought it would be
becoming to you, so I went inside. But the dress was too
large for you. The proprietress showed me several samples
and suggested that I take them to you. We could then write
her with your measurements and your choices, and you
could have some dresses nearly finished by the time we
get to London. All that would be required would be the
final fittings."

Amanda fingered the colors and fabrics, none of them
anything like what she had been accustomed to wearing.
True, there were greens, and yellows, and blues, but not in
the same tones as had been selected by their London modiste with Penny's coloring in mind. She was especially enchanted by an orchid shade, and hastened to the mirror to
drape it around her shoulders. The effect was gratifying.

"I have often suspected that what became Penny did not
become me, but . . ."

"Let me guess. You did not like to hurt your sister's
feelings. Or was it your mother? Or the modiste?"

She smiled. "Mother. She always wished us to dress
alike." Amanda lowered her eyes; her voice grew wistful.
"I daresay you hope I may improve with better costuming."

This was what Jack had feared: that suggestions of a new
wardrobe would reawaken her worries about her looks. "It
was something the modiste said. She remembered you, actually. Apparently you and Penny purchased some clothes
from her in the spring. She said, "I remember *la petite.*"
He mimicked a false French accent. "Nevair for her the
same coleur as for her seester, I theenk. But that Maman!
She must 'ave eet so. *Eh bien, la petite* is the married lady
now, monsieur. She must dress accordingly. Not for her the
clothes of the ingenue, eh? Non! Non, I say. For her, different coleurs and styles *le plus sophistique.*"

Amanda laughed at his antics, for he had assumed the
posture and gestures of a dressmaker. "Jack, neither you
nor your modiste need fear that I will resist gowns more
suited to my figure and coloring."

Relieved, he drew her back to the mirror and began

draping the swatches over her shoulders one by one. When he asked him his preferences, he scolded her. "Now, none of that. You will dress to please yourself. I expect you have excellent taste, and I never want to worry that you are wearing something unappealing to you for my sake."

Amanda turned her eyes back to the mirror. It was a bit frightening, the thought of having responsibility for her appearance. In matters of household management, she would have felt quite at home. But in fashion?

Then she remembered her harrowing climb the night before. *I did that! I can do whatever I set my mind to.* She turned to him, a challenging look in her eyes. "I do not intend to wear a wig. I have decided I quite like my hair like this. It feels ever so good without all that weight atop my head. And I like not having to go through that horrible curling process each time I dress."

"Good!" Jack relaxed. *Heavy ground, m'boy,* he told himself, *and we have gotten over it very lightly.* He turned back to the box.

"Oh, surely you haven't gotten me anything else?"

"One more. I saw this in Ackermann's and couldn't resist it." He lifted a folio volume of botanical drawings from the box.

"A Collection of Roses from Nature," she read. "Oh! This is Mary Lawrence's work. We saw some of her drawings at the Royal Society this spring." Amanda turned the pages reverently. "She is truly remarkable."

"Your drawings are as good."

"My too-fond husband," she whispered, and leaned forward to stroke his cheek.

He caught her hand and began kissing it from each finger tip to her palm. When she sighed with pleasure, he looked up at her as he began laving kisses on the other hand. "Are you by any chance feeling 'cooperative' again, wife?"

It was an unfortunate reminder. Suddenly as effusive as her sister had ever thought of being, Amanda cried out, "Oh! Your poor arm. I had forgotten all about it. However did you pick me up last night? You should have said something." She jumped up. "I know! I shall go down and prepare a liniment for it."

"Thank you, but no. I do not wish to smell of horse

medicine this afternoon. It might drive away the lovely lad
I mean to spend it with." He caught at her hand.

"I have a receipt that will help you without the olfactor
impact of Haskins' preparation." She looked everywher
but at him.

"Hmmmm. That sounds most tempting, particularly
you rub it in very slowly. Then, perhaps, I can find som
way to return the favor. But let us postpone those particu
lar delights for this evening. My strongest need right no
is to take you in my arms and kiss you from head to toe.

"Oh, Jack, I don't know. It just seems so . . . wicked . .
in the daylight."

"Nothing is wicked between two people who love eac
other. Or did I hear wrong, for I could swear you sai
those words to me this afternoon." He wrinkled his brow
and put his finger to his lips, as if trying to remember
"Though to be sure, the tone of voice in which you sai
them hardly convinced me."

"I do. Oh, yes, I do love you, Jack, but . . ."

"There are qualifications on your love for me? For
tell you true, my love for you is without qualification o
stipulations." He pulled her into his arms and began a sen
sual assault to which she raised only the feeblest resistance
Then he carried her to the bed and laid her down, tenderl
removing her clothes item by item, kissing each newly ex
posed area ardently.

Jack's busy hands soon put it out of Amanda's power t
deny him. With a deep sigh, she allowed her husband t
undress her, and saw his eyes darken with desire as h
did so.

When he felt her surrender, and knew that the last bas
tion had been breached, her last defenses abandoned, h
felt a thrill of triumph, of joy that he knew would neve
leave him.

And as he rose over her, hands intertwined with hers
Amanda saw his eyes adoring her and sensed the love i
his every move, and she knew at last that she was beautiful

Epilogue

〰️

"Lord Maitland! A pleasure, sir. Haven't laid eyes on you since you left for your little adventure on the ontinent."

Viscount Maitland returned the bow of the mincing Sir eginald Frompton without any sign that this meeting with ne of the *ton*'s foremost gossips gave him any pleasure. o have Waterloo called a "little adventure" was bad nough; to hear such from a dandified man-milliner filled m with disgust.

"You walk remarkably well, sir, for a man with a wooden g, I must say." Frompton opened his snuffbox and held out to the coolly reserved viscount. "No? My best stuff, r, mixed especially for me by the Prince Regent's own bacconist." He took a pinch and inhaled it ostentatiously.

"You have been misinformed, Sir Reginald," Lord Maitnd said. "I received a slight wound in the leg, long nce healed."

"Ah. To be sure, to be sure." Frompton winked conspirarially at him, having no doubt that shame caused the visunt to hide his condition. "I wish to compliment you pon your latest conquest, sir."

"My . . . ?" Maitland had been about to turn away. "I eg your pardon, Sir Reginald, but to whom do you refer?"

"Why, to the charmer you had on your arm in the park esterday at the fashionable hour. Such a piquant little face. uch a lovely complexion. Hallo, Richard. Just complimentng our friend on his latest acquisition."

Richard Dremel lifted a curious eyebrow. "What's this? ought Charles' black, did you? Drat you, Jack, that cost ne a monkey."

"Anyone who would bet five hundred pounds on which orse I would purchase deserves to loose his blunt. But I

do not think it is to a horse that Frompton refers." F
turned back to the dandy. "I am at a loss to know . . . O
You must have seen me with Penelope Garfield. She is n
sister-in-law, sir, not my mistress."

"As if I would not recognize the magnificent Penelop
Pity you had to marry the plain sister. Left her in the cou
try, I'm sure, and I cannot blame you for it. Quiz of a gi
Met her at the first of last Season, before her parents re
ized it was hopeless and sent her home. Only way she cou
get a husband is by trickery, so it serves her right if y
disport yourself with the fair ones, eh?"

Jack drew a deep, composing breath. It would not be
his wife's interest to plant Frompton a facer at Almack
as he longed to do. "You are mistaken again, sir," he sai
"Lady Maitland and I are inseparable. I expect you sa
me with her, for we walked in the park yesterday."

"No, by gad, I'm not mistaken. I danced with Mi
Amanda Garfield several times last spring. It seemed
please the beauteous Penelope. So you see, you cann
gammon Sir Reginald Frompton. Miss Amanda is nothi
like the fashionable beauty I speak of. I see I have ha
pened upon a liaison that was meant to be secret. My di
cretion is legendary, my lord."

"Oh, indeed." Jack wondered if killing the man as
stood there would be considered murder or merely a s
cial solipsism.

Blissfully unaware of his danger, Sir Reginald plunge
on. "But I do hope when you tire of the fair incognita . .

Richard turned accusing eyes on Jack. "Wouldn't hav
believed it of you. Not if offered odds of a thousand
one. Thought you doted on Amanda."

"I do. I haven't the slightest notion whom you are spea
ing of, Sir Reginald, and I wouldn't care, except that su
talk would upset my wife, who is the only woman oth
than Penelope that I strolled with yesterday."

"Huh! You can't pull the wool over my eyes. I wou
give just such odds as Richard named, that this fair inco
nita was not your wife."

"Done!" Richard reached out and shook Sir Reginald
hand. "Ten guineas to your cow!"

"Huh? Ah . . ." Sir Reginald did a quick calculatio
"Ten thousand pounds if I—that is, if you—lose?" Nev

ry plump in the pocket, the horrified baronet jerked his
nd away. "No, no, Mr. Dremel. I never bet on a sure
ing. Not fair to you, sir. Not fair at all."

Jack's eyes narrowed. His hands curled tightly with the
ge to strangle the gossip. *Frompton is starting just the sort
rumor that can ruin a marriage. It'll get back to Amanda,
itably embroidered, and all the confidence her recent suc-
ss has given her will be for naught.*

"Dick, you are taking advantage of Sir Reginald's ab-
nce from society these several months. Do not persist in
is wager!"

Richard had but to look at his friend's expression to
now he had trod on dangerous ground. "Oh, no. Just jok-
g. Forget I said anything. Wouldn't want to take your
unt, Reggie. Know for a fact Jack isn't seeing one of the
uslin company."

Jack threw a strong arm around Frompton's shoulders
nd began propelling him across the ballroom. "You've
en on a repairing lease, for some time, have you not, Sir
eginald? Duns after you, I expect."

"Why, no indeed!" Frompton shook his head vigorously.
In France, savoring our victory. I say, where are you tak-
g me?"

"I wish you to meet my fair incognita."

"Ah! I knew it." Sir Reginald grinned at Jack, displaying
o awareness of the cold glitter in the viscount's eyes.

Jack led him to a small cluster of people laughing and
lking while waiting for the next dance to begin. The knot
pened up as he approached, revealing at its center a young
oman of somewhat less than medium height, her light
rown hair cut short and layered like petals from her
rown, barely fringing her forehead and exposing a pair of
napely ears. Tiny opal eardrops trembled in those ears,
nd were echoed in the dainty diamond and opal tiara she
ore. Her pale aqua gown was trimmed at the scooped
eck with layered petals of the same fabric, and a single
arge opal on a silver chain brushed the delicate swell of
er bosom.

Amanda's smile froze on her lips as she saw her hus-
and's approach. Her sister-in-law, Sarah, leaned over to
hisper in her ear. "Now, don't let him off easy. A man

who has taken a mistress before he has been married
year deserves . . ."

"He has not taken a mistress," Amanda hissed. "I kn
my husband very well, Sarah, and . . ."

"Then challenge him!" Sarah Stratford's hoarse whisp
carried well enough that the closest people heard her, i
cluding Penelope, who glared at her.

"Stop trying to make mischief," Penny said, entirely c
loud, causing a stir all around them.

"Penny, please! Let us not have a scene. I can fight r
own battles, remember?" Amanda looked Sarah directly
the eye. "Whether or not he was with another woman ye
terday matters not to me. I know he loves me, and hon
his wedding vows."

"Then confront him. That man he is dragging with hi
is the one who told me of your rival. Ask him in front
Jack and see what he says."

Before Amanda could reply, her husband had reach
them.

"My lady," Jack said, bowing formally to her. "Here
someone I wish you to meet." He turned to Sir Regina
frowning at the eager way the dandy ogled her. "This
the fair incognita you saw me with yesterday, is it not, §
Reginald?"

"Indeed it is! Please do present me, that I may reque
this waltz."

Ignoring the titters from the group around them, Ja
flashed even white teeth in a less-than-friendly smile. "R
grettably, she has already promised this waltz. To me. N
love, may I present an acquaintance of mine, Sir Regina
Frompton. Sir Reginald, my wife, Lady Maitland."

"A bold attempt, sir, though foolhardy in front of
many witnesses. But I repeat, I met the younger Miss Ga
field last year." Frompton wagged a scolding finger und
Jack's nose. "A veritable quiz of a girl, nothing at all li
this lovely creature." He offered Amanda his hand. "No
do tell me your name, my dear, and let me rescue you fro
this trickster."

A few stifled gasps and snickers caused Sir Reginald
poise to slip a little. Amanda slanted a glance at Sara
who looked decidedly crestfallen at this development. Ta
ing the dandy's outstretched hand, she smiled up at hi

I remember meeting you last year, Sir Reginald, though I cannot blame you for not remembering me. But I am indeed Amanda Garfield, now Lady Maitland."

Sir Reginald turned as red as the embroidery on his yellow waistcoat. "I . . . beg your pardon, my lady. Of course, I jest . . . That is . . ."

Jack laughed out loud, which gave the embarrassed onlookers their cue. In the sudden shout of ridicule, Sir Reginald would have retreated, but Amanda still grasped his hand, and she closed her fingers, preventing his escape.

"I think I shall give you this waltz, after all, Sir Reginald, for you have paid me the finest compliment I have received since returning to London." Amanda shot her suddenly astonished husband a mischievous look. "How unfair of everyone to laugh at your mistake. I did, indeed, look a veritable quiz last year, yet no one else mistook me for a different person. You, sir, have shown me just how successful my transformation is!"

Sir Reginald stammered a little, then collected himself and carried her off to the dance floor, leaving a husband behind who was torn between delight at his wife's spirit, and annoyance at seeing her dance with such a dirty dish. Admiration for her graceful movements as she danced overcame his irritation. *She looks so slender and elegant, no one would guess that she is increasing.* This knowledge, so recently confirmed, made his heart swell with pleasure.

"What *will* she do next?" Penelope asked Jack, a note of pride in her voice as she stood by him, watching the dancing couple. "First, she steals my suitor, then shears her hair off and takes the ton by storm. Will she next take Hippolyta to Hyde Park and bring riding mules into style?"

"Oh, I say, Jack. Don't answer that, if you know." Richard's face lit up with joy. "I am sure I can cozen Gerrard into giving me high odds on that one!"

"I'll give you odds that you'll end up in the punch bowl if you don't stop involving my wife in your madcap wagers!" For a moment Jack looked as if he would carry through on his threat on the instant, but his expression gradually shifted into a puzzled frown. "I wonder if she will?"

"Ride the mule in Hyde Park, you mean?" His sister

Sarah shuddered. "It would be just like her to try. But y[o]
must forbid it, Jack. I couldn't stand the disgrace."

Turning his shoulder to his sister, Jack looked at Penn[y]
who only opened her eyes very wide as she responded, [I]
don't know. But she *did* bring Hippy with her."

"Yes, but she brought Aurelia, too." Jack looked spec[u]
latively at his wife on the dance floor.

"You don't know? You really don't?" Richard, who h[ad]
not been the least intimidated by Jack's threat, studied [his]
face carefully. "You'll not forbid it, will you?"

Jack shook his head. "If she wishes it, I don't see why [I]
should object."

"Well!" Sarah threw up her hands and stalked away [in]
disgust.

"He doesn't know! I say! Must find Gerrard. Just Ge[r]
rard, Jack? A private wager?" He looked pleadingly at h[is]
friend, who smiled and nodded.

"I will venture ten guineas that she won't," Penny sai[d.]
"Since it is to be a very private bet, I may, mayn't I?" S[he]
looked to her brother-in-law for his approval.

He nodded, his brow still wrinkled in puzzlement.

Not staying to give his friend time to reconsider, Richa[rd]
started across the ballroom.

"Wait." In three strides Jack intercepted him. "I've [a]
hundred guineas that say she will."